This is a work of fiction. Names, characters, places, and incidents either are the product of the author's imagination or are used fictitiously. Any resemblance to actual persons, living or dead, events, or locales is entirely coincidental.

Copyright © 2023 by Katie Flanagan

All rights reserved. No part of this book may be reproduced or used in any manner without written permission of the copyright owner except for the use of quotations in a book review. For more information, address: katherine@katherinegrantromance.com

Cover design by Julia Gerbach

ISBN 9798986125978 (paperback)

ISBN 9798986125916 (ebook)

www.katherinegrantromance.com

ALSO BY KATHERINE GRANT

The Countess Chronicles:

The Ideal Countess

New Year's Masquerade

The Duchess Wager

The Husband Plot

The Prestons:

The Baron Without Blame
The Viscount Without Virtue
The Governess Without Guilt
The Charmer Without a Cause

Northfield Hall Novellas

(an unordered series for the mood reader)
The Hellion of Drury Lane
It's In Her Kiss
Three Nights With Her Husband

Plus, a free short story, The Spinster, available exclusively at www.katherinegrantromance.com

The Charmer Without a Cause

Katherine Grant

CONTENT RATING

THIS BOOK CONTAINS ON-PAGE physical intimacy and minor violence, as well as themes of grief, systematic oppression, and family separation.

LONDON, 1817

CHAPTER ONE

I N THE SLUDGY SPRING of 1817, ten thousand pounds changed Benjamin Preston's life.

He knew, of course, from the moment he learned about his uncle's bequest that with ten thousand pounds, he would be a different man. A freer man, one who was no longer reliant upon his father and Northfield Hall for money. A more powerful man, one who could take those ten thousand pounds and wield them like a sword against the onslaught of injustices in the world.

He hadn't reckoned that his experience of a musicale in the middle of March would be any different. At the age of twenty-five, he had been attending musicales for seven London seasons already. Sometimes, he attended alone; others, he accompanied one of his sisters or Papa, as he did now.

Never before had the entire room hushed at his entrance.

Never had he walked through a crush and heard whispers from behind ladies' fans that were about him.

What a difference ten thousand pounds made.

He and Papa had barely removed their cloaks before their hostess, the famous actress Mrs. Atwood, rushed over to greet them. "How glad I am you could join my little soiree. Lady Howson was just wondering if she would have the opportunity to be introduced to you this evening."

She whisked them across the room to where a matron in swaths of silk waited with two debutantes, and before Benjamin could even realize what was happening, he was introduced to both young ladies and begged to give his opinion on the music they anticipated that evening.

It was not that no hostess had made an introduction for him before. But Benjamin wasn't sure it had ever been done so eagerly, and certainly not to a marchioness such as Lady Howson, whose husband often publicly called Papa a nuisance.

Ten thousand pounds, apparently, was enough to smooth over political differences.

"I must offer you my deepest condolences on the death of your uncle," the young Miss Kirby said, pressing close enough that the peacock feather in her hair bobbed against his forehead. "I hope you are not too overcome with grief."

Benjamin didn't quite know how to respond. *I am not* would be the truth, but it would not be fair. He could not be overcome with grief. It was only ten years ago, when Benjamin's mother died, that he had even met his uncle, the earl. The countess was Mama's sister, estranged until Mama was so ill from her wasting disease that it was time for final farewells. The earl and Aunt Charlotte had arrived at Northfield Hall in outfits of imported silk and rings encrusted with Indian jewels, a chest of tea tucked in their carriage to keep them comfortable during their stay.

They were kind people, but not principled. Not the way Benjamin and his family were. They did not mind spending more money than a man's yearly wages on a piece of art or keeping shares of the East India Company. Still, after Mama died, they let the Prestons stay at their townhouse when necessary. Aunt Charlotte hosted parties to introduce them to likeminded people in London. She told stories of Mama as a girl and always had a coin purse with her to hand money to urchins on the street.

And now the earl had bequeathed Benjamin ten thousand pounds. Without a single string attached.

He replied to Miss Kirby with a different version of the truth: "I wish I'd had more time with him."

Her companion, Lady Philippa, huddled in. "Do tell us if there is anything we can do to comfort you."

"Now, now," their chaperone admonished, but with such a twinkle in her eye that Benjamin half expected her to rush them off for a private romp in the garden. "Do not overwhelm Mr. Preston with your womanly care, young ladies."

Benjamin wasn't about to complain. Miss Kirby seemed lovely, compassion written across her every expression. Lady Philippa, too, was beautiful, if a little young. Benjamin didn't feel the familiar, exciting flutter of new love for either of them, but still. If these young ladies wanted to cozy up to him—even if all they saw were his ten thousand pounds, and not him—Benjamin didn't mind at all.

Beside him, Papa cleared his throat. "It is lovely to make your acquaintances, but you must excuse us. I promised the Duke of Berkwell we would pay him our regards, and I see him across the room."

As they moved through the crowd, Papa warned, "Don't get carried away by all the excitement. It worked for your mother and me, but it is better to know your spouse well before marrying them than to end up committed to a woman who can't accept the way we live."

As if he needed the warning. Benjamin had no intention of marrying for any reason other than love, and his father damn well knew it. "No one even whispered the word marriage. We were only getting acquainted."

"Caution is your best friend, even when only getting acquainted. Your heart is very large, after all."

Before Benjamin could defend himself, they reached Robert, the Duke of Berkwell. A man only ten years Benjamin's senior, he was both an ally to Papa in Parliament and a friend to Benjamin when in town. He was also wealthy and unmarried; as usual, a dozen women hovered nearby, waiting for his notice.

Benjamin fancied that, for the first time, a few of those women perked up at his arrival, too.

"Ah, my favorite radicals," Robert greeted them. "Good to see you back in the thick of it."

"If you can call a Mayfair musicale 'the thick of it.'" Papa shook the duke's hand.

Robert grinned at Benjamin. "Spent all that money yet, Preston?"

"I still have a few shillings left."

In reality, Benjamin had it in an account at the Bank of England, and he woke up nightly in sweats of dread, afraid of what to do with it. The Prestons were a titled family, but they were not wealthy, particularly not since Papa had divested from colonial and slave imports thirty years ago. Everything they consumed came from their country seat, Northfield Hall, and any profit they earned from their surplus was split among the family, the household, and the laborers.

Benjamin had never imagined possessing ten thousand pounds of his own. Ten thousand pounds was enough to break off into his own household. It was enough to buy private carriages and a whole stable of horses and still have remaining funds. It could pay for a run to win a seat in the House of Commons. It could feed ten thousand children for half a year. It could fund a hundred volunteers to round up signatures for a petition to set a minimum wage for weavers, or for a lecture campaign to gain energy around abolishing slavery, or to establish schools in London for orphans and urchins.

In short, it was more money than Benjamin knew what to do with.

"You'll be getting an invitation from me in the next few days for an afternoon review of my investments" Robert said. "I thought you might be interested in sharing some of that money with one or two of the causes closest to my heart."

"Ah. Thank you."

A footman paused, offering up a tray of drinks. Benjamin followed Robert's lead, accepting a cut-crystal glass of ratafia.

Papa declined anything. Even though he didn't comment, Benjamin could hear the critique: *There is rum in that punch, and you know how rum is manufactured, don't you?*

Benjamin believed in avoiding slave imports as much as the next Preston, but if the punch had already been made and the alternative required some poor maid to go in search of a glass of milk especially for him, then he considered ratafia a perfectly fine choice.

"You'll be particularly interested in the plight of the chimney sweeps," Robert continued. "Have you ever considered how a chimney is cleaned?"

Benjamin had, in fact, and he knew all about the chimney sweeps. He opened his mouth to reply when his attention was stolen: there, in the far corner, the most arresting woman he had ever seen. So tall that her hair, styled high atop her head, nearly brushed the door lintel. Her dress offered the impression of a long torso and even longer legs. She waited on the threshold between the parlor and the corridor, even as two lords passed through. When he first noticed her, she was looking far off in the distance, at something Benjamin felt sure didn't exist in reality. As he watched, she blinked, turned her chin, and disappeared into the corridor.

Benjamin couldn't say what it was about her exactly that caught his attention. The confidence with which she carried her height. The impression that even among a crowd, she had carved herself a private moment. Whatever it was, Benjamin knew, even in that instant, that he needed to meet her.

Mrs. Atwood rang a chime to collect the crowd's attention, then invited everyone to take their seats for the performance. Benjamin followed Papa and Robert, but not before looking again for the woman. His eyes roamed the crowd, searching for her golden head rising above the rest. There: moving towards the seats on the far side of the room, neck bent in a slope as she conversed with a man who barely rose to her shoulder. Benjamin watched long enough that her gaze rose and collided with his.

He looked away first, but not before he recorded the shape of her face in his memory: eyes set close together; a small, solemn nose; lips the color of pink summer roses.

The music began. They were treated to a chamber ensemble of violins, viola, and cello playing a selection of Bach, followed by a German flautist, and finally a furious solo by the first violinist. Benjamin tried to attach his attention to the instruments, or at least to the thick brown eyebrows of the flautist, who swept deep glares across the audience at the start of every phrase.

Yet his mind wandered back six rows and over seven seats to the woman he had never met. The vision of her was already burned into his memory. He hadn't spotted a mother or sister or friends, but a young woman like her wouldn't come to a musicale alone. He wondered who she sat with, and whether they were her relations or friends or—God forbid—her husband.

Benjamin turned his head, just an inch, to see if he could glimpse her over his shoulder.

She was beyond his field of vision. He saw instead the elderly Lady Leighster, a few rows behind, pointing her fan at him as she murmured something to her neighbor. And a whisper from someone else carried over the decrescendo of the flute: "He's still a Preston. Ten thousand pounds doesn't change one's blood overnight."

Benjamin straightened, joining in the applause for the flautist. Papa and Robert both leaned in to murmur advice in his ears:

"I wish *I* were a Preston," said the duke.

"The only opinion that matters is your own," said Papa.

Hearing them together, it came into Benjamin's head as something like, "The only opinion that matters is a Preston's."

The violinist began his solo before Benjamin could deliver a rebuke. He didn't care about gossips; he had walked into the musicale expecting that, as always, people would spurn him because he was a Preston. He had known for years now what he hunted for: a woman who could love both him *and* what his family stood for. A partner who would cherish him as much as she shouldered his burdens with him. A soulmate who cared for the parts of him no one else could know.

Whoever that was would not care about the direction of Lady Leighster's fan or the content of the whispers about him.

He wished his father could understand that, instead of always assuming Benjamin would fall in love at the drop of an elegant hat. He yearned for Robert to know it, too, to stop acting like he was some fragile lamb who needed protection from circling wolves. Giving his heart easily did not make him weak. Being vulnerable did not mean he could not shield himself from blows.

If he were ever going to marry, he must first fall in love. Perhaps this time, he would fall in love with a woman who would marry him.

The music ended, to another burst of applause. Benjamin followed the cues of the crowd: standing, turning to each other to comment on the music, waiting for the ladies before filing out of his row. The whole time, he cautioned himself not to look towards the back. He didn't want to signal his interest too early, not when all eyes in the room seemed to be tracking his movements. He wanted to learn her name before she saw him through the veil of ten thousand pounds.

But when finally he filed into the parlor where refreshments awaited the crowd, he couldn't spot the woman anywhere. Her golden hair didn't extend above the heads of any men; her slender arms didn't fold against any chairs; her rosebud lips didn't purse against any punch cups.

She might be in the courtyard for a breath of fresh air. She might be in the retiring room, seeing to a personal need. She might even have left.

Papa touched his arm. "Time for our farewells. Oliver will be waiting at the coaching inn."

Oliver Chow, just arriving from Northfield Hall for his first trip to London. Oliver, who was practically his brother.

Oliver, Benjamin repeated to himself, tearing his attention away from the crowd. Oliver deserved his focus more than some nameless woman who might or might not care that Benjamin Preston existed.

And yet he looked behind him once more, before taking leave of Mrs. Atwood. And he knew himself well enough to predict he would be looking still, in every theater, in every assembly hall, in every alleyway, until he found once more the woman he didn't know.

WORD SPREAD THROUGH LONDON like typhus. Lydia heard it first from her friend Claudia, Lady Chatteris, the morning after the musicale. By that afternoon, Aunt Camille and Mother were discussing it over tea. At a dinner party of twenty people the following evening, even Father and his windbag friends were dissecting the potential meanings of it:

The Honorable Benjamin Preston was back in London with ten thousand pounds at his disposal.

To Father and his friends, the topic was a source of both amusement and preoccupation. Amusement because apparently, they considered Benjamin Preston under the thumb of his father, Baron Ashforth, who refused to purchase imports from the colonies and funneled every ounce of energy into progressive policies on behalf of the downtrodden. Preoccupation because they worried Mr. Preston might use the money to do something even more radical than his father, though they couldn't fathom what that might be: purchase bread for every man in London? Buy the freedom of a hundred slaves?

To Mother and Aunt Camille and even Claudia, the topic had more immediate consequences. For a man with ten thousand pounds to his name—even if he was still a little green at twenty-five—in addition to a title and entailed estate was a rare marriage prospect.

Lydia considered both points of view with a certain sense of optimism. A man with ten thousand pounds certainly could make a good husband. Even better, once married, a Preston might allow his wife to influence how he spent those funds.

She dressed with care for Lady Gresham's breakfast the following week, for rumor had it that Mr. Preston might be present. Cotton and silk, both imported from various colonies, were banished to the back of her wardrobe. The breakfast was to be outdoors should the rain hold off, so Lydia opted for her blue linen dress with yellow flounces at its hem, a wool petticoat underneath for warmth. Orla, her maid, arranged her hair in curls with a lace cap pinned atop. They decided together that Lydia should wear only the most modest of jewelry, a set of amber earrings and a matching necklace. The only part of her outfit that was not for the benefit of Mr. Preston was the green ribbon pinned in a bow onto her bodice. Her silent declaration to Ireland and Seamus's memory that she would honor them.

The rain did not hold off. Almost as soon as the Devereaux carriage pulled up to Lady Gresham's townhouse, the London drizzle turned into a heavy downpour. A footman rushed out with umbrellas to protect their outfits—if not their poor slippers—as they crossed the black-and-white tiled courtyard into the foyer. Her sister, Adelaide, moaned, "Oh, but it is too warm in here for all these people!" just as Lady Gresham swept across the room to greet them.

"I am so glad you could join us, Lady Devereaux." Their hostess beamed, pressing Mother's hands between her own. Lady Gresham was the stuff of legends: the great beauty of her generation, she had first been married to the elderly Duke of Surrey and spent years following him around Europe; upon her husband's death, she hurried back to England to marry the love of her life before he married another lady. Beyond that, she hosted salons for ladies to discuss political topics and was rumored to be behind several major bills passing through the House of Lords in the last handful of years.

"It is indeed warm in here," she agreed, turning to Adelaide, "but I have ordered the garden doors open to admit fresh air, never mind the rain. Let me introduce you to some of my dearest friends."

It felt as though the introductions lasted an hour. While Adelaide had been to London for two of her own seasons in a fruitless search for a husband, this was Lydia's first visit to England, let alone the capital city. Knowing this, Lady Gresham introduced them to a dozen people: matrons, fellow debutantes, a cleric, three eligible men, and a handful of married couples.

To Lydia's disappointment, Mr. Preston was nowhere to be seen. Yet he was present in nearly every conversation. "Preston the younger is out spending his money before the marriage mamas can set their sights on him, no doubt," pronounced one of the married men.

"Oh, but he is eager to be married," argued Lady Gresham. "Has he not courted at least one young lady each of these past three seasons?"

One of the matrons warned Lydia—with her arm protectively hovering above her own daughter's shoulder—"He is a little young for you, my dear. You'll want a man who is more established in London, since your own family is in Dublin for most of the year."

The comments were enough for Lydia to build an idea of the man in her head. His face would still be youthfully round, perhaps clean-shaven by virtue of his not yet being able to grow a full beard. He would shine with eagerness, since by all accounts he was anxious to please both his father and the young ladies. He might be cocky, too, now that all the attention of London had been squarely on him for a week.

Lydia could work with whatever he looked like, so long as he was a considerate human being at his core.

They had all sat down to eat the lavish buffet when the man himself arrived. The buzz of a hundred conversations dimmed to a hush as he made excuses to Lady Gresham for his tardiness. Lydia tilted in her chair ever-so-slightly so that she could see him for herself.

After all the chatter, the first thing she noticed about Mr. Preston was how average he was. Average brown hair, average height, average build. Even his voice was neither profoundly low nor surprisingly high: it was exactly as one might imagine an Englishman's voice to be. Other than the band of black on his arm—out of respect for his departed uncle—his suit appeared to be the same one the Savile Row tailors made for all the wealthy gentlemen.

Then he looked away from Lady Gresham and across the room. Directly at Lydia. He did not nod or smile or wink, nor make any gesture that would suggest they knew each other. Yet he settled his attention on her as if he had been expecting her. Hoping for her. As if she alone were the reason for his attendance at Lady Gresham's that day.

That didn't feel average at all. Neither was the thrill—strange, sudden, and pleasant—that shot through her body in reaction.

The party resumed its previous buzz as Lady Gresham steered Mr. Preston towards the buffet. Mother leaned closer to Lydia to whisper, "Stop looking so sour, dear. Honey catches flies, not vinegar."

Lydia bristled. As far as she was aware, she looked neither sour nor sweet. She only looked the way she looked, which apparently wasn't good enough for Mother. Fastening a smile onto her lips, she turned to her sister Adelaide and said in her crispest *ton* accent, "Will I catch flies in my teeth now?"

"Spiders, too, I should think." Adelaide slid a tea cake from her plate onto Lydia's, in the silent way the Devereaux children always comforted each other when their parents disappointed them. As the eldest—five years senior to Lydia—Adelaide had most often been the one doing the comforting.

There never had been any pleasing their parents. The Devereaux children were English nobility born in Ireland, a sin for which Mother could never forgive them even though she had done the birthing. She had spent their childhoods fleeing to England for most of the year, while Father had entrusted them to governesses who would make them more British than Irish.

"If you would only take this seriously," Mother hissed through a false smile of her own. "I will not have two spinster daughters."

"I have no intention of remaining unmarried." Lydia had never allowed herself that fantasy, not even for an instant. It was far too tempting. "We have been here a mere month. You must allow me at least another week or two before you declare me a failure."

"I was only in London a fortnight before suitors lined the entire block at my father's townhouse waiting to pay a call."

Lydia slid the tea cake back to Adelaide, who had been forced to hear this speech a hundred times already. Each telling grew more vicious, because Mother couldn't fathom why Adelaide—who, everyone claimed, was the very picture of her most beautiful mother—had only ever attracted a few suitors while she herself had been the coveted diamond of the season. Nor could Mother forgive Adelaide for losing her fiancé to another woman, with the result that she was now a twenty-nine-year-old spinster.

They had lived this drama for half a decade, at least. Now, Lydia could at last script the ending: a successful society marriage for herself and an invitation to Adelaide to live with her at her marital home. The legacy of their parents, the Earl and Countess of Kilkenny, would remain intact without casting Adelaide as some sort of villain.

And, if Lydia could manage it, she would end up in a position to fight with money and power for Ireland's freedom.

Teacup to her lips, Lydia sought out Mr. Preston again as surreptitiously as possible. He wasn't within sight; if she wanted to find him, she would have to twist her neck, or her whole body, or walk directly to his side. Any of that would make it clear to everyone at the party exactly what her intentions were. Yet there were a dozen other debutantes more beautiful and experienced than she who might keep Lydia from securing a natural introduction to the man.

She lowered the teacup, deliberating, when a light hand landed on her shoulder. "Lady Lydia, may I introduce you to Mr. Preston?"

The teacup rattled against the saucer as Lydia turned too sharply. Lady Gresham stood behind Adelaide with Mr. Preston by her side.

He was less average up close. More handsome. Not take-one's-breath-away handsome, but the kind of looks that made one want to lean closer to learn more. A set of brown eyes framing a nose a little too large to be fashionable. One ear slightly larger than the other, making one want to smile, as if he had made himself lopsided as a joke. Lydia went back to those eyes: his gaze was so steady, so kind, that she was loath to look away.

"Lady Lydia Devereaux," Lady Gresham was saying, "and her mother the Countess of Kilkenny and her sister Lady Adelaide."

They all stood; Mother held her hand out for Mr. Preston to kiss and fluttered her eyelashes. "May I offer my deepest condolences to you on the loss of the Earl of Pemberly. We are all the worse off for losing such an esteemed man."

"Did you know him well?" Mr. Preston asked.

"No, I did not have the pleasure of more than a brief acquaintance." Mother hesitated for all of half a breath before adding, "He courted me when we were both young, but alas, Lord Devereaux won out."

"Fate had other things in mind, such as making him my uncle and bestowing you with a happy family." Mr. Preston's gaze drifted briefly over Adelaide before landing on Lydia. She was taller than him—as she was most men—by almost half a head. Nearly as wide as him, too, with thick bones inherited from her father's maternal line. She kept her smile small, as if that would diminish the rest of her, too. "I understand this is your first trip to London, Lady Lydia. How does it suit you?"

"There is so much to see and do here, Mr. Preston, that I feel I can hardly conclude an opinion yet. Except to say there is no comparison to the natural beauty of our home in County Kilkenny."

Mother tittered. "Once you have visited the English country-side, Lydia, you will see there is no comparison between Ireland and England at all."

Lydia knew well enough what Mother meant: they weren't supposed to find Ireland superior in any way to England, the center of the entire world.

Mr. Preston tilted his head, an elegant gesture that managed to acknowledge Mother's sentiment without agreeing with it. "I haven't yet had the honor of visiting Ireland, but I have heard wonderful descriptions of it."

"If you do make a tour of it, I hope you will stay with us," Mother responded.

"I certainly will." He looked at Lydia again. "Perhaps you will allow me to share my meal with you now, and you may tell me more about your experience of the country?"

His gaze did not light her insides on fire, the way a simple glance from Seamus had, yet Lydia felt Mr. Preston's eyes as if they were his arms outstretched. An invitation to speak. An invitation to make herself at peace.

An invitation to be herself.

Lydia didn't plan on falling in love with her husband. That was for Seamus, and it was buried with him, too.

Still, Mr. Preston asked the very question that she wanted every-one in the world to ask her. As Adelaide scooted her chair away to make room for him and Mother fussed over how kind he was to honor them with his company, Lydia had to keep herself from sliding her hand directly into his.

She hadn't realized she felt alone, until this very moment, when she didn't anymore.

"It is a beautiful country, yet there is so much more to it than that," she began, promising herself she would not say too much. That she would not feel too much. Yet, when she looked into Mr. Preston's eyes, she found she could not stop.

Chapter Two

B ENJAMIN COULD HARDLY BELIEVE his good luck. Here was his mysterious woman, the one who hadn't left his imagination for days, and all he had needed to do to secure an introduction was ask. And both she and her mother seemed delighted to have him sit with them.

Lady Lydia Devereaux. Benjamin soaked her in as she told him about her childhood in Ireland. Blond, fair, and tall, as he had observed in his first glimpses at the musicale. Bright blue eyes slicing through small talk followed by a slim, solemn nose. Hers was not a face that smiled easily at a joke. Yet she didn't need to smile, not when her whole countenance was softened by a pair of perfect pink rosebud lips.

That mouth had anchored his daydreams this whole week. He couldn't help but fantasize about running into her at Hyde Park to earn a smile, about dancing with her at an assembly and seeing those lips part with exertion, about whisking her into the garden for a kiss.

"There never was a people more eager for an education. Why, the children will gather wherever a teacher is to be found, even in the hedges by the road, if only for an hour lesson." She shone with emotion as she spoke, a mix of warmth and ferocity that rippled against Benjamin's skin.

"Now, Lydia, no need to get carried away." Her mother grimaced. "She has not yet spent much time in our own great country, Mr. Preston, as you can see. Do you find your tenants at Northfield Hall interested in education?"

Lady Lydia shut her lips as tightly as a castle gate. Benjamin wished he could refute her mother entirely. But he was no rogue: he had been raised to treat people with respect, even when he disagreed with them, and especially when he wanted something—such as permission to court their daughter—from them. He limited his response to, "They are not our tenants, Lady Devereaux. They are paid for their labor in currency, room and board, and supplies. In any case, my mother was very proud to start a school for both Northfield Hall and the town of Thatcham. Nearly every soul over the age of ten in the neighborhood can write their own name, do their sums, name the kings of England, and show you on a map which territories Britain has colonized."

"An impressive feat, especially as I have read that many of your laborers do not speak English natively." Lady Lydia leaned ever-so-slightly forward as she said this, the lace trim of her bodice swaying with the movement.

Benjamin looked up to her blue eyes, so as not to start speculating on the breasts beneath the lace. "That is a challenge in Ireland, too, I understand. How many of the Irish in County Kilkenny speak English?"

"Lydia surely wouldn't know. If they don't speak English, we have no dealings with them," Lady Devereaux responded, a knife's edge lining her words.

Those lips parted for a half second, then closed. Benjamin waited, silently urging her to continue with whatever it was she wanted to say. After a slight nod to her mother, Lady Lydia countered, "I have read about it. I'm afraid I have an unhealthy appetite for newspapers of all kinds, Mr. Preston. The tradesmen and day laborers near the towns usually speak both English and Irish, but most of my father's tenants understand only the most basic of English."

"And you?" Benjamin couldn't help asking, though he suspected Lady Devereaux would object. "Do you speak any Irish?"

Lady Lydia blushed as pink as her lips. "A few words, here and there."

Amazing how even a blush could ignite him so. Benjamin felt like a magnet pulled helplessly by the gravity of each of Lady Lydia's movements. Even her flitting her gaze towards her mother, as if expecting a punishment. Even her reaching for a cup of tea—imported tea, the kind Benjamin would never touch—to distract them all from her reply.

She was beautiful. Eloquent. Passionate—and trying desperately to keep anyone from noticing. Benjamin's breath came fast, waiting for her to say something more.

It was his bad luck that Robert interrupted. "Begging your pardon, Preston, but do you have a moment to become acquainted with a few of my associates?"

He couldn't refuse the duke, not even when his entire being yearned to stay at Lady Lydia's side. Benjamin rose, leaving his plate of barely eaten food on the table between Lady Lydia's and her sister's. The Devereaux women stood as he did, giving him another chance to take in Lady Lydia's long legs, longer torso, and heavenly head rising far above his own.

His heart pounded in his ears as he threw out his parting words: "Perhaps I may call on you this week, Lady Lydia, to learn more about your experiences in Ireland?"

There was no reason to be nervous. He had survived far worse rejections than a lady's declining his offer to visit. And this time, he had ten thousand pounds to recommend him, if she hadn't yet found his conversation entertaining or his appearance appealing.

He knew he shouldn't expect to be rejected. Yet he did, flinching even as Lady Lydia's perfect lips smiled. She bent her neck modestly. "I would be honored, Mr. Preston."

Benjamin's hopes soared.

B Y THE TIME BENJAMIN turned twenty-four, he had been in love eight times.

The first time he lost his heart to a singular woman was at the age of seventeen, to the governess of his youngest sister, Caroline. Miss Lockhart had worn spectacles that caught the light, no matter where they were, and she uttered multisyllabic words like whispers in the night. She had also been thirty-two, a widow, and far too intimidating for Benjamin to do anything other than watch her with moon eyes.

The next year, he had fallen in love with Miss Amanda Fairchurch, a proper London debutante in pastel gowns with a fluttering hand fan. All season, he followed Miss Fairchurch from garden party to opera to ballroom, drawing her away for dances or promenades around the room or just murmuring in her ear that he was glad to see her that afternoon. She had returned his attentions; Benjamin knew he hadn't made that up. She and her mother called on his aunt, at whose townhouse he was staying. She always accepted dances with him. She told him when she would be at Vauxhall Gardens and asked him to meet her there.

Until she announced her engagement to the Marquess of Thorne, beaming up at her fiancé at a midnight waltz, without so much as a word of apology to Benjamin.

That had been his first heartbreak. For nearly a year, Benjamin had believed he would never love again. She had been his soulmate, and he had lost her forever.

Then he had met Arabella, who served ale and pies at the Thatcham pub. They had never done more than flirt, but she had consumed Benjamin's thoughts, had given him a reason to smile, and he realized Miss Fairchurch was not the last woman he would love.

From then, there had been Mrs. Littleton, a widow visiting from America; Miss Emily Sharpe, another London debutante who had discouraged him as soon as he showed up with flowers for her calling hours; Miss Belinda Edgeworth, who had stayed at Northfield Hall for a house party and promised to wait for him, then got herself engaged to a naval captain before the next season even started; Isabella Costellini, the opera singer who had helped him forget all about Miss Edgeworth; and most recently Miss Jeanette de Vere, whom he had courted all throughout the previous spring, whom he even asked to marry him on a quiet afternoon in her drawing room, and who had rejected him with the charm of a banker: "I admire you, Mr. Preston, but you are not the kind of man a woman like me can marry."

Benjamin had recovered from Miss de Vere more quickly than he expected. Her attraction had been in the way she listened to a person, as if each word was more important than the last, and Benjamin discovered once she turned him away that his thoughts didn't linger on her, nor did he lose sleep wishing to turn back time. He felt very little, actually, and had done so for the last year.

Which was, in part, why he was so excited to have noticed Lady Lydia. Whether or not she returned his interest, the very fact that his heart stirred—that he couldn't keep a whistle from his lips—made Benjamin feel more like himself.

"You have that look about you," Papa said that evening as he poured them each a glass of Northfield cider. This was their custom at the end of a day. When he was younger, Benjamin would find himself quizzed on what he had learned from following Papa around: why things operated as they did, who was important to keeping Northfield Hall running, how he had interpreted certain exchanges between certain people. Now, more often than not, they simply shared the pertinent details of their days. "Has a young woman caught your eye already?"

In a perfect world, Benjamin would have kept his love affairs to himself. This wasn't the case, however. Perhaps because his family cared for each other and tracked each other's lives, even as his elder sisters married and his brother Nate disappeared into the Navy. Perhaps because he himself was an open book, unable to keep any secret. Perhaps because love was too grand: when it seized him, it changed him, carving its essence into his thoughts, altering his appetite, filling him with such hope and buoyancy that he couldn't sleep at night.

In any case, he had never yet succeeded in keeping his feelings secret, so he did not try to begin now. "I am enraptured by her, as always." Benjamin offered this up as a joke because if he didn't, his siblings would soon. "There is more to discover about her, of course, but she and her mother have already invited me to call on them later this week."

Papa raised his eyebrows at this.

"She is Lady Lydia Devereaux," he added, in case Papa didn't believe him. "Her father is the Earl of Kilkenny. She is quite passionate about Ireland."

"What about it?"

Benjamin hesitated. Lady Lydia had limited her conversation to topics that did not betray her to be either for or against Catholic emancipation, which was the primary question remaining to be settled about Ireland. In 1801, Ireland's Parliament had been made one and the same as the Westminster Parliament. The country followed British laws and civil codes, and the Church of Ireland ruled as an extension of the Church of England in all things ecclesiastical. Yet most of the country was Roman Catholic, and they were punished for it by being excluded from voting, serving in the government, holding long-term leases, or even hiring more than two apprentices.

"She did not quite say, but I sense that she is sympathetic to the Irish national identity."

Papa took this in with a twitch of his lips. "Lord Devereaux opposes Catholic emancipation and makes no secret of it."

"It would not be the first time a daughter disagreed with her father's politics." Benjamin referred to his mother, who had been disowned by her parents when she decided to marry Papa and assist him in his vision for turning Northfield Hall into a safe haven for the downtrodden.

Papa acknowledged this with a smile. He did that more now: beam at the memory of Mama, rather than retreat into sadness.

"In any case," Benjamin continued, "I hope to learn more about her ideas when I pay her a call tomorrow."

"I wish you great success." For a moment, the conversation lulled. Benjamin hardly noticed, his mind racing with clever things he wanted to say to Lady Lydia. He would begin by asking her which of the newspapers were her favorites; or, perhaps, he would bring her a particularly interesting clipping; or he would tell her the story of how Ellen's husband Max had posed as a carpenter in an effort to write a secret exposé about the Prestons.

Papa broke into the silence. "Have you considered what you will do with your inheritance?"

"Considered it, yes. Decided, no."

Papa passed his cider from one hand to the other. "There are plenty of people telling you what to do with that money."

"I should like to think I am wise enough to listen to advice without being susceptible to it."

Papa smiled at his turn of phrase. "Your fashionable wit will get you farther than those ten thousand pounds, mark my words."

The ten thousand pounds would get Benjamin rather far, though. Of course, he wouldn't invest it in the East India Company or any other shipping ventures, nor would he offer it up to a government fund as most people did, since that interest was earned on the industry of colonization. Still, Benjamin could stretch that ten thousand pounds out to provide a more comfortable existence for himself and a wife—with a solemn nose and rosebud lips, perhaps—for the length of his life.

"If you are open to advice from your humble father," Papa continued, "I would recommend a tour of the empire."

That possibility hadn't even crossed Benjamin's mind. As soon as he heard it, he dismissed it: that was what Papa had done at his age, and the tour had famously been his impetus for finding ways to divest from the colonial economy.

Benjamin wanted to break free of Papa's path, not follow directly in his footsteps.

"There is much to see, and I'm sure it has changed since my travels thirty years ago."

"I'll think on it," Benjamin lied. Finishing his cider, he set the glass on Papa's desk. "For now, I'm off to dinner at Lord Solander's."

"Benny—" But Papa didn't finish his thought at first. He sipped from his own glass, leaving Benjamin in suspense at the threshold.

"What is it?" Benjamin asked at last. He could tell it was some fatherly wisdom, probably the type he didn't want to hear. Papa would warn him against getting too involved in too many causes, or to be mindful of the company he kept, or something like that. He almost hoped that Papa would decide not to say it.

"Your uncle's bequest is common knowledge," Papa said at last. "I hope you are able to tell the difference between a person who finds you interesting and a person who finds your money interesting."

"I'm being mindful."

"Particularly in the case of Lady Lydia."

That pierced the ebullience that had been carrying Benjamin all afternoon. Of course, he knew Lady Lydia might only have smiled at him because she saw ten thousand pounds trailing him around. He chose to believe it was because she was as entranced—or even half as entranced!—as he was by her.

He didn't need Papa casting doubt this way and that.

"I am not a fool."

Papa smiled. "It is more likely that she is besotted with you. What woman wouldn't be?"

Benjamin had a list about a dozen long. He took leave of Papa, however, before doubt could consume him.

CHAPTER THREE

Their next at-home day was two afternoons after Lady Gresham's breakfast. Lydia woke early with a stomach tied in knots. She didn't know if Mr. Preston would come. The duke had introduced him to a few of the other debutantes at Lady Gresham's, all of whom were beautiful and witty and smart. Lydia couldn't tell whether she had made a lasting impression on him, even though he had asked for permission to pay a call.

There was a part of her—an indulgent, secret part of her—that did not want him to call. For if he visited that afternoon, then she would need to flirt with him to get him to invite her on a walk or ask for a dance at an upcoming ball or something else to move the courtship forward. And she would need to keep doing it until he married her.

And then she wouldn't be Seamus's Lydia anymore. She would be the Honorable Mrs. Benjamin Preston. A more powerful woman with a thicker purse, to be sure.

But no longer a girl whose loyalties lay purely with the man who held her heart.

There was no point in indulging those thoughts. No matter whom she loved, Lydia had months ago pledged her life to a cause larger than herself, and she would not stray from it.

Lydia dressed with the assumption that Mr. Preston would call. Her buttercream linen woven in County Kilkenny, with green ribbon laced through the trim of the neckline and puffed sleeves, and a matching green linen sash tied below her bust. An outfit entirely sourced from the countryside near her home at Balise House, to show she wasn't afraid of the Preston family's politics.

Mother was far more elaborately outfitted in a mix of silk and velvet flounces, hair curled stiff by hot irons, and thick clusters of pearls on her ears. Aunt Camille, who joined them almost every day at almost everything they did, was even more resplendent, with a diamond necklace sparkling from her neck. They both frowned upon Lydia's entrance. "You look like a country parish girl," Mother said.

Adelaide—who wore a beige silk afternoon gown—came to Lydia's defense. "You can hardly expect her to catch a Preston wearing imported goods. If you're really serious about this suit, Mother, you should buy up all the Berkshire linen available and redo our outfits for the season."

Mother sniffed. "Mr. Preston, I hope, is only the first of many suitors for dear Lydia."

"Won't you at least wear a necklace?" Aunt Camille pleaded as Lydia took a seat by the window. "They'll think you a fortune hunter otherwise."

"Or my bare neck will trigger their innate male need to provide for an unprotected woman, and they will marry me simply to shield my neck with the biggest jewels they can find."

"These girls are impossible and always have been," Mother muttered to Aunt Camille.

Lydia tuned out the diatribe, one that would last until Aunt Camille chose some other topic to gripe about. She turned her attention instead to the street below. The townhouse—rented for three months—sat on a side street off Berkeley Square. The road ended after only two blocks, and the buildings were all houses for fine families or mews for their horses and carriages. Still, tradesmen came and went with deliveries, servants rushed out on errands, and stable hands and tiger boys leapt here and there to tend to horses.

It was busy enough for Conor Devlin to report to her about their scheme without her family noticing.

So far, he had only come the once, to confirm that he had found someplace to stay in London. He was due again soon to tell her how the rest of their plans progressed.

Lydia's nerves came alive again as she watched the street from her perch. She told herself she was hoping to spot Conor, that all the anticipation churning her stomach was from the wait to begin their plans.

Yet it was Mr. Preston turning the corner who made her heart leap into her throat.

It was unusual for a gentleman to arrive on his own two feet, especially since their street was unpaved, which meant it was packed dirt pocked with manure and trails of litter. Lydia wondered if it was part of the Preston ethos, a type of austere living to keep them closer to the common man whom they swore to represent.

Or perhaps Mr. Preston simply didn't like horses.

He strode with purpose—and mindfulness, for she watched him diverge from a straight path in order to dodge several obstacles of an unsavory nature—up to the townhouse door. Just before he disappeared from her sight, Lydia spotted a bouquet of violets in his hand.

Lydia smiled. Not because she was flattered that Mr. Preston was so eager. Nor because he cut a handsome figure, with or without a horse. Her heart belonged to Seamus, and nothing in this world or the next could change that. She was only happy her plan was working.

Mr. Preston looked nervous as he entered the room. With too much energy, he thrust the violets at Mother, and he tripped over his words to say, "If you will permit me, ma'am, I brought these for Lady Lydia."

"How kind of you." Mother gestured him towards Lydia, her smile fading into a grimace as soon as his back was to her. Lydia knew this moment would be pinned in her memory like a favorite jeweled brooch to pull out and recount in private. *He offered the flowers to me! How gauche!*

Perhaps little exchanges like this—too small to be faux pas, yet not quite the right thing to do—were why people always seemed to be laughing a bit at Mr. Preston as they mentioned him.

Lydia didn't mind a man who wore his emotions on his sleeve. Besides, by the time he had crossed the room to present the bouquet to her, he had mastered his embarrassment. His smile was rueful, as if he were laughing at himself. "A governess once scolded me for picking her flowers without her permission, and I have been anxious ever since not to make the same mistake."

"That governess sounds particularly joyless." When she accepted the flowers, the bottom of Lydia's little finger brushed against the length of his thumb. She wore linen lace gloves from an Irish convent; through the filigreed rose pattern, she felt every inch of Mr. Preston's smooth, sizzling skin.

Anyone might have warm hands, Lydia reminded herself. Especially anyone who had just walked through Mayfair on his own two feet.

It meant nothing at all that his heat spread instantaneously from her little finger to her core.

"Won't you sit, Mr. Preston?" This invitation came from Adelaide, who followed with a raised eyebrow at Lydia, insinuating that she should have been the one to say it.

"Yes, please do." Lydia patted the pillowed window seat beside her. She had chosen this spot purposely: it prevented them from forming a circle with Mother and Aunt Camille, and it also forced them to sit slightly closer than they would if sharing a sofa.

If she was going to solicit Mr. Preston to court her, then she might as well do it as expediently as possible.

He sat. They had to angle themselves awkwardly on the window seat in order to face each other, so that instead of their thighs approaching, as Lydia had imagined, their knees bumped.

Clumsy though it was, the collision still sent heat rippling through her body.

"I searched *The Morning Chronicle* for an interesting article about Ireland to bring for you," Mr. Preston said. He was close enough for her to smell the honey in his cologne—an aroma that made her want to lean in. "All I could find were reports on the trial of the criminals involved in last year's terrible tragedy in County Louth. Do you find that disturbances are increasing, as the newspapers all seem to believe?"

From the other side of the room, Mother interjected, "I hardly think that a polite topic of conversation, Mr. Preston. Would you like some tea?"

Lydia wished Mother on the other side of the ocean. It was ridiculous that somehow the two of them were supposed to collaborate to find Lydia a husband. Mother, who had spent every moment of Lydia's childhood flocking back to England and cavorting with the Prince Regent and otherwise claiming a life she felt had been stolen from her, would never charm the same person that Lydia would. Not when Lydia wanted a husband who would respect her intelligence and afford her pin money without asking how she spent it.

Mr. Preston blushed a little at the admonition. "I apologize. I forgot myself."

"There is much to puzzle one about Ireland," Lydia said, hoping he could tell that she herself didn't find the question about the disturbances impolite at all.

Tricky, perhaps, but not impolite.

She added, "I know many Irishmen felt deeply betrayed when the Act of Union was not followed with Catholic emancipation."

Seamus had harped on that. How they had put their trust in the likes of Lydia's family after the 1798 Rebellion in the expectation that the Irish Catholics would be given the vote. Yet all the Act of Union had done was abolish the Irish Parliament and force British law on the country. That was why it was time for the common Irishman to take his fate in his own hands.

"Tea, Mr. Preston?" Mother repeated.

"No, thank you."

"Nor for me," Lydia added, looking down at the violets in her hand rather than at Mr. Preston. She declined for his benefit, and she hoped both that he noticed and that he didn't suspect her of playing a role on his behalf.

"If tea pleases you, don't abstain on my account," Mr. Preston said, shattering her illusion that she could get away with the performance. "It has already been purchased and brewed. In fact, it is rather a lost cause at this point."

"Oh no, but I don't want any."

They smiled awkwardly at each other for a moment, both trying to pretend they believed the other.

Perhaps both trying to pretend not to be aware that their knees still pressed together, too. At least, Lydia was trying desperately not to think about that fact, or the way Mr. Preston hadn't even tried to shy away from her touch.

The only question she could think of to move the conversation forward would not garner Mother's approval. She asked it anyway. "Do you find it difficult to be in London surrounded by so many imported goods?"

"It requires more vigilance, to be sure, but I never acquired a taste for tea or sugar or any of that, so it does not require very much willpower."

This surprised Lydia. Even dressing for the morning had required such care that she imagined Mr. Preston must always be exhausted, weighing what he could or could not consume on his family's moral scale.

She wasn't sure whether she was relieved to discover he did not find it a burden or if that made it all seem a little less impressive.

As he adjusted in his seat, Mr. Preston's ankle brushed against hers. For just a half second, yet long enough for her to feel it. "Do you have any causes close to your heart?"

"Lydia cares deeply for poor children, of course," Mother replied. "She and Adelaide attend a sewing circle every week to raise money for parish schools."

Acknowledging this with a nod, Mr. Preston returned his soft gaze to Lydia. "Do you find that cause to be isolated, Lady Lydia, or do you consider it to be a symptom of other injuries in our society?"

"I do not believe one can look at any one problem in isolation." She ventured her own foot forward. She found the instep of his boot; almost breathlessly, she continued, "As soon as one begins to suspect one has discovered the source—such as that there are more orphans because their parents are being transported for sedition—one must then consider a hundred others. Why are seditious individuals transported? Why is there no consideration for their families? Why are they partaking in sedition in the first place?"

"Really, Lydia," Mother scolded. But Mr. Preston was smiling, a new kind of smile that looked neither overeager nor polite. Lydia felt it, too, that sensation of kindred hearts meeting.

The sparks flying across her body were only an extension of her performance, not actual attraction. They couldn't be. That part of her had died with Seamus. Lydia couldn't fall in love with her husband; she didn't think she could even want to kiss another man.

This feeling was real, though. A new kind of hope, one that hovered above her plans for Ireland and independence. One that offered a silver lining. She couldn't marry for love or lust. But perhaps she could hope to marry for friendship.

Surely a friendship was a stronger foundation for marriage than the traitorous heat building in her body.

T HEY WERE CHANGING FOR supper at Aunt Camille's when a kitchen maid rushed up to whisper with Orla, who in turn came to murmur in Lydia's ear: "My cousin is here to visit, Miss. Do you mind terribly if I have a few words with him?"

If possible, Conor was supposed to leave notes for her in care of Orla so that no one in the house would be any the wiser that Lydia knew him. When notes were impossible, they had planned for him to claim to be calling on Orla, so that the English servants would simply assume he was Orla's relative. The Irish, after all, had too many children.

"I had better come with you," Lydia replied so that the kitchen maid could hear. "Otherwise you'll spend all night talking with him and forget about finishing my hair."

In her dinner gown—a pastel green poplin printed with a vine motif in darker green—with her hair half-down and bare of any jewels, Lydia followed Orla to the kitchen. Thankfully, it was empty save the scullery maids finishing their cleaning, since the family wasn't eating at home that night. Conor Devlin waited just inside the door, hands tucked in his pockets and a nervous frown fixed to his face.

At first glance, Lydia always thought he was Seamus. He had the same height, same broad shoulders, same sandy blond hair sprouting thick like a halo above his head. Conor's face was narrower, though; his eyes were dark instead of Seamus's ever-changing hazel. And when he saw Lydia, he only frowned more deeply, where Seamus would have lit up like a summer's sunrise.

Sorrow washed over Lydia as her body realized once again that Seamus was gone forever. Dead in the ocean, never to come back.

"Cousin," Orla greeted him, "how good it is to see you again. Have you news of the family?"

They had agreed on this script before leaving County Kilkenny. Conor could say two things now: that everything was just fine, indicating there was no change to their plans, or that their aunt was ill, which would mean he needed help. "Everything is the same as it was before, as far as I can tell," he responded. His gaze shifted to Lydia. "I had a devil of a time finding a position, but I finally got myself hired with a stonemason."

If Lydia already had pin money, Conor would have spent the last few weeks collecting petition signatures instead of looking for work. She pushed away her frustration, reminding herself: soon, she *would* have pin money, if she had to marry herself off to the Prince Regent to get it. Soon, she could bankroll Conor and three dozen more of the men from Kilkenny eager to do something for Ireland.

In the meantime, Conor had found himself a position. And they might be the better for it, since one of the reasons she had convinced Conor to join her in London was to meet fellow Irishmen living in the capital city. She asked, "Have you very many countrymen working with you?"

"Aye." He ducked his head, looking at the cap in his hands instead of her. "None of them much want to discuss the family, though."

That was another code: Conor's first task was to see how many of the Irishmen working in London would sign the petition—or do more, such as solicit signatures themselves.

Lydia struggled to find an appropriate response that would ask her question without being too plain. "They have no sympathy for your troubles?"

He shrugged. "They have sympathy, but they have their own troubles. Most of them are sending money back to their own families or saving up to sail elsewhere. Helping me is a good way to catch bad attention."

Lydia touched the letter tucked between her corset and her breastbone, as if Seamus's words alone could imbue her with the necessary strength. Conor looked to her because he believed she knew what she was about. Now was hardly the time to fail him. "Let me see to the money for your family, then. Keep your companions close, however. We'll need their friendship soon enough."

There was no code for the next part of the plan, so she lowered her voice to a murmur. Conor and Orla both leaned closer in order to hear.

"Our best hope is the petition. We'll need men to help us collect signatures. I'll let you know when I can afford to pay you and them, so that the burden is not so dear."

"Aye," Conor said. A shadow crossed his face, one that Lydia couldn't read. Uncertainty flickered through her stomach. Seamus had been the planner, the one who had issued directions and offered inspiration to keep the movement alive. Lydia was only his substitute, and a poor one at that. Conor must feel his brother's absence most keenly in these moments.

But she worried that the shadow meant more. She didn't quite know why Conor looked to her as a leader, only that from the very moment he showed up in her kitchen, begging her to stop Seamus from being loaded onto the transport ship, she had been the one to come up with the plans. Plans that had been unsuccessful in helping Seamus, that hadn't yet been any more effective than the Ribbonists in claiming independence from England, that hadn't yet even found a group of Irishmen willing to contribute funds. Perhaps that shadow on Conor's face was the same worry that crossed Lydia's heart every time he showed up: that she was leading them to failure instead of to revolution.

"Here." She couldn't let him leave on such an uninspiring note. Reaching into her velvet coin purse, she pulled out a handful of shillings. "Take your friends out to a pub when you have spare time."

Conor tucked the coins into some hidden pocket faster than Lydia could say, "Be careful." He nodded at her once more in acknowledgment.

"You'll stop by next week at the latest, won't you?" Lydia added. "To check on your favorite cousin?"

"Next week," he agreed, and ducked out of the kitchen without further discussion.

Lydia watched him go, anxiety rushing in now that he wasn't there to pretend for. Stopping the Insurrection Act was important, that much she knew. With it in place, the county officials in Ireland could search any man's house or arrest and transport a man for being out after sunset. It was uncivil; it was inhumane.

But stopping it from being renewed by Parliament didn't seem like it was enough. And Lydia didn't know how she was going to bridge the gap between relieving Ireland from the Act and relieving Ireland from England's control entirely.

All she knew was that her plans were going to require money, and a lot of it. If Conor couldn't raise it from his countrymen, then she would have to keep her focus on a surer bet:

Mr. Preston's inheritance.

CHAPTER FOUR

"**B**ENNY IS IN LOVE."

This was how his sister Sophia greeted him when Benjamin joined the family for supper that night. She was in town for the week with her husband, John; Benjamin should have known she would start the evening with teasing. It was her favorite occupation when siblings were nearby.

They were gathered in the cramped drawing room across the hall from the townhouse dining room. The family did not own property in London. For a time after Mama's death, they had stayed with Aunt Charlotte at Partridge House whenever they came to town. After a season or two of that, Papa had decided to lease a separate house where he could hire servants to his own satisfaction and eliminate imported goods as much as possible in a metropolis. And so they were here, in a narrow, four-story townhouse on Peter Street, on the less fashionable side of Soho.

45

Benjamin smiled, choosing to feel the affection in the tease rather than bristle. "That is a lazy guess, even for you, Sophia. Everyone knows I am always in love with *someone*."

"But it isn't a guess. Papa told me himself you've fallen in love with someone new again."

Oliver Chow, who was back in town on his own tumultuous journey with love, turned from a conversation with John to ask, "Oh? Who is it this time?"

John was kind enough to suggest, "Perhaps it is too new for him to want to discuss."

"That goes to show what you know," Sophia retorted. "Benjamin always wants to discuss the woman he loves."

It wasn't so much a want as a need. The ebullience of his heart being captured by a woman so beautiful and smart and interesting—as Benjamin always believed the object of his affections to be—bubbled up so that there was nothing else he could think about but her.

Except with Lady Lydia, Benjamin wished he could protect himself from the conversation for a little bit longer. There was something about her that felt different. More special.

She had made room for him at her window seat when he called that afternoon. Benjamin didn't know why that stuck with him, yet it did. And she had clung to his violets throughout his entire visit. After her mother cleared her throat and declared she couldn't believe it had already been an hour, Benjamin had taken his leave—but looking up at that window seat from the street, he had seen Lady Lydia still there, her nose bent into the violets, a smile on her lips.

And there had been that moment, halfway through the visit, when her delicate silk slipper slid against his boot. A touch that, through the leather of his shoe, Benjamin couldn't even feel. Yet it was the most erotic moment of his year. Even now, remembering it, his face heated, his mind dissolving into white hot bliss.

Benjamin knew better than to believe himself a paragon match. He was not quite handsome, nor was he witty, charismatic, or athletic. The best that could be said about him was that he came from a powerful family; with the earl's bequest, he could add to that a certain amount of wealth. Miss Fairchurch and Miss de Vere had both pretended to return his affection before without interest in a long-term match. He had been a passing amusement for them, while his heart had burned with intense passion for them.

There was a chance he was misreading Lady Lydia, too. She liked violets more than any other flower, perhaps. Or she might enjoy flirting, and not particularly care with whom she did it.

Still, there had been something a little magical about their visit that afternoon, and Benjamin wished he could keep it from his family.

"Shall I run out for a special license for you, too?" Oliver pressed. "We could share a wedding trip back to Northfield Hall!"

Papa said, "No need to get ahead of yourself, Oliver. Benny has a few years yet before he need worry about marriage."

Sophia scoffed, "Isn't it charming how girls are rushed into marriage as soon as they fill out a dress, while grown men are allowed to decide when it is the right time for them personally?"

Benjamin didn't quite register her words. He was still caught on Papa's comment. Of everyone in the room, Papa was the only one in whom Benjamin had already confided about Lady Lydia. He knew she was a debutante, that Benjamin was enchanted, and that she and her family weren't opposed to Benjamin calling on her.

Why, then, would Papa say that Benjamin needn't worry about marriage?

"How do you propose we change that?" Papa responded to Sophia.

"Abolishing the institution of marriage would be a start," Sophia replied. "Though I certainly haven't the energy to do anything of the kind. How about giving women our own money and not stipulating that a father or husband or brother must control it?"

A sliver of Benjamin wanted to rake Sophia over the coals for this debate. She was the one who always bemoaned the fact that their family had to be radical; she didn't believe that avoiding imported goods did an ounce of good and in fact wore silk and cotton without a hint of guilt. If their elder sister Ellen were there—or their younger siblings Nate and Caroline, for that matter—Benjamin would be joining a chorus teasing Sophia for turning out to be just as much a Preston as the rest of them.

He didn't have much energy for that part of him, though, because he was still stuck on why Papa didn't think Benjamin's feelings for

Lady Lydia reason enough to consider marriage. Or perhaps Papa didn't find it credible that Lady Lydia returned his feelings. None of the eligible women Benjamin had loved so far had, after all.

Still, one liked to think that one's own father believed one worthy of marriage, even if no one else in town did.

It was true that at twenty-five, Benjamin was a little young for marriage. Lady Lydia, however, would likely have only this season to find a husband. Perhaps even less: she was a pretty woman from a good family, and there would be suitors lining up for her within days, no doubt.

If Benjamin had any hope of earning her as his wife, he had better strike now. And he would think Papa would understand that, instead of assuming failure before Benjamin had even put the matter to the test.

Oliver's voice rose above everyone else's. "You still haven't told us who the young woman is, Benny. Or perhaps she isn't young at all. Have you fallen in love with a matron this time?"

Benjamin wished Oliver at least had remained his ally. It would seem he would have to stand up for himself, instead, to make his family see that he was in earnest. So he swallowed his remaining ale in one go, rose, and declared himself once and for all: "The lady in question is Lady Lydia Devereaux, second daughter of the Earl of Kilkenny, and I intend to ask her to marry me."

I T WAS AN EASY declaration to make, but not so easy a task to complete. Benjamin couldn't simply walk up to Lord Devereaux and ask for his daughter's hand in marriage, not without first having some degree of confidence that Lady Lydia returned his affection.

Benjamin called again on her family's next at-home day. This time, he borrowed the family phaeton so that he could invite Lady Lydia for a drive in Hyde Park. Purchased secondhand from a carriage dealer in Reading, the phaeton had none of the flash that most other gentleman sported while courting. Benjamin wasn't often one to feel poorer for not having the most expensive items, but as he waited on the steps for the Devereaux major domo to carry his card to Lady Devereaux, he spotted every patch of peeling paint and warped wood. At least the horse, Phoenix, boasted a shining mane and a happy demeanor, though she was neither a thoroughbred nor a particularly attractive beast, since she lacked an eye from the ill-treatment of her previous master.

When Lady Devereaux walked Lady Lydia to the phaeton, Benjamin could feel her judgment rake over every inch of vehicle, horse, and man. Whatever she saw did not make her smile. "No fast driving, Mr. Preston. We are going to the Marquess of Thorne's ball this evening, and I can't risk Lady Lydia being overexcited."

It had been seven years since Miss Amanda Fairchurch had chosen the Marquess of Thorne instead of him. On the average day, Benjamin didn't think about her at all. Yet at the mere mention of the marquess, pain still skittered across his body, stealing his breath. He held out his hand to Lady Lydia to anchor himself back in this moment; she flashed him a smile as she placed her palm in his, leaned her weight onto him, and stepped up into the phaeton.

That was enough to spark him back to life. Benjamin didn't need to earn Lady Devereaux's esteem, so long as he could win Lady Lydia's heart. And she didn't seem at all fazed by a secondhand phaeton.

He helped her maid onto the rear seat, which faced the opposite direction as the driving bench. The poor woman gripped the chair railing with white knuckles. He assured both the maid and Lady Devereaux, "I will drive as carefully as if I am carrying the most precious cargo."

"A word of advice," Lady Devereaux sniffed. "Never compare a lady to a piece of cargo."

But again, Lady Lydia was smiling when Benjamin joined her on the driving bench. A small, delighted smile that made him want to steal a kiss from her lips. When he had spurred old Phoenix into motion, she asked, "What do you consider the most precious cargo, Mr. Preston?"

Even sitting, she was taller than he. She tilted her narrow face a little bit downwards, perhaps so that he would not be looking directly into her nostrils, which gave Benjamin a most enchanting view of her glittering blue eyes.

He turned his attention to the road as he considered an answer to her question. The afternoon was not particularly beautiful, the sky muddy with clouds, and so traffic towards the park was light. "The question is what do I define as precious, and what do I define as cargo? The traditional definition of cargo is goods that are being transported from one place to another, which is why Lady Devereaux wisely objected to my comparison. In that case, I suppose I would define precious by what is most needed wherever I am transporting it. If I were on my way to a battlefield, for example, then bandages and medicine would be most precious. If I were on my way to a famished town, then food would be most precious. Although, the truth is, the most nervous I have ever been driving a gig is when my passenger was my three-year-old niece, who kept trying to launch herself from the seat whenever she saw a pretty flower or distracting cloud."

It was a bit of a soliloquy. He rushed through the last of his words, glancing over to see if Lady Lydia was yawning in boredom yet.

She wasn't. Her gaze danced away only as he looked over, and she returned her attention to him quickly enough with another smile. "Your reasoning seems very sound to me."

"What would be your most precious cargo, Lady Lydia?"

She parted her lips. This, Benjamin had already discovered, was her habit when she was thinking: an open mouth and a far-off gaze, her chin turning away as if to shield her thoughts from any intervention. When she had her answer, she returned to perfect posture like a dancer resuming a pose. "My answer is a bit obtuse, I'm afraid."

He grinned. "It cannot be as obtuse as mine was."

"You'll think I am refusing to answer."

Her face was pink with a blush, which only made Benjamin enjoy the exchange more. He adored philosophical conversations; they were how he formed his closest friendships. To decorate one with flirtation made his blood race. "It is cruel to tease, Lady Lydia."

She smiled a little. "Very well. If you insist on hearing my answer, you must promise not to think the less of me for it."

"I swear it on my honor as a gentleman."

"The only answer I can think of is this." She twisted away again, her eyes landing on the trees of Hyde Park a quarter mile ahead of them. "The most precious cargo I can carry is the trust of another person."

When Benjamin grinned this time, it wasn't because she amused him or because of the fun of the game. It was because she literally charmed him. "You call that obtuse, Lady Lydia. I call it wise."

Her blush deepened, and her eyes dashed around instead of looking at him straight on. Still, Benjamin suspected she was pleased with the compliment.

He turned towards the maid in the back. "And what of you, miss? I'm sorry, I forget your name. What is the most precious cargo you could carry?"

"Me, sir?" The maid gawked at him.

In the same moment, Lady Lydia said, "Orla is her name. Orla Maher."

"Miss Maher, then." Benjamin could have called her Orla, since she was a lady's maid, but it felt too informal for a woman of her age—at least ten years older than he—and whom he hardly knew. "We are debating what might be the most precious cargo in the world. What is your answer?"

"Why..." She thought for a moment, her eyes darting furiously this way and that at the passing townhouses. "I suppose a basket of eggs, sir."

"The wisest answer of all," Lady Lydia declared. Her smile had broadened; Benjamin hoped that what he saw in her now was true delight. "I rely on Orla for all my common sense, Mr. Preston. She has been with us...what, is it ten years now, Orla?"

"Fifteen, miss. Since Lady Adelaide turned fourteen."

The maid spoke with a thick Irish accent that Benjamin could only barely understand. When Lady Lydia replied, he heard a hint of it in the way she ended her words. "You've been doing for me ten years, anyhow. I understand your family values long-term relationships with servants, too, Mr. Preston."

"I suppose that is one way to describe it." They had entered the park, and both Benjamin and Lady Lydia paused every now and then to nod at passing carriages. "Northfield Hall could not operate without our servants and farmers and laborers. I generally consider them to be the true owners of Northfield Hall, while my family is there just to...I don't know, provide direction, I suppose, or to shield them from forces that want to strip away their power."

Again, Benjamin stole a glance at Lady Lydia to see whether he had said too much. In general, he tried not to discuss Northfield Hall, since most people found the concept of an estate that shared its profits with its laborers too bizarre. But if he really thought Lady Lydia was the woman for him—as he had already declared so brazenly to his family—then he needed her to understand how he lived. He needed her to want to live the same way.

A tall order. No wonder his family expected him to end the season unmarried still.

Lady Lydia was thinking about something again, her lips parted, her gaze somewhere past Benjamin's ear. "I think..." She stopped herself and darted a look at him. He nodded in encouragement. "I confess that I think a great deal about power. It is striking to me in Ireland because the power sits with a very small minority of people. And I wonder how that can sustain itself, when there are so very many people living there without any power at all. I suppose the question is: where does power come from, and can a government maintain its power when so many of its people are unhappy?"

Benjamin grinned. An inappropriate response to her senti-ment. But an inevitable reaction to her soul. His heart raced with excitement. In his rosiest daydreams, he hadn't dared hope for a political theory debate on this carriage ride.

If this was what they spoke of as mere acquaintances, he could only imagine the soul-fulfilling conversations they could have in the cocoon of marriage.

For now, he selected a response that would—without advo-cating for sedition—indicate his own personal sympathy with the Irish cause. "We Englishmen like to think we settled the question of tyranny with the Civil War, but it seems to me we only settled it for the landed gentry of England."

They understood each other; Benjamin sensed it like the ringing resonance of a perfect harmony.

"Do you suppose change is possible?" Lady Lydia asked.

"To believe the opposite is to give up hope. It might be more realistic, but it is not the way I want to live."

"You have the example of your parents, too. From what I have heard, they have changed the world, at least within the confines of Northfield Hall."

His parents set an excellent example. The question Benjamin struggled with was if he could effect change, too, or if he would only keep his father's legacy from crumbling. "I should like to find a way to impact the world myself."

Again, Lady Lydia hesitated, a thought clearly formed in her mind yet not quite leaving her lips.

"Do you have any ideas for me?"

She blushed. Looked down at her hands in their kidskin gloves. "Perhaps you would take up the Irish cause."

"Perhaps I could." Benjamin didn't want to mislead her, though, so he confessed something he couldn't quite bring himself to say to anyone else: "The trouble is that one day, I feel committed to one cause. Ireland, for example. Then tomorrow, I'll be walking down the street and see a woman dying in the gutters, and I will resolve to do something about making sure everyone has a safe place to live. The next day, I'll meet a fellow from the West Indies who convinces me my energy is best spent advocating for the end of slavery. And then I'll learn about something terrible happening in Calcutta, and I will declare *that* is the cause I must champion. I am inconstant."

Lady Lydia tilted her chin downwards. "You are overwhelmed."

"I am ineffective."

They broke away from the conversation to greet a cousin of Lady Lydia's. The small talk—a comment on the likelihood of rain, a compliment on Lady Lydia's hair ribbon—made Benjamin's teeth ache. When at last he could pull the phaeton away, he worried that they wouldn't recover the intimate nature of their conversation.

Lady Lydia waited until they were out of earshot to say, "Perhaps it is impertinent of me to ask, but did your uncle the Earl of Pemberly have a specific cause he cared about? I understand he left you a bequest, and I wonder if he hoped you would do something particular with it."

So she did know about the inheritance. Benjamin was a little relieved that it was in the air between them, rather than worrying about whether she knew. "He left no instructions. It is up to me to use as I see fit. The wisest course is probably an independent income. My father wants me to put some of it towards a trip across the empire." Benjamin almost didn't ask the next question. He thought it through twice before saying: "What would you do, if it were your ten thousand pounds, Lady Lydia?"

This time when she hesitated, it wasn't because she was looking off into the distance conjuring up an answer. Lady Lydia looked at him directly, twisting her lips against each other, and he could feel her deciding whether or not to trust him with her reply.

He willed her to say it. He didn't know what he wanted her to answer, but he knew that if she parroted something that anyone in polite society might say, his heart would sink.

At last, she decided to speak. And it was clear her reply was the truth, for otherwise, she would not dare to say it. "I would use those ten thousand pounds to secure Ireland's freedom as an independent republic."

Miss Maher gasped, even though all along she had been pretending not to listen to the conversation.

She needn't worry that Benjamin would take offense or carry Lady Lydia off to the authorities for seditious speech. He didn't feel her passion for Ireland's independence, but the fact that she felt it was exactly what he wanted to hear.

He had never realized it before, but Benjamin wanted to marry a revolutionary. And at last, he hoped, he had found her.

CHAPTER FIVE

LYDIA TRIED HER BEST not to get caught up in dancing at the London assemblies. The trouble was she liked dancing too much; she was liable to put too much of a jump into her hops and too much of a sway into the promenades around her partners. She did not want to give the impression of being a frivolous, silly creature by dancing with abandon. Whichever husband she caught needed to understand that she was serious minded, that she harbored independent goals, and that she intended to borrow his suit of armor rather than rely on him entirely as her white knight.

It had been a week since her ride through Hyde Park with Mr. Preston. A week since she had laid bare exactly what her goal was. Fool, she had called herself, remembering in horror that she hadn't even cloaked her words in any sort of code. And then in the next moment, she went wild with hope, for Mr. Preston hadn't recoiled in horror. He had, in fact, smiled before changing the topic, as if her words had never existed.

His smile had sizzled all the way through her skin.

Still, Lydia had not yet won him. When she looked at it from a practical perspective, she decided she could not relax until she had signed the marriage register. And so she continued to cast her net, especially at these balls where Mr. Preston seemed not to be invited. At the moment, she danced with the new Duke of Berkwell, whose cousin had famously freed all the slaves on the family's Jamaican plantation. The duke was older than Lydia by at least a decade, was a full head shorter, and kept laughing off everything she said instead of engaging in conversation. All that aside, he was handsome enough, and he certainly had the money she needed to stay involved with Conor Devlin.

"You dance very well, Your Grace," she said as they waited to rejoin the dance at the top of the line.

"Not half as well as you, Lady Lydia." He was a little breathless from the exercise, and very red in the face. "No wonder you have caught the eye of my friend."

Lydia didn't know what he meant. She feared he was about to be horrid, perhaps spew something lewd at her under the guise of an anonymous "friend." All she could think to say was, "Oh?"

"Mr. Preston." The duke smiled, as if he could see how much his response relieved her.

It was relief, after all, not delight, that lifted her so.

"I see much of myself in him, and I make a point of keeping in touch with him. Just yesterday he was waxing poetic to me about a woman so beautiful she could make the sun weep, so intelligent she could fill libraries with her thoughts, so mesmerizing she could make Don Juan himself commit to monogamy."

The duke recited the words with a blend of drama and sarcasm. Lydia felt sure that if Mr. Preston had said them himself, they would be flattering, not hackneyed.

"He must have been speaking of someone else, Your Grace. The only titles of those that I boast any claim to is intelligence."

"Ah, the lady is modest. I am glad to see it, for too often Mr. Preston has so turned the head of an admirer that she ends up seeing another man entirely."

They had to rejoin the line then, taking up the dance from its opening figure. Lydia could barely focus on the steps—balance, allemande, promenade, and balance again—as she swirled the duke's comments around in her head. She couldn't quite make out the purpose behind anything he had said. It wasn't to court her: there had been too much of an edge to his words for flirtation. It wasn't to vouch for Mr. Preston: he had said nothing by way of recommending Mr. Preston to her. If anything, it seemed His Grace wanted to warn her against misusing Mr. Preston.

How a gentleman of the peerage with income and an estate entailed to him could possibly be misused, Lydia didn't quite understand. Yet, as the duke reclaimed her hand for the next balance, she decided not to prickle at His Grace's presumption. If he was willing to protect Mr. Preston, then Mr. Preston must be a friend worth protecting.

"I admire Mr. Preston very much," she said, hoping her words were loud enough for the duke but not so loud that the entire line of dancers could hear. "He and I share many thoughts about how life should be lived. The same principles, if you will, which I have always believed must be the basis of a sound marriage."

The duke pushed her away for the promenade. It was getting to the end of the set; soon, their conversation would end when he returned her to Mother, who beamed from beside the garden doors at the sight of Lydia dancing with a duke.

It was obvious now that he was not considering her as a match for himself. Lydia knew she should be at least a little disappointed, for he was one of the few prospects she felt confident would afford her the money she needed. If Mr. Preston did not ask for her hand, or if Father turned him away for some reason, then Lydia needed to have another suitor, and she didn't have the patience to wait for another season to find him.

She had learned from Adelaide's mistake of counting chickens before they hatched. Early in her second season, Adelaide had struck up an understanding with the second son of a marquess. Like her, he had believed himself incapable of falling in love with a person eligible for marriage, and so they had agreed on a marriage in name only, to satisfy their parents and protect each other from rumor as they went about separate love affairs.

Then he had married a richer heiress, leaving Adelaide to the mercy of gossips and family.

Lydia was playing the game with more strategy. If the Duke of Berkwell did not consider her a potential match, then she need not waste time inviting him to call on her or trying to solicit another set of dances at tomorrow's ball. But she would use him as her emissary to Mr. Preston, if she could.

"If I may confess, Your Grace, every night I look for Mr. Preston at these balls, yet every night I am disappointed. Does he not dance?"

The duke's hand was sweaty even through both their gloves as he led her through the final balance. Then their arms intertwined so he could escort her back to Mother. "Mr. Preston is selective about the company he keeps, or perhaps it is the other way around. A principle, as you say, that his wife will have to bear as well. I am sure, however, that if you asked him to dance with you, no force of nature or human strength could stand in his way."

It was as Lydia had suspected: Mr. Preston wasn't attending the balls because he wasn't invited, or because he objected to some aspect of the hosts. A peculiar life for a peer. One that might be lonely if they spent very much time in London.

Lydia smiled at the duke. "It is a good thing that I too am selective about the company I keep. Or at least, I desire to be, once I have more autonomy in such things. Your Grace, of course, will always be welcome to pay me a call. Perhaps you can join Mr. Preston tomorrow and help me encourage him to hold a private ball?"

The duke had an easy grin, that much could be said for him. He deposited her hand into Mother's with a bow. "Lady Devereaux, I am indebted to you for introducing me to your charming daughter. Are you at home tomorrow to callers?"

Mother let out a great, nervous titter that had everyone nearby looking at them. "To you, Your Grace, we are always at home."

"I shall see you tomorrow afternoon, then." And he left Lydia with a wink that only she could see.

"A duke, Lydia," Mother breathed. "Just think!"

For once, they agreed. Having the Duke of Berkwell—particular friend to Mr. Preston—join them for tea tomorrow could only lead to positive outcomes.

THE QUEUE OF CARRIAGES and single riders waiting to dismount at the Devereaux townhouse crept all the way to Berkeley Square. Benjamin thought at first Lord Devereaux must be holding an emergency political meeting, until he noticed that most of the gentlemen ahead of them held extravagant bouquets of flowers in their hands.

"Did you happen to mention you intended to call on Lady Lydia to every person at that ball last night?" he asked Robert, peering out the window of the ducal carriage.

"Only to Lady Devereaux herself." Robert, damn him, grinned in the face of Benjamin's consternation. "You don't want Lady Lydia to choose you from a dearth of suitors, do you? Much better to be her selection from a wide field of contenders."

"Except I am hardly the prime choice from a wide field of contenders." Just comparing himself to Robert reminded him of all he lacked. With only a barony, his family was among the lowest of the peerage. The profits from their land were split among hundreds of farmers and laborers, leaving them with only a modest income. Neither did Benjamin have the duke's easy humor or social standing.

"Oh, my mistake. I thought you admired Lady Lydia for her intelligence and beauty, not because you thought she would be an easy prize."

Ordinarily, Benjamin appreciated it when Robert disputed his nonsense. Right now, their carriage ten deep in a line to call on Lady Lydia, it only blackened his mood even further.

No matter how many confidences she shared with him or how many smiles she slipped him, she wouldn't consider him for her husband when she had so many options available to her. She would choose a duke, or a man with a hundred thousand pounds to his name, or the champion of Gentleman Jackson's boxing club who could lift her above his head with his littlest finger.

"It is inconsiderate of everyone to arrive ahead of me," Robert said after Benjamin failed to reply. "After all, I'm the one who put the idea in their heads. Let me see what we can do about that."

He stuck his head out the window to confer with the driver. Benjamin slid to the middle of the bench, drawing his cape around him like a child trying to hide inside a blanket. It had been Robert's idea to go together to Lady Lydia's; he had come to their breakfast meeting on supporting the Manchester weavers crowing that she was besotted with Benjamin and that arriving in a ducal carriage would be just the thing to earn the approval of Lord and Lady Devereaux.

At least Benjamin didn't actually have to contend with Robert. He would never stand a chance against a rich, handsome duke.

"We're walking," Robert announced as a groom opened the carriage door for them as solemnly as if they had arrived at Clarence House.

Benjamin kept his fingers curled tightly around the edges of his cloak. "They will only make us wait in the parlor for the sitting room to clear."

"No one makes me wait for anything." This Robert emphasized by raising a single eyebrow. Because he was handsome and a duke and able to do things like that. If Benjamin ever tried raising just one eyebrow, his whole face contorted into a horrifying mask.

"Very well, then I'll be left waiting while you are invited in to flirt and compliment and take up an entire hour of her time."

Robert leveled him with a look rarely seen from the duke: one of impatience. "I thought you wanted to marry this lady."

"I do."

"It doesn't seem like it, if you are surrendering so quickly at the first sign of resistance. How were you planning to react the first time you and your wife disagree? Run off and sulk?"

It was hardly a fair comparison. If Benjamin did ever manage to marry, it would be to a woman who loved him as fervently as he did her. Their disagreements wouldn't be about whether one had time to see the other.

Still, he took Robert's point. He was being monumentally unfair to Lady Lydia. It wasn't her fault that all these suitors were suddenly crowding her door. All this week, she and Benjamin had shared lovely visits together. Their conversations hadn't come close to any topic as dear as her political views on Ireland—mostly because her mother or aunt were always chaperoning—but whatever they did talk about, it felt like a conversation with an old friend. Except more exciting than that, because there was the thrill of discovery: that racing heartbeat, that feeling that one can't get one's words out fast enough, all because one has discovered a new someone whose soul resonates in harmony with one's own.

She always smiled when he arrived. Benjamin watched them overtake her face, first crooking her lips, then crinkling her eyes, and finally lifting that solemn little nose a little closer to Heaven. He didn't think those were polite smiles; his whole heart believed she truly was delighted to see him.

And then there was the way she always found some reason to touch him. Her fingers lingering as she accepted flowers from him. Her shoulder brushing his as she leaned past him to pour tea. Every now and then, when her mother was looking the other way, her foot slipped up his ankle again.

Benjamin didn't dare push the game too far. But there was no doubt in his mind she *was* playing the game with him.

None of that was erased by a new line of suitors. As much as any lady was at the mercy of marriage-matching logic, Lady Lydia had a good head on her shoulders. She asked him questions about Northfield Hall that suggested she respected his family's principles; she engaged with him about topics published in the more forward-thinking newspapers; the only time she had ever mentioned money was when they had discussed what he might do with his inheritance. The qualities that Benjamin considered his weaknesses might not be liabilities at all.

He followed Robert out of the carriage. The violets he had brought—purchased always from the same flower girl, Tessa, who fed herself and two brothers with the proceeds from each day's flower sales—were wilting in his fist and looked paltry compared to some of the bouquets they passed as they marched around the corner onto Dover Street. Benjamin refused to allow those comparisons in. He was now resolute: he would visit with Lady Lydia as if it were any other afternoon. He would bask in her smile, enjoy her conversation, and make her feel cherished. He would be himself, in other words, and he would have to hope that was enough.

As predicted, Robert's title worked like magic to allow them to jump the queue. Lady Devereaux rose from her seat within the crowd to coo over the duke. To Benjamin, she said only, "How lovely to see you again, Mr. Preston," and directed the maid to take his violets.

He sought out Lady Lydia's gaze. The furniture in the room had been rearranged to form an oval, and she sat at its apex on the far end of the room in an ornate mahogany chair. She was more decorated than usual in a blue silk gown, a white organza fichu, and a gold necklace with a diamond pendant, with a pearl net in her hair. This was the daughter of an earl, while the other lady he had come to know and admire—who wore simple linens and relied on ribbons for adornment—must be plain Lydia. She looked stiff in her chair, her chin held unnaturally high, a false smile on her lips.

Then she looked up, at him. With a blush, her expression softened. She rounded her eyes, as if to say *Can you believe this nonsense?*

Benjamin knew in that moment what to do. There was no point trying to pry his way through the crowd to get to her side, only to conduct an awkward conversation overheard by a dozen competitive suitors. If he wanted to win Lady Lydia, he had to play the game his own way.

He gave her a wink. Then, he went in search of her father.

CHAPTER SIX

LYDIA TRIED TO COUNT her blessings. She had gone from one solid marriage prospect to a dozen potential suitors, all of whom seemed desperate to fill the sitting room that very afternoon. The son of an earl in a tight black coat; the fourth son of a duke in red regimentals; a viscount with powder over his age spots; a recently-returned nabob wearing an orange turban to signify his new Indian fortune. Their perfumes, colognes, and sweat vied in the air for dominance. Lydia breathed through her nose, trying to present herself as the impeccable young woman who had caught the Duke of Berkwell's eye.

She wished Mr. Preston had remained in the room. Even though he would distract her from her main goal, which was to cultivate one or two of these men as new suitors. If he were there, he would say something clever to deflect the viscount's old-fashioned compliments (*Your eyes shine like the diamonds I should like to cover you with*). He would know how to ask a question of the nabob to reveal his politics without coming across as pointed or political. When it all felt so very overwhelming—as it did right now, with Mother greeting yet another newcomer—Mr. Preston would give her a little wink, and the world would feel small and manageable again.

Instead, she looked to Adelaide for help. Her sister perched on the settee on the other side of the oval, chatting with a handful of callers who were waiting their turn to make an impression upon Lydia. But Adelaide never had been any good at this part: she was beginning to look like a drowned cat, her hair wilting in its coiffure and desperation haunting her eyes. Adelaide wasn't the one to save Lydia from the officer's lecture on battle strategy.

Her rescue came from the most unlikely source: Father. That he was at home was surprise enough, since ordinarily he went off to White's club in the morning. Mother had cajoled him to remain since they were expecting the Duke of Berkwell, and at first, Lydia thought he had come down to greet their visitors. Except rather than enter the sitting room, he gestured for Mother to join him for a private word.

Even more curious. Unless they couldn't help it, Lydia's parents avoided being in private together.

When Mother returned, her eyes were bright with excitement. Too loudly, she announced, "Please excuse Lady Lydia, gentlemen. Mr. Preston has requested a private word with her."

The Duke of Berkwell grinned. The nabob sputtered. The viscount smirked.

Lydia's stomach flipped in a somersault both hopeful and painful. There was only one reason her parents would be so publicly granting her time with Mr. Preston: a marriage proposal.

It was exactly what she wanted. Yet her mouth went dry. Her ears rushed with her pulse. When she stood, following her mother's beckon, the room tilted and for a moment, all she could see was black.

And Seamus in the night, his eyes shining like beacons in the moonlight. *Say you'll be mine, Lydia. That's all I want.*

Lydia took a deep breath, and her body righted itself. She followed her parents out of the sitting room, down the corridor, and upstairs to the more private family drawing room. She was doing this for Seamus, she reminded herself. For Seamus, and for Ireland, and for her own conscience.

"Did you see how Mr. Sewell went white?" Mother said as they climbed the stairs. "He'll be next to propose, mark my words."

"Next?" Lydia echoed.

"Yes, of course. You won't accept Mr. Preston. Not when you can make a much better match."

Father added, "His income, when examined, is paltry beyond the ten-thousand-pound inheritance. We shall find you a much more suitable husband, with better political connections. You must let him down gently, however. It does not do to hurt a man's ego."

More suitable in their terms, of course. They wanted her to cling to status instead of morals. Lydia nodded along like an obedient daughter. She allowed Mother to pinch her cheeks pink before the footman opened the door. And she accepted a stern, emotionless "That's the way," from Father.

Then she entered the drawing room. The door shut behind her. And she was alone for the first time with Mr. Preston.

He looked nervous. He stood by the window, hands folded behind his back, which should have been a calm posture. Only his elbows weren't still, for he was worrying his fingers behind him. He looked pale, too, his dark eyebrows standing out more than usual on his forehead. When she entered, he smiled, then straightened his mouth as if it were better to be solemn, and then he smiled again as she approached.

A handsome man. The kind of man any woman should be proud to call her husband.

"How nice it is to be in a quiet room again," Lydia said to break the silence. Her voice sounded tinny and false. She remembered how it had done that the first time Seamus kissed her, too. That time, it had been from excitement and a little bit of danger. This time, it was from pure, unadulterated anxiety.

She wished she could slip away to read Seamus's letter one more time. To remind herself why she was doing this.

"It was a bit of a zoo down there, wasn't it?" Mr. Preston cleared his throat, erasing his smile again. "Your father has been kind enough to grant me a few minutes alone with you, so I won't tarry. You see, the thing is, Lady Lydia…"

She waited. He wasn't looking at her anymore, casting his gaze instead behind her, then down at the floor, then out the window.

"I'm trying to find the right words. Well, I suppose, here it is: I am captivated by you, Lady Lydia."

Now he looked directly at her. There was no smile. Only his eyes, brown and endless and full of an emotion she knew but did not feel.

"You have perhaps heard of how my parents married for love. For my whole life, I have hoped that I would have that opportunity as well. My father could not have achieved what he has without the support of my mother, and she achieved a great deal as well because she had him by her side. Since meeting you, Lady Lydia, I have dared believe that perhaps I have at last found the person who could be my wife in just such a way. I am charmed by you, as I said, yet even more than that, I believe we can forge a life together on shared values the way my parents did. My fortune is not large, and there are certainly some sacrifices involved in being a Preston. However, I can promise to make you comfortable and to do everything in my power to make your own visions come true. Lady Lydia, would you do me the honor of becoming my wife?"

The sting in her eyes surprised her. Lydia had not expected to feel emotional about marriage. She was arranging it so that she might feel as few emotions as possible. And yet, tears blurred her vision.

Perhaps because it wasn't Seamus in this drawing room. It wasn't Seamus with his beautiful hazel eyes and lumbering shoulders she was about to accept. It was someone else, and that was all her fault.

Mr. Preston waited for her response. He was doing his best not to look terrified, Lydia could tell, and yet his eyes were so wide, his breathing so shallow. She had to say something soon, or the poor man might faint.

"My parents have advised me against accepting your proposal. They think I can make a better match. I daresay they don't approve of your politics, either." She hadn't meant this to sound so ominous, but she could see him rearing backward, receiving her words as a rejection. "I only want you to know that they will not greet this news with joy. If you are willing to bear that, though, I would be honored to say yes. I feel the same as you: we can build a beautiful life together."

Mr. Preston grinned. Laughed a little, too. "Oh, Lady Lydia." Hands flying forward, he came closer in a delighted stumble. "Do you really accept? May I really believe this is happening?"

Lydia surprised herself with a giggle. From relief, surely. She had been hoping for this outcome, and here it was. Why shouldn't she be happy? "You may, Mr. Preston. I am truly going to be your wife."

Their hands found each other, quite without Lydia realizing it. He still wore gloves, soft kidskin ones that felt like velvet on her fingers. His grasp was firm, like a dance partner who would never let one spin off beat. Lydia found herself squeezing back.

"We can marry in Ireland, if you like," Mr. Preston offered. "Next spring, perhaps. I have heard spring is beautiful there. Or the summer. Whenever you like, wherever you like."

"I don't want a long engagement. Let's marry soon, before the season is out. At St. George's—that will make my parents happy."

Mr. Preston's eyes widened a little in surprise. Still, he grinned, "Whenever you want. Your wish is my command."

"I am so very happy." It was a lie. One she felt bad about, especially because it made Mr. Preston look that much more delighted. Lydia squeezed his fingers again.

When she had imagined the physical side of marriage—which she tried very hard not to do—Lydia had pictured holding Mr. Preston's hand the way she held Adelaide's. A friendly, comforting grip.

She hadn't expected it to be like touching a hot iron. She hadn't anticipated that his fingerprints would light a fire across every inch of her skin.

He opened his mouth, as if to say something more. Lydia didn't want to hear him say how happy he was, and she couldn't bear to say it again herself. So she followed the heat in her body and kissed him.

It was brief. A surprise to them both. It could have ended there, a solitary moment of flesh against flesh.

Except that first brush of the lips wasn't enough. They both leaned in for another, this one a little longer and a little firmer. Lydia inhaled the scent of Mr. Preston—and wanted another gulp. He smelled like a grassy meadow and butterflies dancing across the sky. What a heavenly place to be.

She should have been the one to finish it. She should have remained in control. Yet the kiss ended because Mr. Preston backed away, desire deep inside his eyes.

"You have made me the happiest man."

Lydia tried to summon an appropriate response. One that assured him she wanted this just as much as he did. But he wasn't Seamus; she hadn't made Seamus the happiest man even though he was the one who deserved to be; and now—worst—she had enjoyed a kiss that wasn't Seamus's.

Mr. Preston didn't notice the guilt breaking across her like a cold sweat. He lifted her hands and kissed her knuckles. "Let us tell your parents, shall we?"

Lydia nodded. Her hands released, she pulled them to her sides and wiped them on her skirt, as if that could remove the desire from her body. She inhaled, sucking in the stuffy air of the drawing room as Mr. Preston crossed to the door to fetch her parents. This was all part of the plan. She was doing this for Seamus and for Ireland. She was not a horrible, miserable wretch.

And yet, no matter how she tried to summon Seamus's face to her mind, Mr. Preston's kiss lingered on her lips.

Chapter Seven

Benjamin couldn't believe it. Not as they announced the engagement to Lord and Lady Devereaux; not as the cluster of gentlemen in the sitting room gaped at him; not even as he sent out letters to Ellen and Sophia and Nate and Caroline and everyone at Northfield Hall.

Lady Lydia had said yes.

Lady Lydia wanted to be his wife.

Lady Lydia wanted to marry him as soon as she could.

"Are you sure you don't want a longer engagement?" Papa asked when Benjamin told him the good news. "You could take a tour of the East Indies first, then marry Lady Lydia when you return."

"A tour of the East Indies would take years!"

"It would afford you more time to get to know Lady Lydia. Even you must admit you don't know her very well yet."

Benjamin was too excited to let his father's skepticism deflate him. Still, he noted it. "How well did you know Mama before marrying her?"

"Our circumstances were different."

Different because they had been compromised and forced to marry, even though they were all but strangers to each other. "I know Lady Lydia much better than you knew Mama, so you have nothing to worry about. A swift wedding is what she wants, so a swift wedding is what she will get."

Papa looked away to say, "I am more concerned about *why* she wants a swift wedding."

"Her sister was disappointed by a long engagement. The cad went off and married someone else." Benjamin didn't quite remember all the details. Lady Lydia had shared the story with him on one of his afternoon calls, her voice hushed so that Lady Devereaux wouldn't overhear.

"If she knew you better, she wouldn't worry about the same thing happening." Papa phrased this with an apologetic grimace, as if he thought he were winning the debate.

The bubble of perfection that had surrounded Benjamin since Lady Lydia accepted his suit began to quake. All because Papa couldn't believe a respectable young woman would find Benjamin suitable for her husband. More than suitable: she wanted to marry him, and she didn't want to wait any longer than they had to.

"I do not need your protection, Papa. Only your blessing, if you don't mind giving it."

His anger must have bled into his voice because Papa cleared all dismay from his expression. "Of course. It is a blessing to bring someone new into the family. And, after all, yours will be the most respectable wedding yet of all your siblings."

So wedding planning overtook the household. Lord and Lady Devereaux arranged for the announcement in the newspaper; Benjamin clipped it himself and framed it as a wedding present. He worked with Mrs. Trim, who looked after the townhouse, to prepare a suite of rooms for Lady Lydia, and sent instructions to Mrs. Chow to do the same at Northfield Hall.

And now, two weeks later, the Devereaux family was coming for supper with as many of the Prestons as Benjamin could assemble: Papa, Ellen and her husband Max, Sophia and John, and sixteen-year-old Caroline. Nate—Benjamin's only brother—was somewhere at sea with the Navy.

It was Lady Lydia's first visit to the Preston household. Benjamin had visited her every afternoon since the engagement. Mostly, they talked about the future: when they should retire from town to Northfield Hall, how often Lady Lydia wanted to visit Ireland. Benjamin had spared a few moments, however, to prepare her for the Preston way of life. In an effort to curb slavery and exploitative colonization, Benjamin and his family didn't use any imported goods. What that meant for the evening was that they would be eating food sourced from local butcher shops and vegetable markets. Anything sweet would be made so with honey, rather than cane sugar. Instead of French wine and brandy, their spirits would be elder wine and ale made at the Northfield Hall brewery.

Benjamin hoped this first taste of their lifestyle wouldn't make Lady Lydia regret accepting his suit.

His siblings assembled in the sitting room wearing their best London outfits. Ellen, who despite being a viscountess spent most of her days at her carpentry work, had swapped her usual work dress for a delicate linen evening gown. Her husband, Max, wore a black suit with his long hair falling about his face. Caroline, who at the age of seventeen was visiting London for the first time, wore a white linen dress with pink ribbons and a silver filigree pendant around her neck. Meanwhile, Sophia had, as usual, bucked the family collective to wear silk—imported from Damascus—and her husband John was in a black cotton suit.

Benjamin inspected them as he waited for the Devereaux carriage to arrive. Lord and Lady Devereaux had made their shock—and dismay—very clear when Lydia accepted him. He did not want to make apologies for his family; he did not want to feel shame about the family he belonged to; yet Benjamin felt the need to somehow make them a little bit less objectionable for this first dinner.

After all, Lady Lydia could still cry off, if she realized that life as a Preston did not suit her.

"I think it's all very romantic," Caroline was saying, clearly defending Benjamin to the crowd. "A lady who cannot wait another month before marrying. That shows it is true love, doesn't it?"

"True desperation, anyway," Sophia said. Then, catching herself, clarified, "Oh, Benny, I didn't mean it like that. Desperation is good. Lord knows I was desperate when I married John."

Benjamin didn't think she had meant to imply that Lady Lydia was desperate to tear off his clothes, though. Her tone had not been crude; it had been worried. It was the same anxiety that had leached into Papa's words these past few weeks and that even now had Ellen frowning in that maternal, thoughtful way of hers.

"I cannot wait to meet the lady," Ellen declared for peacekeeping. "She has a good head on her shoulders to choose you for her husband, that much I know."

Max, with his big imposing smile, said, "As for myself, I am excited to see Lord Devereaux squirm as he is forced to break bread in the infamous House of Preston."

"We will not agitate him," Ellen promised. "By the end of the evening, he will be so charmed by the Prestons that he'll be begging for an invitation to Northfield Hall."

Papa himself scoffed at this.

But there the family banter had to end, for the Devereaux carriage at last rattled around the corner.

Standing on ceremony, Ellen rose to play hostess for Papa at the threshold of the sitting room. Benjamin took up his post beside them. His palms were growing sweaty; he was glad to be wearing dinner gloves so that no one would know. He was not so lucky about the sweat on his forehead. It beaded just beneath his hairline, threatening to drip down to his nose as his nerves worsened in the moments of waiting.

Then they arrived. Lord Devereaux in his old age—for Lydia was his youngest, at least forty years younger than he—walked in as solemnly as he might enter a wake. Lady Devereaux in glittering diamonds and ruffled muslin followed him with a haughty refusal to look anyone in the eye. There was Lady Adelaide, too, and the brother, Lord Alistair, whom Benjamin hadn't yet met.

But even though she was the last to enter, Benjamin had eyes only for Lady Lydia. Desire—which he tried to keep at bay except in the dark of night—crashed over him as soon as she stepped into the room. Her shy little smile. The way she bowed her head as Papa kissed her hand in greeting. The curve of her spine disappearing into the linen column of her gown.

Their first kiss had surprised him—her answer had surprised him—and he had fumbled his way through it. Yet it was all it had taken to addict Benjamin to Lady Lydia. Even now, his hands twitched on their own, impatient to touch her some way or another.

If she tarried a moment longer with Ellen, he would catch fire and burn to ashes in front of everyone.

"Mr. Preston," she said at last, as if they were strangers. As if she didn't reach for him each time they were left unchaperoned, her fingers as eager to explore as his. She bent her knees for a small curtsy, one that brought her down to his height for only half a second.

"It has been an eternity." Benjamin didn't think about the words, only spoke from his heart.

"It has been a little more than a day," Lady Lydia corrected, but her lips twisted into a smile. Echoing what Benjamin felt: that his heart drummed twice in each moment they were apart, once for himself and the second time to hold a place for her.

They made small talk for the half hour before dinner was served. Ellen engaged Lord Devereaux on the topic of horses, one of the few subjects to which no one in the room would object. Max flirted with Lady Devereaux. Caroline, Lydia, and Lady Adelaide formed a group. As for himself, Benjamin made a point of engaging with Lord Alistair.

On the surface, he and Lord Alistair should have gotten along famously. They were both heirs to a peerage, both looking forward to a political career, both responsible for significant estates with farmers and livestock and crops. Though Alistair was a few years older than Benjamin, they had overlapping social circles—Robert, the Duke of Berkwell, being one key linchpin—and should have at least been able to muster up some friendly gossip to exchange.

Alistair was determined to play the protective brother, however. "My sister won't be expected to burn all her clothes and give away her jewels."

"Only if she wants to." Benjamin meant it as a joke. They were not that fanatic; they simply tried to be conscious about whose labor was involved in what they purchased and whether that laborer was treated fairly.

Alistair did not laugh. "She is desperately fond of chocolate, you know."

Benjamin didn't know. She had never said as much to him. "To drink?" The truth was that Benjamin didn't know much about chocolate at all, other than that it came from cocoa beans imported from the Spanish colonies. He had once tried hot chocolate, a favorite breakfast drink in town, only to find it caustically bitter.

"To eat. French bonbons and the like." Alistair glared at Benjamin, as if he had already failed as Lydia's fiancé for not knowing this. "I always bring her fresh ones from Madame Meunier when I visit."

This was another way that they differed: Alistair lived apart from his family, even now when they were all in London at the same time. Benjamin supposed it allowed him a more independent lifestyle, one that included returning foxed at dawn or dallying with inappropriate mistresses.

It was strange to think of visiting a younger sister when she still lived at home and he could do the same.

"Our chef makes wonderful desserts," Benjamin offered. "For example, tonight I believe we are having strawberry cake."

He couldn't help looking at Lydia; it had been almost a whole minute since he had last glanced at her. This time, she was watching him in the same moment. She smiled—still just a small one—before returning her attention to Caroline.

"I know about you, you know." Alistair sipped his elder wine after saying this, as if the statement alone were supposed to put Benjamin on alert.

It confused him, that was certain. He replied, "I have heard many compliments on your character from our mutual friends."

"I have heard that you have a habit of falling in love. That you always declare yourself to be recklessly, hopelessly in love with one girl or another. And then, after a few months—after she has spurned you or gone to a richer protector—you find someone else whom you are convinced is the woman who is meant to be your wife."

A blade as cold as steel wedged between Benjamin's lungs. It was not a pastime, like Lord Devereaux considering which horse to back for the season's races. The governess he had adored at age seventeen was not the same as Miss Amanda Fairchurch, who was very different from Mrs. Littleton. The fascination, the adoration, the desire—they had all been facets of love. Sometimes they had felt similar, but never had they been the same.

"My sister is the first one to accept your attentions."

That wasn't true either—Benjamin had shared something real with Mrs. Littleton, who had visited Northfield Hall for a summer from her home in Boston, though they had always known it couldn't last. It hadn't quite been love, but it had been affection edged with obsession, and they had both felt it.

"Your pattern must therefore end. She believes you to love her with your whole heart. However you feel about her now, it must not end. For you have convinced her to marry you. She is now your one and only." Alistair towered over him, losing all appearance of friendliness. "You understand me, don't you, Preston?"

"Perfectly."

Alistair put down his cup with a grimace. "This tastes like piss." He stalked off, joining his father and Ellen, before Benjamin could say anything else.

Benjamin looked for Lydia. She had moved, now laughing at some joke of Sophia's. It was the most relaxed she had looked all night, her head thrown back, her smile wide, her brow crumpling in delight.

Alistair had it all wrong. Benjamin did love easily. But when he loved, his love was true. He had eyes for no one else. And now that he had Lady Lydia—now that he had found the person whose soul rang in harmony with his own—there wasn't any risk that his feelings would change. Not now, not ever, not even if the worst happened and she didn't marry him after all.

He was hopelessly, helplessly hers.

No matter how carefully Ellen, Viscountess Berwick, had planned the seating chart, there was no perfect arrangement around the dinner table for this group of families. Lydia watched with unease as Father took up the seat beside the red-haired viscountess, while Mother was paired with Lord Preston. That followed precedent, yet Lydia could already hear Mother's complaints. *He didn't once compliment my jewels!* Or *That is the most boring man in all of Britain.*

With a deep breath, she tried to let the worry go. It was of no concern what Father or Mother thought of the Preston family. They wouldn't be the ones living with these people, day in and day out, for the rest of their lives.

Marriage had sounded good and dandy as a plan from the cold distance of Balise House. Find herself some rich lord, offer herself up as his wife, and solve all her problems.

Only now, each day drawing her closer and closer to her fate, did Lydia think of all the reasons why she might be running foolishly into a catastrophe. She had never acquired a taste for more than a few glasses of French wine with her meals, yet now, she would never have the opportunity to. She might never eat chocolate again. Lord Preston would be the head of her household, and she had only just met the man, with his thick eyebrows and severe countenance.

She liked the Prestons so far. Mr. Preston's siblings were all going out of their way to be lovely and welcoming and to try to find common ground with her. But she hardly even *knew* Mr. Preston, let alone the rest of his family. Yet here she was, handing over her body and spirit to them.

Lydia took her seat. She was at the center of the table between the two brothers-in-law, Viscount Berwick and Mr. Anderson the accoucheur. Across from her was Mr. Preston. Smiling at her. As he had done all night.

Guilt displaced her unease. Or perhaps it was the source of it, the gushing spring from which unease and fear and sadness spilled out as natural-born creeks. Mr. Preston was so very excited to marry her. Every time he visited—which was each afternoon, always with a fresh posy of flowers for her—he rhapsodized to her why theirs was a match made in Heaven, how he looked forward to spending every day with her, how he knew their love would only grow deeper and truer.

Lydia tried not to lie to him. She tried to turn his declarations towards plans. *Everyone will love you at Northfield Hall* led to *How can I make a difference at Northfield Hall?* And *You make me the happiest man* could become *How shall we spread our happiness?*

Still, she lied to him. If not in outright words, then in omissions. She never corrected him when he said things that implied she loved him back. She never hinted to him that each morning, the idea of marrying him brought her more dread. She never told him about Seamus, and she certainly didn't suggest that she was not the innocent, pure young woman everyone believed her to be.

Most visits, the easiest solution was to kiss Mr. Preston. They were never alone long enough for the kisses to deepen, which meant Lydia disappeared into a fugue of desire. Instead of facing up to the reality that she would marry Mr. Preston, she imagined his hands on her breasts. Instead of worrying how her family would react to his, she pictured him naked and hard. Instead of hearing herself lie to him, she fantasized about how he would feel inside her, easing the ache that built more every day.

She couldn't kiss him now, however, nor take refuge in an endless fantasy. Which was why every time Mr. Preston looked at her, Lydia's stomach twisted with guilt. She didn't know how she would get through an entire meal, not when he was there across the table, beaming like the cat who caught the canary.

"Well, John, what do you think Lady Lydia should most be afraid of?" Viscount Berwick asked as footmen placed the soup course in front of everyone. He was a tall man, broad shouldered, with a devastatingly handsome face and gold hair falling past his ears. Worse, with a booming voice and an air of confidence that made him seem absolutely impermeable. If Lydia were afraid of anything or anyone, it was probably him.

Mr. Anderson took his question seriously. He regarded his soup as if it were a puzzle as he thought up his answer. He was about as opposite the viscount as a man could be: slender, with dark hair and brown skin, and a hint of the trade in his Londoner accent. Lydia knew he and Mrs. Anderson had married three years before in the midst of scandal—but Mr. Preston had smiled this off, saying, "Mr. Anderson has had a calming effect on my sister. I daresay she is actually happy now. Marriage to the right person, you see, can do that."

Now, Mr. Anderson replied, "The hardest adjustment for me was to believe it when everyone said they were so pleased to have me join the family. The Prestons say what they mean. Except my wife; she often says the opposite of what she means, which gives me the pleasure of puzzling out the truth."

Brightening, he turned slightly to seek out Mrs. Anderson. She flared her eyes at him flirtatiously before turning back to a conversation with Alistair.

"Lady Berwick is painfully earnest, that is true. As for me, I like to keep one on one's toes." The viscount pinned his gaze on Lydia.

"And you, Lady Lydia? Do you speak honestly, or do you keep the truth closely guarded?"

The viscount was not asking if she was a liar. Lydia understood that. Yet the question gutted her. She thought the soup she had just swallowed might come up again. The way he watched her—steady, confident, all-knowing—she was sure he could tell that she did lie, that every word she had said to Mr. Preston had been false.

Well, not every word. At least she had told the truth about how she wanted to use his money. And she did intend to marry him.

Just not for love, as Mr. Preston seemed to believe.

"I should like to believe I am sincere," she answered the viscount.

"That response leaves room for doubt." He directed his next comment across the table to Mr. Preston. "Lady Lydia is too clever for you, Benny. She will be running circles around you while you stare in amazement, mark my words."

She hadn't heard this nickname before. She would have to ask him if he wanted her to use it. She hoped he didn't. It felt too young, like a leash keeping Mr. Preston tied to his youth. Lydia would prefer to call her husband by his full name, the more dignified *Benjamin*, than by some infantilized version from his childhood.

And there spouted the even deeper spring of guilt. That she was even planning this future. That she was thinking about any man but Seamus as her husband.

"Then we'll be just like you and Ellen," Mr. Preston responded to the viscount. "What meeting was it that you attended today?"

"The Society for Products of Free Labor. A worthy cause."

Mr. Preston smirked. "Not one you would have supported before you married Ellen, though."

Lydia couldn't take another moment of the family basking in how happy it was and how glorious it would be for her to join it. She seized the opportunity to steer the conversation towards something less dangerous. "Where do you stand on the Insurrection Act, my lord? I know it is up for renewal this year in the House of Commons."

From the head of the table, Mother inserted, "What an inappropriate topic! Lord Berwick, I do hope you'll forgive my daughter. Her nerves are at all ends with the wedding. Why, she has quite forgotten herself."

Lord Preston himself replied, "We are not afraid of a little friendly debate in this family, Lady Devereaux. You might even say we encourage it."

This did not satisfy Mother, who looked to Father, who looked down at the plate of fish that replaced the soup.

From the other end of the table, Adelaide said, "I can see why Lydia and Mr. Preston are so taken with one another, then. There is nothing that pleases her more than a debate, friendly or not."

That was not quite true. Lydia didn't care for debates, nor did she care for any old political topic. She wanted to discuss Ireland, and she wanted to persuade everyone that it needed its independence just as desperately as France had needed freedom from the Bourbons and America had needed freedom from the Hanovers.

Still, she appreciated Adelaide's intervention. It kept their parents from saying something that might insult the Prestons. And it allowed the viscount to reply: "I am in favor of the Insurrection Act, Lady Lydia, for without it, the rabble-rousers in Ireland might never cease their intimidation and murder."

A disappointing answer. Though not surprising. Most of the English viewed Irish rebels as lawless, uncivilized men roaming the countryside, rather than a specific group of people fighting for a specific cause. Lydia tried to craft a reply that would challenge the viscount's view without completely revealing her own, more dangerous beliefs.

"One man's rabble-rouser is another man's army."

The viscount raised an eyebrow. "An army, Lady Lydia? And what do you suppose these Ribbonmen are fighting for, then?"

She didn't dare say it. There would be too much defiance in her voice, or a gleam in her eye. The whole party would see where she stood on the topic.

Mr. Preston answered for her. "Independence, of course."

The viscount scoffed. "The country has been unable to govern itself for centuries. Even its best leaders couldn't put together a winning rebellion in 1798. They would do better to learn trades and help build roads and canals to bring the country into the nineteenth century than to keep fighting a battle that should have ended with the Tudors."

"On that we can agree, Berwick," Father chimed in. "If these Ribbonmen really want to see their country grow, they will join us in improving it, instead of burning their own crops and killing their own people."

Lydia tried desperately to hide the emotion from her voice as she objected, "How can they join in improving it when they cannot build businesses with more than two apprentices, nor even own a horse worth more than five pounds?"

Father answered as he always did: "They need only convert to the Church of Ireland. That is not so much to ask."

Perhaps not for him. He only went to services for christenings, weddings, funerals, or holidays. The Church of Ireland was an obligation, not a part of his identity. But Lydia knew that for Seamus and Conor, and other families like the Devlins, Catholicism was wrapped up in everything they did. They could not simply abandon one church for another.

And neither should they have to.

"Even if they could vote, I do not see that it would calm things down," Lady Berwick said from the head of the table. "The unrest in Ireland reminds me of the unrest of the Luddites in Nottingham and York. Those are Church of England men, many with apprentices and horses. Yet they are so desperate for fair pay—to afford bread, mind you—that they are driven to destroy property and even to murder."

"They even meet in the dead of night, just like the Ribbonmen," Viscount Berwick added. "Which is why the Insurrection Act is necessary, to provide the police here and in Ireland with more power to catch men in these societies before they commit violence."

"Or," Lady Berwick replied, an edge to her voice, "the government could pass laws that actually help the common man afford to live, such as a minimum wage for weavers or the right to vote for Catholics, so that no one would be driven to violence."

The viscount grinned at Lydia. "My wife and I hold opposing views of human nature. She believes the best of people, and I believe the worst. What is your philosophy?"

Lydia replied—in a mix of honesty and facetiousness—"I believe the worst of people in power and the best of the rest of us."

Father and Mother exchanged a look of alarm. Viscount Berwick laughed. Lydia looked across the table to her fiancé. He raised a glass of elder wine to her in a toast. "That is why I am so excited to marry you."

For a moment, she wasn't filled with dread or guilt or shame. Lydia felt a glimmer of hope. The same hope that had propelled her to claim him as her future in the first place.

She accepted the toast as everyone else raised their glasses, too, calling "Hear, hear!" or—from Adelaide and Mrs. Anderson, who perhaps were having too much wine—"Huzzah!"

Lydia touched her goblet to Mr. Preston's. "To our marriage," she said, and she vowed to herself that she would do her best to be earnest as his wife, if not honest.

CHAPTER EIGHT

AND THEN THEY WERE married.

The ceremony was swift, only an hour or so. Benjamin tried to soak up every moment of it: the meaning of each prayer, the whisper of each psalm, and most especially the beautiful hope emanating from his Lady Lydia. She was resplendent in a green, flounced linen gown and a veil of thick Irish lace. Benjamin couldn't see the details of her face, only the cut of her forehead, the dip of her nose, and a hint of her chin as she spoke her vows.

His fingers itched to tear away the veil. His palms burned to clasp hers, and his feet very nearly started moving on their own to spirit her away from the church and their families, to claim this marriage as a private union between two people. Between just the two of them.

He resisted all urges. He did everything that was expected of him: signed the register, returned to the Devereaux house, smiled his way through the wedding breakfast even as it lasted hours and hours longer than he wanted it to.

But though it felt interminable, the day did eventually come to an end. Benjamin and Lydia left the party in his secondhand phaeton, decorated with festoons of lilies, and returned to the Preston townhouse.

And then they were alone in the family parlor with nothing except a tray of chamomile tea and a crackling fire.

Benjamin was nervous. About everything. His throat felt tight from the nerves, his tongue swollen; he couldn't think of a single thing to say. He didn't want Lydia to feel the pressure of the wedding night. Yet she was so beautiful, with the firelight casting stories across her face, that every word crossing Benjamin's mind seemed heavy with innuendo.

He wanted her. Desperately and primally. But he also loved her. He would be as happy to sit beside her, lapping up her attention, as he would be to tear off her clothes and taste her skin.

He couldn't tell what was going through her mind. She sat perched at the edge of the settee, her hands folded calmly on her lap. She had changed from her wedding gown into a more sedate brocade dress, the kind she might wear at home when no one was visiting. Which was exactly where they were now: at the home they now shared, with no company. Her hair, too, had been simplified from an elaborate maze of curls adorned with pearls; now it lifted from her neck in a twist.

Benjamin dearly wanted to untwist it. To run his fingers through each tendril and discover whether it felt as silken as it looked. To tenderly sweep it aside so he could make her shiver with kisses along the slope of her neck.

She looked at him. Perhaps she could sense the heat in his thoughts. Benjamin shouldn't feel embarrassed, but he did. He reached for his cup of tisane. "How would you like me to address you in private? Mrs. Preston? Lady Lydia? Or..."

"Lydia, I suppose. Just Lydia." She angled her chin his way. "And you? Shall I call you Benny now?"

"If you like." He didn't mind the name when his family used it. On his wife's lips, however, it felt incorrect, as if she were looking at the wrong man entirely. "I'm named after Benjamin Franklin, you know. Seditious though that may be. My mother admired his strength of character and his sharp mind. I don't think anyone ever called him Benny, though."

"Then you don't like the name Benny?"

He didn't, not as a husband. But he was babbling: "Preston could do. Most men go by their surnames, don't they?"

"What do *you* like? It's your name."

He had never stopped to consider it before. He liked how she leaned towards him, her hands now loose at her sides rather than clasped primly in her lap. He gave the honest answer that popped into his mind: "Benjamin."

"Benjamin, then." And his wife smiled.

Gorgeous. Benjamin's body filled with that same delicious mix of fascination and hope and excitement that had first hooked his attention on Lydia from across the room at Mrs. Atwood's musicale.

How he ached to take her into his arms. He *could* now, since she was his wife.

Except in the emptiness of this room, it felt like she was more a stranger than his helpmeet. They had stolen dozens of kisses these past weeks—heady, dizzying, wonderful kisses—but they had always come in stolen moments, after a long, silent dance of his hand creeping closer to hers on the sofa, their toes touching. Now they were on opposite pieces of furniture, and there was no threat of interruption.

Benjamin's lust felt demanding instead of natural. "I'm not in a rush, if you're nervous."

"Not in a rush about what?"

Benjamin's heartbeat raced. He shouldn't have said anything. "The..." There was no term for it that wouldn't make him blush, not with Lydia looking him straight on as solemnly as a parishioner listening to her vicar. "The physical part of marriage. It seems to me we could get to know each other before...fully..."

"Oh." She tilted backward. Benjamin couldn't tell if she was relieved or disappointed or confused. "You're not in a rush about that."

Somehow, from her lips, the words made it sound as if he weren't attracted to her at all. "I'm not in a rush about the entirety of it. I don't think we should ignore it completely. What I am trying to say is tonight does not need to be a night you dread. We can ease our way into it."

Benjamin had introduced this conversation to comfort her. Yet now Lydia looked more distraught than ever. She rocked backward and then forward in her seat, and her right hand worried the thumb of the glove on her left hand. She wouldn't look him in the eye. "Perhaps..."

Now she was the one who trailed off. Benjamin resisted the urge to rush in and suggest words for what she had been trying to say. He had no idea what was on her mind, anyway.

"Perhaps I should be honest with you. Benjamin." His name she added as its own thought, as if reminding herself with whom she spoke.

Benjamin braced himself. He could only imagine what confession she was about to make that she felt the need to preface it so. That she was actually Lord Devereaux's by-blow; that she had been warned by physicians that she could not have children; that she wasn't sure she ever wanted to be physically intimate with him.

Whatever she said, he promised himself in that half second of waiting for her to continue, he would respond kindly. Calmly. With the grace of the husband he had just vowed to be.

Lydia looked up now, her eyes fixing on Benjamin as if weighing his receptiveness to what she had to say. He tried to look encouraging but not eager.

Then she dropped her gaze to her fingers again. A softness swept over her as she finally said, "I do not dread tonight. In fact, I am...overtaken by the need to experience it. With you. If that's all right."

And Benjamin suddenly didn't feel shy at all.

LYDIA ACCEPTED HER HUSBAND's kiss. More than that, actually. Even though she had meant it as a lie, the instant he rose from his settee, her desire leapt like a flame reaching for the Yule log. It shoved away the parts of her that loved Seamus. It turned her into a siren whose arms wrapped around Benjamin's neck as soon as he was within reach. She kissed him as much as he kissed her. They both kissed as if they had been waiting a thousand years for this very moment.

She had almost confessed that she was not a virgin. With Benjamin being so considerate and the air between them filling with awkwardness, the truth had welled up in her. But Benjamin had looked at her with so much trust. And Lydia had realized she could not confess without also telling him about Seamus.

So she had lied with a different truth. And now Benjamin's palms were running across the front of her gown, cupping the shape of her breasts, and she was loving it.

Blindly—eyes still closed, mouth still encouraging his—Lydia reached for his neck. She fumbled with his cravat until its knots dissolved and she could throw it free across the room. How she had longed to do that all these weeks. She moved on to his coat, pushing it off one arm, then the other. She wanted to remove all the outside trappings that made him Mr. Preston so that she could discover the Benjamin yearning from underneath.

His kiss traveled from her mouth. "This perfect neck," he whispered, dotting kisses from just beneath her ear all the way down to her collarbone. Lydia shivered, but not from the cold. She lost track of her own movements. Her husband knelt before her, nestled in between her legs, so she wrapped her calves around his torso to pull him closer.

"You make me lose all sense," he growled, both hands plunging beneath her to cup the curve of her buttocks.

God help her, she loved it. She sought his mouth again. His lips were ferocious against hers; his tongue a torch that made her burn ever hotter. Her nipples and belly and legs chafed against all the clothes she still wore. She wanted to be naked, and she wanted Benjamin naked, and she wanted him to plow into her as if they would never have another chance to do this.

Piecemeal, in between kisses that lasted for eons, Benjamin said, "We should go upstairs."

Lydia knew he was right. But moving upstairs meant parting—for literal minutes!—in order not to inflict their desire on the poor servants finishing their evening duties. It meant a break in their kissing. It meant returning her mind into her body, which Lydia was very loath to do.

"Why not stay here?" She looked around the room, letting him work her neck again. "Lay me down on that settee. Or on the floor. Or hold me up against the wall. I'm not particular."

He groaned. A delicious groan, one that vibrated across Lydia's skin. "You're my wife. You deserve a bed."

"Don't I deserve a choice?"

They lost the thread of the conversation for a bit as they latched onto each other's mouths again. Lydia started undoing the buttons on his waistcoat. There were only three, but she couldn't figure them out, distracted as she was by the friction of his fingers skating along the back of her neck.

"I never want to stop touching you," he murmured, his lips moving into her hair this time. Even her scalp responded to him, setting her shivering with lust again.

Seamus had never talked when kissing her. Except to say *Are you sure you want to do this?*

"Don't stop," Lydia responded to Benjamin, desperately pushing away the memory of Seamus. He was dead; she was married; this was what she had to do for the cause. She tried to follow her husband's lead. "I can think of nothing but you touching me. I want your lips on every inch of my skin."

"Yes." His breath landed like a caress on her neck. "I want to explore each and every part of you."

They couldn't possibly wait until they retired upstairs. Lydia needed release, and she needed it now. Untying the ribbon at her bodice, she said, "Take it off. Please, I can't bear to wear it anymore."

He hesitated. She tugged at the dress herself, dropping her feet to the ground so she could stand and pull it over her head. Before she had even finished, Benjamin swept her into his arms, lifting her first into the air before lowering her onto the carpet in front of the hearth. He untangled her wrists from the dress, then untied her petticoat shift and removed that from her as well. Now she was naked, except for the wool stockings held up with ribbons just below her knees.

"You are so beautiful, Lydia." He made it sound like a song. He ran his fingers along the outline of her skeleton: from her wrists to her shoulders, in a loop around her breasts, down to her waist, then along the outside of her thighs and calves until he had reached the tips of her toes. "How lucky we are. Can you believe it? The two of us, in love, in such desperate need of each other, and at the perfect time and place to marry. We are luckier than a hundred thousand others, Lydia. I will never stop counting my blessings that you chose me."

"Kiss me." She didn't want to hear about love. She didn't want to lie to Benjamin any more than was necessary. And she didn't want to ruin this moment with guilt. "Kiss me and take me. I want you inside me."

He didn't exactly obey. He kissed her—but on the inside of her left thigh. His mouth drew a trail all the way from her knee to the nest of hair covering her quim. Then—just when Lydia thought he would kiss her at her little peak—he skipped over to the other thigh. "You tease," she cursed, but it felt like heaven as he worked his way down the right leg, ending with a kiss on the side of her knee.

"Oh, did you want me to do something else? Something like this?"

Now he kissed the perimeter of that triangle of hair. He was so close to her quim that his nose brushed against her peak for one tantalizing second. Lydia gasped. He still didn't indulge her, moving along just as quickly to finish his inspection of the border.

"Take off your clothes and get inside me already," Lydia demanded.

"So impatient." Benjamin eased her thighs apart a little further. "I will only remove my clothes when I have earned the right. One piece of clothing for each moment of joy I give you."

"I have already had a dozen moments of joy."

He only grinned. Then, nestling onto his elbows, he kissed her directly on her peak.

It was a strange sensation. Seamus had tried to give her this treatment once or twice, but Lydia had always felt so afraid of what she must taste like that she could never enjoy it. She preferred him inside her, when she knew she was doing it right.

With Benjamin, that very first lick erased all her rational thought. She didn't care that she must taste strange or that his mouth must be cramping or that he wasn't getting any mutual pleasure from the act at all. She felt only the coil of desire wrapping ever hotter and deeper inside of her. She wasn't even aware of *what* he was doing with his tongue, only that it felt good, that it evaporated everything around them, that it distilled her existence into a pure plane of pleasure.

And then she erupted. In great waves of joy, just as he had promised. When it ended, she lay still, overwhelmed.

Overwhelmed, and a little sad.

How she wished she could have experienced that with Seamus, instead.

BENJAMIN ROSE TO HIS knees to admire Lydia. His wife. The woman he would love and cherish for the rest of his life. Spread naked on the ground like some kind of nymph. Her orgasm had not been loud—more like a sudden void of breath—yet he had felt it rippling through her, and now she lay limp, her lips stretched in relaxation, her eyes closed.

He was as hard as a rock. Hot, too, and ready to pump himself inside that delightful quim. Even though he had seen to the little monster between his legs that very morning, so as not to be an overeager bridegroom.

It was just that Lydia was so ready. She responded to his slightest touches as if he were delivering her to ecstasy. It awakened every nerve in Benjamin's body.

He would have taken her right there on the floor, except for two things. First, his wife needed a moment of recovery. She still had not opened her eyes; she had, in fact, covered them with one of her palms, as if overwhelmed by the light from the fire. Benjamin would let her spirits return to her body before touching her again, no matter how desperate he was to press against her.

And they were still in the drawing room. The family was gone; the servants were hiding somewhere below; yet this was a public space within the townhouse. Benjamin just didn't feel right about taking his wife on the wool carpet. They would reserve the full act for the privacy of their own rooms.

"That must count for three moments of joy, at least," Lydia said on a puff of breath. She still covered her eyes. "I forgot myself entirely."

"You are a poor negotiator. If you underplayed how joyful it was for you, I would be compelled to do it again...and again...and again..." Benjamin teased his fingers up her body again—naked! And her skin so smooth!—and bent to steal another kiss from those perfect rosebud lips.

She responded with the lightest of puckers, then turned her chin away. "A deal is a deal. Remove your clothes."

"If you insist, my darling wife." How thrilling that he could say the word aloud. "First, we really must move upstairs."

At last, Lydia peeled her palm away from her eyes. "Is that an order? The first spousal decree that I must obey?"

"It is a request, most humbly submitted. You may extract sacrifices as payment, if you must."

She grinned. Over the past month, Benjamin had spent so much energy trying to memorize every moment of Lydia, but before tonight, he had never seen this version of her: lustful. And unguarded. And a little silly.

He loved this version of Lydia the most—at least, so far.

"I shall contemplate your payment as I follow you to our chambers."

They reassembled their clothes as best they could, then proceeded upstairs in pretend solemnity. From the kitchen—on the lowest level of the townhouse—came the sound of a fiddle and singing, suggesting the household was keeping itself busy with its own merriment. Still, as Benjamin led Lydia by the hand to their adjoining suites, they were discovered by Orla, Lydia's maid.

The Irishwoman flushed an immediate, bright red at the sight of Lydia, whose gown hung so haphazardly that it was very clear she and Benjamin had not merely conversed over a nighttime tisane. Still, Orla managed an unemotional delivery of "Will you be needing me tonight, ma'am?"

With even more composure, as if discussing which gown to wear the next day, Lydia replied, "No, I'll ring for you in the morning. Thank you."

And then they were alone in Benjamin's bedroom.

Lydia looked around. Benjamin's nerves prickled, feeling her attention sweep from the old wooden armoire to the four-posted bed to the painting of Northfield Hall on the wall. It was not a luxurious or sumptuous room; it was even a little chill, despite the healthy fire at work in the hearth.

She made no comment kant, except to move to the bed. "I believe, sir, that you wanted me on a mattress."

"And I believe you, madam, wanted me to remove my clothes." He folded them over the valet stand as he went: jacket, waistcoat, cravat, shirt, then his shoes and stockings, and finally the formal wedding breeches.

He hesitated before turning around. He had heard from friends that young ladies could sometimes be a little horrified at their first sight of an erection, being so unfamiliar with male anatomy. Yet, too, he had been warned his wife might be shy or withdrawn on their wedding night, and so far, Lydia hadn't been shocked by anything.

Benjamin turned to face his wife. Naked, on full display, with his cock as hard as it ever had been.

She neither gasped nor recoiled. Her gaze raked over him, and then she raised her solemn brows. "Hadn't you better come over here and make me your wife?"

"Ah, I knew I was forgetting something."

Lydia rose to her knees on the mattress as he joined her so that they could together pull her dress and shift over her head again. They almost didn't; she nipped his lips, and he retaliated with a full-blown kiss, and their hands got tangled in the billowing fabric overhead. Her torso was silky and warm against his. At this angle, they were almost equal in height, and his cock pressed naturally against the inner curve of her hip. It jerked, almost bursting with its need to get inside her.

Benjamin paused their kiss, running a finger along her jaw to sate his need to touch her. "You might feel some pain this first time."

Her breath caught. But she raised her eyes to meet his. "I am not afraid of that."

"I hope you feel some pleasure, too. If you don't this time, then the next time you will."

Now she smiled. "That's a big promise, Benjamin." Lydia captured his lips in another kiss. "You had better prove these claims."

They eased together onto the mattress, sparring in kisses the whole time. She wrapped her legs around his waist. His cock brushed against the tapestry of hair at her nexus and jerked in excitement.

"Are you ready?" He hoped her answer was yes.

"I shall expire if you don't take me soon," she huffed against his neck.

Benjamin loved her spirit. Maneuvering onto his knees, he took one last kiss from her lips. "You make me want to tease you more, wife. But I cannot wait much longer, either."

With his thumb, he checked her slit and discovered a fountain of wetness. She shivered at his touch. Slicking some of her desire over his erection, he positioned his cock at her sacred circle. And then there was nothing to do but thrust forward.

The feeling was exquisite. Like he was sailing across a lake of pleasure. Any minute now, he would fall overboard and drown in it. And how he wanted to drown.

Belatedly, Benjamin remembered poor Lydia. "Are you in pain?"

Her hips bucked in rhythm to his. "Not to speak of," she replied between breaths. "Keep going. Get deeper."

Her words only added wind to his sails. He obeyed, seizing her legs so he could position himself at an even sharper angle inside her. "Tell me how much you want me."

"I want you so much I would suck your cock if it weren't already inside me."

That image enthralled him too much for him to be shocked by her coarseness. "How long have you wanted me to fuck you?"

"Always. Forever." She wrapped her palms around his forearms, her fingernails digging into his wrists. "I want you to fuck me until I can't think at all."

The idea of it made Benjamin moan. He was going to come soon. "I love you, Lydia. I love you." It became a chant, as he focused his energy on that lake of pleasure, on the feel of her hot and soft beneath him, on her heels pressing into the flesh of his buttocks.

"Fuck me, Benjamin," she hissed in reply.

That wasn't enough. Not now, not in this crucial moment, when he was about to drown in her lake. "Tell me you love me. I love you. Tell me you love me."

"I love you fucking me."

He was so close. And yet. "Tell me you love me."

She met his frenzied pace with her hips. She dug her nails into his flesh. This perfect wife of his. And then, at last, "I love you."

Benjamin came in a great crash. His mind spilled into a hundred colors as the release rushed over him. He fell into Lydia's arms, realizing he was crushing her only when his consciousness returned to his body.

"I love you so much," he laughed, pulling her into a curl against his side. Sleep was coming fast, and he wanted to cuddle her through the night. "How lucky are we."

"So lucky," she agreed.

His wife's words were the last thing he heard before passing into slumber. And they were perfect.

Chapter Nine

They did not have much time to themselves the following morning, for which Lydia was grateful. She woke in her husband's bed, her ankles tangled with his, completely naked, and nearly feverish from the shame that washed over her.

She had always known she would marry someone other than Seamus. Never had she thought she would behave so wantonly. Or enjoy it. Lydia had been determined to submit like a dutiful wife; instead, she had all but demanded Benjamin slake her lust.

And she felt guilty for lying to him, too. She could never love him—not like that. She would be his friend, his partner, even his admirer, but never would she say *I love you* the way he wanted her to and mean it.

She hadn't planned on saying it at all. But she had, and now she felt guilty about it.

Lydia slid out of bed without waking Benjamin. Slipping into her petticoat and gown, she tiptoed from the room, down the corridor, and into her own set of rooms. There—thank God—Orla waited by the vanity.

Upon her entrance, Orla hustled a teacup out of sight. "Don't tell them you caught me drinking this, my lady. Only I don't know how anyone gets a thing done with neither tea nor coffee in the morning."

Her own head buzzed at the idea of going the whole day without some sort of morning drink. Except Lydia could not make exceptions. She was Lady Lydia Preston now, heir to the barony. This was part of the deal she had made: she would eschew anything touched by exploited labor, just as she would lie with Benjamin, in exchange for the freedom to do what she wanted with her pin money.

She pictured a person far off in China forced to pick tea leaves from sunup to sundown without fair pay. That was enough to turn her away from sniffing longingly at Orla's cup.

"Was it...did you sleep well, ma'am?" Orla set out a basin of warm rose water, then began helping Lydia from her clothes. "Perhaps you want a full bath today?"

"There's no time." Perhaps there was. Lydia didn't want to sit in a hot tub of water with nothing to do but contemplate her own actions. "A sponge bath will do, and then my pink linen. Did you send my message to your cousin?"

Orla eyed her for a full ten seconds without moving, as if silence would get Lydia to say something more.

It worked, of course.

"I'm fine. It was fine. More than fine. I shall not be miserable as Mr. Preston's wife, if that is your concern. As I knew when I accepted his suit, he and I shall be good friends. Now, did you deliver my message to your cousin?"

"I did, ma'am, not to worry."

Lydia worried anyhow. Making sure that Conor knew where to find her was the least of her problems. She needed to get him the funds necessary to capture thousands more signatures on their petition.

The funds, however, were locked in her pin money. Lydia wasn't sure when she could ask Benjamin for her settlement without betraying herself to be more interested in his fortune than in him.

She took the washcloth from Orla to scrub her own legs. It was as if Benjamin had added new nerves to her skin; for the first time, she was aware of the soft down of her thighs, and the touch of the cloth made the primal part of her yearn to climb back into Benjamin's bed.

Shameful. She threw the cloth back into the basin and accepted the towel from Orla, instead. "Let's do the yellow linen, actually."

They left soon after for the royal picnic at Kensington Gardens. Benjamin collected her from her room beaming. "Good morning, Mrs. Preston!"

He looked more handsome today. In a private way, for those lips hooked into that smile just for her. And his brown eyes glowed only with her in the room.

Guilt clawed at Lydia. For making him feel that way. And for finding him handsome at all.

They rode together in the same old phaeton. Benjamin filled the air between them with a narrative about the horse, who apparently wasn't licensed from some stable for the season but instead had been purchased by the family from a horse trader who rehabilitated maltreated animals. Then—as they queued up for the stables at Kensington Gardens—he asked, "Did you sleep well?"

The question alone reminded her of his arm wrapped around her naked body, his palm loose and soft on the mattress just beneath her breast.

The sleep of lovers, not spouses.

"I woke early," she lied. "I hope I didn't disturb you."

"No. I must admit, that was the best sleep of my life." And he grinned again.

A groom came forward to see to their phaeton. Lydia accepted his hand, then waited to the side on a patch of green grass as Benjamin negotiated with the groom to mind the vehicle and horse for the duration of the picnic. There was a cold whistle to the wind; Lydia hoped they wouldn't stay long. Yet at the same time, she hoped she and Benjamin weren't alone again until they absolutely had to be.

Benjamin offered his arm for the stroll. Lydia threaded her hand under his bicep and over his elbow, trying not to notice how it awakened desire across her body. He beamed again.

Their families had nominally come to the picnic together, but as they walked up, Lydia could see her parents had quickly abandoned the Prestons for better company. Alistair, too, was mingling elsewhere; only Adelaide waited under a parasol, nodding amiably at something the Viscountess Berwick said.

Lydia went straight to her sister, breaking free of Benjamin's arm to step under the parasol and steal a hug. "How glad I am to see you."

"There, now, it hasn't even been a full day," Adelaide whispered back. More loudly, she said to Benjamin, "Mr. Preston, you must allow me to monopolize my sister for a few minutes. Perhaps you can go find her some lemonade?"

"I shall see what I can find." Because of course he wouldn't bring her lemonade sweetened with sugar from the West Indies. Still, her husband acquiesced with another of those grins: he imagined Lydia to be as happy as he, and so he thought she only had good tidings to share.

Adelaide and Lydia moved to a grove of trees where they could speak privately. "How was the wedding night, then? Was he kind to you?"

"Of course. Very kind." Lydia felt the flush roving across her body at the mere memory of his touch. She didn't know how to explain her reaction to Adelaide. "I never intended to marry a man whom I couldn't stand. I always wanted a husband with whom I could be friends, and with whom my wifely duties would not be...tedious."

Adelaide watched her steadily. She was shorter than Lydia—practically everybody was—but only by an inch or two, and she had the patience to wait in silence until a person ended up saying what they really meant.

"It was fun," Lydia said at last. "Almost like how it was with Seamus."

That still wasn't the truth, but Lydia would never speak aloud the truth: that it had been better with Benjamin than it ever had been with Seamus.

Poor Seamus hadn't had the luxury of a real bed or the time to unspool her one lick at a time.

"And now you're feeling guilty?" Adelaide shifted the parasol from one hand to another. "Really, Lydia, not even widows remain celibate after their husbands die."

"Some do."

"You and Seamus both knew even as you were sneaking off together that you would end up marrying someone else. You've said as much to me before."

Lydia said it to herself all the time. To convince herself this was the right thing to do. But she and Seamus had never actually discussed the future together, not beyond when they could meet again and solemn vows that they would love each other for the rest of eternity. Lydia had known in the light of day that they had no future; she didn't know if Seamus had ever accepted that fact, too.

Adelaide said, "You mustn't tie yourself in knots over the memory of someone you won't see again in this lifetime. He would forgive you, if he knew the circumstances."

"I'm not sure Conor Devlin forgives me for marrying, and he knows the circumstances."

They had drawn closer together to murmur their words, stitching themselves into a private world under the tree and the parasol. At least, Lydia had thought it private. Until her brother surprised them:

"Devlin? That family will come to no good end with the company they keep."

Alistair pronounced this from behind Lydia. The sound of his voice alone made her jump. She turned, inadvertently making room for him to create a circle with her and Adelaide. "What is wrong with the company they keep?"

"Why, one of the sisters planned to marry that Phelan fellow before he and his cousin got caught for administering oaths. Ribbonmen, you know. I wouldn't be surprised if the Devlin brothers are Ribbonists, too, and that's why the younger one was caught out in the fields at midnight."

Any mention of Seamus was a dagger through Lydia's heart. How she wanted to shout in his defense. He had kept apart from the Ribbonists, who swore each other to secrecy with elaborate oaths and practiced military drills by the light of the moon. They played with guns, while Seamus plotted a political revolution.

She forced herself to focus only on the actual information in Alistair's words. "Dominic Phelan was arrested for administering oaths?"

Alistair nodded, eyes alight with drama, the same expression from when he'd told her ghost stories in their childhood. "He and his cousin administered an oath to a fellow who turned around and informed the Crown for ten pounds. They're already halfway to New South Wales by now, I expect."

It made her sick. That men were arrested so quickly. That they were banished without recourse, without any chance to say goodbye to the ones they loved. And that Seamus had died on that voyage, his body tossed into the ocean. Never to return.

And worst was that Alistair—who had the power to do something about it—still looked amused. She tried to cut at him with her response. "Funny to think the government is so afraid of men swearing one oath or another that they'll spend ten pounds and the cost of a transportation voyage on it."

"Be glad we can arrest them for swearing oaths," he responded, sobering into his paternalistic brother intonations. "Otherwise, we would have to wait for them to do something worse. Burn down a barn, or rob their landlord, or murder another dozen people like at Wildgoose Lodge."

"Or we could give them a say in their own government, and they wouldn't need to create their own oath-bound organizations."

Alistair smiled, as if she had said something adorable. "God gave woman a heart so she would care for her people while he gave man a brain to rule them."

Lydia's blood rushed in anger. Adelaide spat back at him, "That's not even Scripture."

But Alistair had already turned away, twirling his empty champagne flute in his fingers as he headed for some other conversation to attack. Adelaide patted Lydia's arm. "Don't mind him. He doesn't even have a vote in Parliament yet. Now you've Lord Preston's ear, you don't need to try to convince our family of anything."

Cold comfort that was. Lydia's hands and lips trembled with an emotion that felt deeper than anger. More hopeless than anger. If the British were willing to send men off to their deaths for nothing more than being out of their homes at night, then how could she wait to find a man in Parliament with whom to reason?

She couldn't limit her actions to debates at the dinner table with men who considered it a philosophical topic rather than a case of life or death. If Lydia didn't take matters into her own hands soon, she would go mad.

Her gaze landed on Benjamin, who stood near the gleaming white marble of Queen Anne's Alcove. He wore the same smile she had first seen on him at Lady Gresham's breakfast. Then, she had known him for nothing but his money.

She knew him better now. Respected him. Even desired him. But it was time she returned to her original goal: to wrest those ten thousand pounds from his accounts and devote them to saving Ireland.

Benjamin was waiting for Mr. Collingwood to take a breath. Or even to pause. But the man must not often have gotten the chance to speak, for once he had begun a sentence, he rushed into all the others, as if he were afraid these were the last words he would ever say.

"So you see, Preston, how poor the conditions are and how maltreated these sailors, who, after all, are not in the country they call home and do not know our customs. Yet no one will pick up their cause. There are other worthy causes, to be sure. I do not mean to suggest any other cause is lesser than this one. Only that these Lascars lack a champion outside their own group. There are no widows collecting funds for them or committees clamoring for them outside Westminster. They need a leader such as yourself, not to mention money for organizing and relief. I did mention the pitiful state of their barracks, did I not?"

At last—an opening for Benjamin to break up the man's monologue. "You did. And I agree, Collingwood, that the cause is in desperate need of help. In fact, a friend of the family manned one of the East India Company boarding houses a few years ago, so I have been aware of the poor conditions. Is there a meeting I can attend to learn more?"

He hoped that would bring an end to the conversation. But Collingwood only took it as an excuse to launch back into a soliloquy.

Benjamin tried not to let his mind wander. It wasn't that he didn't care. The plight of the Lascar sailors—Asiatic seafarers from India and China—was tragic, especially the stories of men being offered passage home only to be forced into labor on the ships as soon as they were out of sight of the harbor. It was just that he knew everything Collingwood said already.

And his mind wasn't quite on the question of how to improve the world that day. It was on Lydia, who was secluded with her sister, as tall and solemn as the chestnut tree under which she stood.

She had said the right things all day long. Smiled, nodded, asked questions. And yet, something felt different. Benjamin had been surprised to wake up alone. After their ferocious coupling the night before, he had expected to spend a lazy, private morning together. Instead, he had awoken cold, the only evidence of his wife a slight impression of her head on the pillow beside him.

The Lydia of today was congenial and polite. But he wanted the Lydia of last night back, the one who confessed her true desires and who kissed him without shame. He wanted to feel like they were blanketed from the world in their own language of understanding. And he didn't know if it was normal not to feel that way when not in the midst of kissing, or if something was bothering his wife.

"A pension fund should do the trick, if I may submit my humble opinion," Collingwood was saying. "Same as any guild offers, only the Lascars haven't the opportunity to create a guild. That should be the first request we make of Parliament."

A hand landed on Benjamin's shoulder: Max, come to save him from Collingwood. "Ah, have you filled Preston in on your relief scheme for the Lascars?"

"I dare not claim it as *my* scheme, my lord," Collingwood stammered.

"Whosever it is, it is a good one. I still remember the pitiful place Martin Chow managed as boarding agent." Max's face screwed into disgust. "We depend on the seafarers for all our precious goods. Without them, the Preston family might rejoice, but our economy would slow until even we aristocrats could not afford bread. The seafarers deserve at least the comfort of safe lodgings as they await their return voyages."

"Well said, my lord," Collingwood said, preening.

"Is that Lord Castlereagh over by the lemonade?" Max pointed to the leader of the House of Commons, who indeed was collecting glasses of refreshment for himself and his wife. "Why don't you go share your thoughts with him, Collingwood? He is interested in learning more."

"Oh yes, thank you, I will."

Once Collingwood had trotted off, Max winked at Benjamin. "Looked like you could use a reprieve from his lecture."

"It is a worthy cause."

"Yes, and one you might consider supporting. But you're a new-lywed. You shouldn't be thinking about anything so gloomy as the unsavory depths of human nature."

Benjamin couldn't argue with that, not when he had returned to watching Lydia. Her brother had joined them now, his head bent as he spoke with a certain intensity to his sisters.

"How does it feel to be a married man?" Max asked. "Is it every-thing you dreamed it would be?"

"It has barely even been a day."

"And how has that barely-even-a-day been?"

Benjamin wasn't about to tell Max anything about the wedding night. That had been too wonderful and too intimate to even hint at. But he was still himself: his emotions always leapt to his tongue, even when he would do better to keep his own counsel. "I think she is unhappy today, but I don't know why or how to ask her about it."

Max joined him in observing the Devereaux siblings under the tree. Lydia was speaking now, her jaw clenched, one hand slashing in the air to emphasize a point. If ever there were a portrait of an unhappy woman, it was she.

"Ellen is probably the better person to give advice than I," Max said, "but as I'm the only one in this conversation, let me offer this: the source of her unhappiness might be you, but it is just as likely something else entirely. It might be the drastic change of leaving her family for another. It might be worry over some friend's trouble. It might be annoyance at something Alistair just said, especially since he has a habit of saying stupid things. So when you do ask her what is wrong, don't make it about yourself. That will only make it worse, in my experience."

As if to illustrate Max's advice, Alistair marched away from his sisters, and both Lydia and Adelaide glared at his retreating back.

"You should ask her about it, though," Max added. "It is tempting not to, but in a surprising way, discussing each other's emotions brings you and your wife closer."

"Why is that surprising?"

Max only chuckled at him. Then he gave Benjamin a gentle shove towards the tree. "Go deliver that drink to your poor wife. She must be parched."

As he approached, Lydia fixed a smile onto her lips. He could see her do it as if she were a marionette doll: first, the up-twitch of the corners; then, the tilt of her neck to invite him to see it; and finally, a little squinting at the eyes to force some natural emotion behind it. All to manufacture a smile that shone with insincerity.

Benjamin hoped she didn't feel she needed to pretend on his behalf.

He handed her the glass of champagne, which was the best option he could find at the refreshment table. "For you." He offered the other glass to Adelaide. "Have you two caught up properly?"

Adelaide nodded. Lydia wrapped her arm around his, with more of that same mechanical vigor. "Yes, thank you. You may introduce me to your friends now, if you like."

Benjamin hesitated, looking her over in the hopes that if he studied her hard enough, he could discover what was prompting this playacting. He far preferred the more authentic Lydia of earlier, even if her attention had been drifting and her words had fallen flat. At least then she had allowed some emotion through, even if he hadn't been able to identify it. Now she was wooden, more like an actress overemoting on stage than a real human being.

But as hard as he tried, he could interpret nothing from the set of her jaw or the clench of her shoulders. And so he took her advice and began introducing her to various friends milling about the picnic.

By every right, it should have been a congenial afternoon. His friend Will Pierce, the lawyer who prosecuted slave traders, was there with his wife, and he told Benjamin and Lydia about his latest case, which had involved hiring a pirate to chase down a slave smuggler. The Duke of Berkwell was there as well and teased them about how he deserved credit for their match. They chatted with Collingwood again—briefly, thankfully—and some fellows Benjamin knew from the Friends of Poland Society. Lydia introduced him to some of her friends, too, including Lady Chatteris, who had also grown up in Ireland, and two dowager countesses who spearheaded a charity to provide relief to war veterans. It was precisely the sort of picnic one was supposed to have while in London; yet by the end of it, Benjamin felt drained and surer than ever that something was bothering Lydia.

As they waited for the groom to fetch the phaeton, he tried to introduce the topic with a guess. "I suppose you wish we had a carriage with a driver so that we could wait in the more fashionable queue." Indeed, the Devereaux family was still by the garden gates, where they would remain until their liveried groom pulled their coach-and-four into the driveway. Meanwhile, Lydia's shoes—dress boots whose leather wasn't meant to get sullied—were sinking into the mud by the stables.

She frowned at him. "I do not care about being in a fashionable queue. Whatever would give you such a poor opinion of me?"

He had no answer except, "You seem unhappy."

She only frowned deeper and turned her head away from him. Benjamin found himself examining the underside of her jaw and the whirligig of her ear as he tried to eke a response from her actions.

The groom arrived with Phoenix and the phaeton. Benjamin handed Lydia up, one palm landing on her waist to make sure she had balance, then pulled himself into the box. For a while, he had to focus on driving, as there was a crush of vehicles already on Park Lane and he had to be mindful not to let Phoenix get too close to any other carriages.

They had turned onto the calmer Windmill Street when Lydia said, "I'm sorry that I seem unhappy. I was trying very hard to be cheerful."

Her apology missed the point entirely. "I don't want you to try to be cheerful or to seem something that you are not. I mind that you *are* unhappy. Especially if I am the cause of it."

Again, Lydia did not respond immediately. Benjamin let Phoenix trot for half a block before he allowed himself to steal a glance at her.

She was looking away, so that mostly, he could only see the back of her yellow bonnet. But he could see her bodice still, and as he watched, a tear dropped from the tip of her chin onto her chest, a dark gray spot on her otherwise pristine white fichu.

He hated that. He hated that so much.

"Do you..." Benjamin had been about to ask her if she regretted marrying him. If everything last night had been too much, after all, and if now she wished she were going home to her parents instead of being stuck with him.

But he remembered Max's words, almost too late. This might not be about him at all.

Benjamin revised his question: "Would you like to talk about it?"

"It's my brother Alistair," she said, her voice shaking a little. "He told me of some of our tenants who have been arrested. Arrested, and transported already. For administering oaths."

"Did you know them well?"

Lydia hesitated. Her chin had turned a little bit back towards him, so that now he could see a sliver of cheek when he looked her way. "I knew them a little. Enough to know they are good people, even if they are Ribbonmen. The law is so cruel to tear them away, without so much as a goodbye. Men die on those transport ships. And they don't come back from New South Wales, not nearly enough for their families to hope that they will ever see them again."

Benjamin's heart stirred—as it always did—at the idea of the law getting in between families. It was too common a theme.

"And Alistair told me all of this as if…it was like he was gossiping. Not sharing terrible news." Her voice changed now. Its tremors no longer wallowed in sorrow. What Benjamin heard now was anger. "He could do something about it. He has his own money, his own connections, his own influence. Even if he doesn't believe in Irish independence, he could be doing something to help our people. He could be agitating here in London on behalf of Irish interests. He could be meeting with Dublin Castle to try to find a solution. But all he does is nothing!"

Even Phoenix picked up on her fury, twitching his head in her direction. Benjamin eased them to the side of the road, drawing the phaeton to a standstill so he could give Lydia his full attention.

She was still crying, angry tears that she didn't even acknowledge as they spilled down her cheeks. "I need my pin money now. I'm sorry if that seems greedy of me. I can't wait any longer for the men who have power to do something. I need to take action; I need to make sure I'm doing everything I can to stop these injustices."

"Of course." Benjamin caught her hands up in his own. That felt right and familiar, the first thing all day that hadn't seemed false. "It's your money. It doesn't make you greedy. And, Lydia, whatever else you need. I'm your husband. What's mine is yours."

She stared at him, her breath catching in a little sob. "Really?"

Benjamin gathered her in his arms. Her head bent against his, her wet cheek resting on his shoulder. And best of all, her elbows wrapped around his torso. She clung to him, in a completely different way from last night. "Really," he promised. "We will make this our cause. Together. I promise. Whatever it takes."

"But you have so many causes you care about." Lydia's voice grew steadier with each word. "You offered your support to a half dozen this very afternoon. You hardly even know about Ireland."

His stomach twisted hearing this fatal flaw of his spelled out so clearly. It wasn't that he *wanted* to be so faithless. He envied her the certainty that the fight for Ireland was her fight. He would have committed his whole self to a cause years ago, if only he knew which one would have the biggest impact.

"Yesterday, I committed myself to you in heart, body, and spirit. Perhaps it is time I did the same for a cause." Being fickle hadn't helped anyone so far, except to prompt him to put some money towards various funds here and there. Benjamin gathered himself, feeling a prickle of fear that even this wouldn't be enough to force him into leading change the way he wanted to.

There was only one way to prove himself wrong.

"Lady Lydia," he murmured into her hair, "in the name of God, from this day forward, I take the cause of Ireland to be my primary cause, to which I devote my time, money, and faith in order to free Ireland of British tyranny, until Ireland is free or until I die."

She pulled back, just enough that their foreheads rested against each other. Her gaze was full and endless. "Whatever it takes?"

"Whatever it takes," he promised.

"You're a better husband than I could ever have dreamed of." Stray tears still stained her cheeks, which must have been why her words rang with a strange, deep sadness. Before Benjamin could brush them away, she pressed her lips to his. "Together," she whispered, the kiss not quite ending. "Until Ireland is free or until we die."

CHAPTER TEN

THE WEDDING NIGHT HAD been a fact, one Lydia had factored into her plans as she and Orla had packed her trunks for London at Balise House. She hadn't thought about the nights that came next. She hadn't thought about the days of breakfasts and dinners and suppers with her husband. She hadn't thought of how he would throw her smiles or vow his heart and money to her cause. She had known he would expect a kiss here and there; she hadn't known to dread her own reaction, which was to claim them from him herself.

Even this morning, she hadn't expected that by supper, she would be craving Benjamin again. Yet there she was, hurrying through the meal. It was just the two of them for one more night; Mrs. Trim had served them a simple soup in the family drawing room, the very place where not twenty-four hours before Benjamin had stripped Lydia bare and licked her into ecstasy. She watched the spoon in his mouth and tried desperately not to acknowledge the yearning between her legs.

"I think I mentioned to you a few weeks ago how much I would love to invite my sister to live with us," Lydia said to distract herself. "She and my mother get along like oil and water. I should like to offer her a space that is more comfortable. Do you think we can afford to do so?"

Benjamin patted his lips with his napkin before answering, which only drew Lydia's attention to them further. She had never noticed before how full and firm they were. He hid them so often—like now—behind a self-deprecating smile. "If there is anything we do well at Northfield Hall, it is making people welcome. The quarters might be tight here at the townhouse, but we can arrange rooms for her as soon as she likes."

"Is there nothing I can ask of you that you wouldn't do?"

"If you are asking it of me," he said, bringing his eyes up to look at her with a sincerity she didn't deserve, "then I trust it is worth doing."

This was why she kept kissing him. His feelings were so big and so transparent, as tangible as if he were handing her a bouquet of roses. And Lydia saw only the thorns on their stems; she didn't know how to accept the offering without breaking the skin on his and her hands.

"I find I'm not hungry anymore," she breathed. The truth, and yet not the full truth.

Benjamin's smile changed. She preferred it like this: a little bit wicked. It made her feel better for being wicked herself. "Neither am I."

She took his hand as they hurried upstairs. As soon as they were in his bedroom, she pressed him against the wall, dipping her chin to claim a kiss. Lydia was dripping with desire, that much was true. But she wanted the control even more than she wanted his body. If she directed their actions that evening, then she could lie to herself and say it was all part of her plan to keep Benjamin's loyalty.

His body fit perfectly with hers. Lydia hadn't noticed that the previous night. Now, as she cornered him against the wallpaper, she appreciated for the first time how his shoulders and hips and legs lined up with hers. How his erection grew harder against her in a perfect, delicious spot.

She did not compare this experience to her memories of Seamus, who had been even taller than her. She did not think of Seamus. She refused to do anything but lose herself in Benjamin. In the way his hands cupped her breasts. In the way his tongue sought out hers. In the way he lifted a leg to hook around hers, pulling her closer than ever.

"You make me lose my head," she whispered, watching her husband's eyes flare. "Undress me, if you please."

He pleased. Benjamin's fingers rushed over her clothes: untying, unbuttoning, removing. Lydia focused on the way each touch rippled through her skin, coiling heat tight between her legs. She watched her husband's desire grow, too, his eyes greedy as he unearthed more of her skin. Without waiting for her to ask, he took her breasts in his mouth, one and then the other, worshipping the nipples with such attention that Lydia fancied she might lose herself from that sensation alone.

But then they would have the whole evening still to reckon with.

"Let me have my turn." Lydia wasn't quite as good at removing clothes: she stumbled over how to unknot his cravat, and Benjamin had to pull off his own coat when she got it stuck on the swell of his muscles. She was the one to unbutton his waistcoat, however, and to unbutton the fall flap of his trousers, and to remove—with great impatience—every last stitch of clothing from his body.

This was her husband. Hers to do with as she wanted. Naked, panting, and with a cock so hard it twitched as she approached.

Lydia had never seen Seamus like this. Theirs had always been quick, furtive trysts. They had only ever removed enough clothes to reach each other.

She liked this kind of lovemaking. With Seamus, Lydia had felt desperate to imbue it with meaning; it was urgent, it was passionate, but it also had to say all the things she didn't have words for.

With Benjamin, she could let it do the opposite. It could simply be two people who enjoyed each other's bodies, finding release together. Building a friendship together, with pleasure at its base. It could erase words from her mind.

She hoped it erased guilt from her heart.

Benjamin claimed a kiss, one hand at the back of her neck and the other at her waist. Chaste, except they were both naked. His erection slipped between her legs, threatening her wet quim to take her right there, in the middle of the room.

This was her husband. For better or worse, the man she had promised her body and soul to. It was time Lydia let the guilt she felt about Seamus slip away.

She tugged Benjamin to the bed, splaying him on his back. Already, her mind filled with possibilities. A hundred ways she could toy with him. A hundred ways he could play with her. A hundred ways they could tease each other until finally, one of them spilled into ecstasy.

"I'm going to have my way with you," she promised Benjamin, a wicked smile on her lips to match his. "And it is going to take all night."

HOURS LATER, LYDIA WOKE from a dream. Or a nightmare. She wasn't sure which. She knew Seamus had been there, as real as Benjamin, whose arm and leg were draped over her body, keeping her safe and warm in their marital bed. Safe and warm, while Seamus drifted somewhere in the depths of the cold Atlantic Ocean.

She tried to hold onto the feeling that it was a dream. A gift from some other realm, one where Seamus still lived. In her sleep, they had been walking through the green fields towards Balise House. Her hand had been tucked into Seamus's elbow, like a proper lady and the man courting her. That moment was dreamlike, and she clung to it. Slipping free from Benjamin, she pulled on her wrapper and found the letter from Seamus in its hiding place in the pocket of her gown. Her only proof that she had been his and he had been hers. It sat in her hand like that dream, rattling with her heartbeat. *If only, if only, if only.*

Before the autumn of 1815, he had merely been one of the many names—dozens, if not hundreds—that appeared in Father's ledgers and the steward's verbal reports at dinner. She knew he was one of the twenty men from the village who had gone off to fight Napoleon. She knew he had a fever upon returning, because the rector's wife reported in a great fury that his mother had turned away the basket of food on account of it being from the Church of Ireland. She had even heard that he was trying to start a hedge school for the local Catholic children.

Lydia hadn't known that he was tall enough to rise above her head, or handsome enough to put the sun to shame, or smart enough to talk circles around Father and Alistair combined. And then, as soon as she knew it, there was no unknowing it. There was no unloving him. There was only yearning—dreaming—that their love could possibly be.

They met because of an accident: Lydia, walking home from tea with the rector's wife, had twisted her ankle on a tree root and tumbled towards the stream, where Seamus happened to be teaching his class of eight children about the natural elements. She had picked herself up, attempting to walk off with the righteousness of a lady who cannot be embarrassed, only to fall down again when she put weight on her weak ankle. "Perhaps you had better join us in our lesson," Seamus had said in a tone that was both stern and tender. It was then, with his hazel eyes piercing her and his gold hair gleaming even on a cloudy day, that Lydia lost her heart to him.

In the bedroom, Benjamin let out a snore and turned onto his stomach. Lydia tiptoed to the window, searching for the moon behind the billows of coal smoke. Guilt swamped the glow of her dream: guilt that she was here in London, without Seamus; guilt that she was thinking of Seamus even now, when her husband slept just a breath away; guilt that her body already yearned for Benjamin again, when once she had thought it would only ever yearn for Seamus.

She hadn't meant to have a love affair with him. At the beginning, Lydia had lied to herself. She believed her own farce that she returned to Seamus's class whenever she could because she wanted to learn Irish. She told herself the thrill in her body was from sneaking out of Balise House or lying to Adelaide and Father about her whereabouts, not from basking in the glory of Seamus. She even meant her own words when Seamus confronted her, telling her not to come around if she was only looking for a bit of excitement with him, and she replied, "I'm here to learn about Ireland. It is my home too, yet all I was taught is that the Normans conquered it and our quest has been to make it English ever since."

They had been the right words for unlocking Seamus's interest. Even now, Lydia felt the power of the smile that crept onto his lips, one that was earnest and excited and a little bit afraid. "I'm the man for that job, then," he had said, words as perfect as a declaration of love.

And he *had* taught her the history of Ireland, more than she had ever learned from tutors or from the books in Father's library. For weeks, that was the sum of their relationship, hidden in the dilapidated stone barn he called a schoolroom. They began with basics she already knew: how the Irish kings had all submitted to the Treaty of Windsor in 1175 and then during the Tudor reign how the English peerage had started taking stewardship of the Irish baronies. But what she had learned as the right and natural order of things, Seamus viewed as a usurpation of the Irish people's independence. He didn't say it in so many words when they first touched on the subject. But little by little, Lydia coaxed it from him. How animated he grew, discussing the rights of the Irish people. Lydia asked him about it first because she loved to watch him grow animated, and then because she knew it mattered to him, and she wanted to matter to him, too.

It didn't take long for her to be infected with his passion. Not when her whole life she had seen exactly what he described: wealth growing for her family and their friends, while the Catholic peasants around them were always too thin, too dirty, and too bedraggled for words. She had been told that was how Catholics *were*; Seamus showed her it was because those were the only options for Catholics. They couldn't grow businesses. They couldn't own land. They couldn't vote. All they could do was work for too little, join the army, or leave.

These were things Lydia had understood the way she knew the sun rose in the morning and set in the evening: immutable laws of nature. It wasn't until Seamus explained it, his fate choking his voice, that she realized how wrong it was. Her first glimpse of his skin was when he showed her a scar from Waterloo, from a saber that had cut through his hip; she felt the horror of a person's life being decided by the accident of birth. Seamus was brilliant, inventive, and kind, yet the best option offered to him was to fight to death.

Before knowing that Seamus had a plan, she'd decided to do something about it. Sneaking into Father's library while he was away in London, she stole his correspondence and discovered a report from the land steward about planned rent hikes. She copied it, returned the original, and presented the information to Seamus. "I don't know what we can do with this," she said, waiting desperately for his unpredictable eyes to flicker in reaction, "but I thought at least the families should know what's about to come."

Seamus read the report, then looked up at her for a long, steady moment. "Are you sure you want to pick a fight with your own father?"

"When will you believe that Ireland is as much my home as it is yours?"

At last, he had smiled. "Lady Lydia, I welcome you to our cause."

Seamus wasn't a part of the Ribbonmen or the Threshers or any of the other organized groups swearing men to oaths of allegiance and collecting weapons for a battle. "I've been to war already," Seamus explained. "That will come in time. We need a better plan than fighting if we are to win our freedom."

And so her evenings had become about revolution. Seamus's plan for the near future was to organize a conference of Irish thinkers and leaders to envision what an Irish government would look like. In the meantime, he needed to make connections, raise the spirits of the countryside, and collect funds. Seamus introduced her to his brother Conor and his cousins, who focused on spreading the idea of a political future to their countrymen. Lydia became the group's chief source of information, sneaking them the Dublin newspapers delivered to Balise House, copying correspondence that came for Father, even plying their land steward with extra food and drink to find out more about his objectives.

It was a report on the fevers in Dublin—a rash of typhoid sweeping through the streets—that earned her that first kiss. Lydia stole the letter, copied it onto her own paper overnight, then brought the copy to Seamus on a frigid February morning. He read the whole thing while she stood there, hoping her efforts were helpful. When he was done, he looked at her—and she felt as if he were seeing her for the first time. "This is a copy?"

She nodded. "You may keep it. Do with it as you will. The original is back on my father's desk."

Seamus folded it into his jacket, eying her the whole time. "What will happen if someone catches you out?"

"I don't know." She didn't worry about it too much, especially not with her parents in London for the season and Alistair in Dublin. "What will happen if someone catches you out?"

"Hanged, most likely."

Lydia had known the answer, yet it sent a shock of fear down her back. "Same for me then, I imagine. Unless Father stepped in, and I can't imagine he would, not if I'm caught planning an overthrow."

Seamus stepped closer, his eyes drifting down to her neck. "I made my peace with death a long time ago. Have you? Are you sure this is worth it to you?"

"My neck is no more precious than yours, and my soul won't be at peace unless I stand up for what I believe in."

She didn't mean it as a seduction. But somehow those words unlocked whatever gate had been keeping Seamus back. The next thing she knew, he was a heartbeat away from her, his hands hovering beside her cheek. "I want to kiss you something bad, Lady Lydia, but I know I shouldn't."

"I want to kiss you something bad, too," she replied, "and I don't know any such thing."

How that kiss had warmed her. It was just a kiss that afternoon, but by springtime, they had moved beyond, Lydia initiating each step of the way while Seamus watched her, caution and hope swirling in his eyes.

They had never had time to luxuriate in each other's bodies the way Benjamin had with her again this very evening. They had never been able to fall asleep afterwards, whispering sweet nothings against each other's lips. They had never been able to promise each other forever and always. Yet they had sworn their hearts to each other as fiercely as they vowed their allegiance to the Irish cause.

The moon emerged from behind the London clouds at last. It was only a sliver, on its way to a dark sky to mark the end of another cycle. Its light didn't reach beyond the windowpanes; it didn't explain why Benjamin stirred, murmuring in his sleep, "Where are you, my love?"

The worst part of it all—what Lydia hadn't prepared herself for—was the part of her that smiled at Benjamin. Already, some invisible gravity tugged her closer to her husband, made her yearn to climb back into bed and burrow into his embrace like a mole finding its winter nest.

Lydia turned back to the moon, instead. She tried to imagine she stood in the fields beyond Balise House watching it with Seamus's arms wrapped around her. Almost a year ago now, it had been a full moon. Watching it rise from behind the hills, Seamus had said, "I should be getting home now," and Lydia had begged him to stay. "I cannot bear to be apart from you," she had whimpered, pressing kisses to his lips and neck and ear. When they finally said goodnight, the moon was as high as the sun in the sky.

Lydia didn't think anything of it until the following morning, when Conor showed up in the kitchens begging to see her: they had arrested Seamus for being out after sunset, and that very day the special magistrates were gathering to sentence him. "They've been keeping an eye on him, you see," Conor explained. "They think he was out on account of his plans. Please, Lady Lydia, can't you do anything to save him?"

She had tried. She had shown up at the sentencing, only to be turned away. She had written Father, asking him to intervene from Dublin.

The moon disappearing again behind the London clouds, Lydia slipped the letter into the folds of her wrapper and returned to Benjamin's bed. He made room for her even as he slept, his lips finding her cheek for an unconscious kiss. "Keep sleeping," she whispered, as a wife should. He snuggled against her, a great warm comfort, and Lydia dismissed the guilt that swamped her once more.

Lydia hadn't had the power to save Seamus from transportation, nor from the cholera that killed him and three dozen other passengers before the ship even rounded the Horn of Africa.

She only had the power to keep his fight going. As long as Lydia kept fighting for Ireland, then Seamus could not be entirely gone. Even if she gave herself to Benjamin along the way. Even if she grew attached to Benjamin along the way. This fight was for Ireland, and it was for Seamus, and she was doing whatever she could for it because she wanted to make Seamus's death right.

Chapter Eleven

The benefit of being a Preston was that once he had decided to commit to a cause, Benjamin knew how to go about supporting it. Those first few days they spent locked away together, Benjamin mostly listened to Lydia as she explained to him the history of the English in Ireland and all the various ways that Irish of all religions were blocked out of power. Benjamin kept scrap paper at hand, scribbling in ink smudges the key points she made, while Lydia paced the room. She summoned the knowledge from somewhere far off, her gaze lost in the upper corners of the room, tossing out famous decrees and breaking down Tudor-era policies without referencing so much as a broadsheet.

On their first afternoon, Benjamin asked her how she'd learned it all. "I can't imagine Lord Devereaux kept tutors in his employ who taught this version of history."

"The truth, not a version." Her reply was as sharp as a saber.

Benjamin tried not to feel a wound. Even though he had only just pledged himself to her cause, he thought he merited a little faith from her.

"The truth," he agreed. "How did you learn it?"

"Oh." Lydia paced away, towards the fireplace. "By reading books. How else?"

It didn't feel like a complete answer. Yet in the same breath, she launched back into her lecture, detailing how the kings had created dozens of new Protestant peers to garner loyalty leading up to the English Civil War, resulting in a bloated Irish peerage of families that had never even set foot on the island. Benjamin let his question retreat to the back of his mind—not quite disappearing but silencing for the time being.

When Benjamin felt he understood the history of Ireland enough to explain in his own words why the Act of Union had weakened the country instead of strengthened it—and when Lydia approved the level of emotion he put behind that explanation—they moved on to planning. A cause such as independence could not be won in a single season or even a single year, which was why for the time being, they would focus on stopping the Insurrection Act from being renewed.

Parliament—and the Protestants living in Ireland—lived in fear of another 1798 rebellion, which had not been fully quieted until 1803 and provoked brutal violence from both the rebels and the government. In 1807, when a group called the Threshers began making trouble in the Irish countryside, the government had passed the Insurrection Act, giving local magistrates the right to invoke it so they could search men's houses for weapons, shut down large gatherings, and even arrest men for being out of their homes after dark. Once arrested, a prisoner was not sent to gaol to await a trial at the assizes; under the Insurrection Act, all it took was three magistrates to sentence the man with transportation for up to seven years.

The Act had been passed again in 1814, and now it was up for renewal once more. Lydia's goal was to stop it from being renewed, so that at least the common Irishman could leave his house at night without fear of being arrested. "We need to get more signatures for the petition, and we need men to collect those signatures."

Benjamin was dubious that a petition alone would make a difference. Just a few months ago, weavers from Manchester had marched with a petition to ask for wage protection. Their leaders had been arrested before they even arrived in London, and Parliament had swiftly handed down the Gagging Acts, a series of laws that suspended habeas corpus and banned gatherings of more than fifty people discussing grievances with the government.

A petition signed by Irish Catholics would not be enough to do anything but get Parliament's attention for the wrong reasons. In Benjamin's view, they needed to win over as many members of Parliament as possible to more moderate measures, such as offering more economic freedom to the Catholic community. That meant dinner parties and debates in ever-widening circles of power.

It was on this last prong of the strategy that they clashed. "There is no point trying to win votes on something like economic freedoms, when our goal is complete independence," Lydia insisted. "It will only make people like Max think they are doing enough to help. It must be independence or nothing."

"You'll never convince Parliament to give up power it already has. Asking them to grant Ireland its independence is like asking them to burn the Magna Carta. It won't happen."

"Then we waste our energy on them."

They had spent hours on the subject already. Lydia sat cradled in his armchair, her legs dangling from her petticoats over its arm. Her hair was mussed from her habit of dragging her fingers through it as she emphasized a point, and she had long since kicked off her shoes, her stockings drooping down near her ankles.

For his part, Benjamin was getting a cramp in his hand and neck from bending over his desk, making furious notes on their plan. He had—with a thrill still, even after a few days of marriage—removed his jacket so that he sat before her in just his waistcoat and sheer linen shirt. Now his cuffs were stained with ink and even a little of the sand he tossed over his paper to dry his scribbles. And his stomach roared with hunger; he was too afraid of breaking this spell of intimacy with Lydia to mention it. They would eat when they had a plan.

Eat, and hopefully other things, too.

"You cannot mean to ignore them entirely," he said, processing her words. "At the very least, think of the inconvenience of family dinners. *How are you occupying your time these days, Preston? Oh, not with much, Lord Devereaux, only trying to remove your government from Ireland.* It ends the conversation before it begins. We can't have any dialogue with anyone in Parliament if we refuse to offer them some way to work together."

"You'll never be able to have a dialogue with my father about it anyway. He is hard set in his prejudices."

Benjamin caught the glint in her eyes as she said this, turning her chin away from him. She wanted him to believe she was not hurt by her father's failure, but there it was, plain as day on her face.

He had never had a chance to ask Mama how she felt about being disowned by her father for marrying Papa. It hadn't occurred to Benjamin how that must have hurt her until long after she had died. Sometimes, he fantasized about how his grandfather would have reacted had they met. He liked to pretend that his very existence would wipe away the acrimony in the family. And that he would have the perfect words to unite his mother and her parents and siblings, once and for all.

It was impossible, of course. His grandfather had died even before Mama. But Benjamin still thought about it, every now and then, wishing for something better for his family.

"Then we won't bring it up with him specifically. No need to create bad feelings if we can help it."

Lydia scoffed. But she didn't say anything more about her father. "We cannot compromise for the comfort of Parliament. Britain has proved it doesn't have Ireland's best interests at heart; therefore, it has lost any right to rule it. Independence or nothing."

Benjamin had heard her all the other times she said it. But he hadn't really stopped to think what she meant. What she ruled out with that declaration. There was, after all, only one way he knew of for nations to demand their independence:

War.

"Shall I add 'organize an army' to the list?" he said, trying to laugh.

Lydia looked at him. Her lips twitched into a weak smile. "We'll leave that to the Ribbonmen, shall we?"

Benjamin let his pen fall to the desktop. He wanted to believe that Lydia hadn't yet thought through the consequences of demanding independence without compromise. But she had been contemplating this far longer than he had.

"These things can go in phases, you know." Benjamin scooted his chair closer to hers. "Compromise first. Like how we have outlawed the slave trade. It is a first step, and we are working on the next one now. Progress by dismantling the status quo piece by piece, rather than exploding it entirely."

She angled her chin away, so that she didn't look him in the eye. "Yet while you take things apart piece by piece, for the sake of compromise, thousands of people remain enslaved."

"What other choice do we have? Would you have us declare war on every man and family that owns slaves? They are too rich and powerful to be removed without violence."

Lydia still didn't look up. "If the status quo is cruel, then perhaps it deserves to be exploded, even if it requires war."

It was the quiet way she said it that scared Benjamin the most. He believed she meant it. And he couldn't stomach that.

"My family believes in progress. Radical change where it is necessary. But not in violence. That can't be the answer. That can only breed more hatred. Worse consequences. It can't be the answer."

Lydia finally looked at him, with a gaze so steady and cool that it chilled him to his core. "It was the answer for Benjamin Franklin and the American colonies, wasn't it?"

"I won't foment violence. I'll do anything else to support the Irish cause, but not that."

His voice didn't even sound like his own: it was too raw and desperate. Benjamin vaulted out of his chair, turning away. He didn't know what he looked like, but he knew he didn't want her to see him like this.

Lydia followed him across the room. Her hand landed on his arm, just above his elbow, and then she leaned into his back, resting her cheek on his head. A warm, steady comfort. A wife, there to catch him if he fell.

She didn't speak. But Benjamin found he didn't need her to. He turned in her arms. They kissed, a silent seal on the argument, and then they held each other in a hug for longer than Benjamin had ever known an embrace could last.

This was marriage. This was love. This was, he told himself, perfect.

The storm within Lydia hadn't disappeared, but it had quieted. Building a plan with Benjamin, seeing in black ink on white paper exactly what steps they would take to stop the Insurrection Act, removed some of the guilt constantly pressing at her heart. Even better was when he took her to the bank and introduced her to the clerks, instructing them to provide her funds from his account whenever she needed them. She began with two hundred pounds, freshly tendered from the bank manager himself in crisp notes of ten- and twenty-pound denominations.

Lydia allowed herself one private moment to imagine how Conor Devlin would thank her when she handed him the money. Then she stored the notes away in the false bottom of her velvet-lined jewelry box.

It was a bit of an adjustment to become a Preston, but all in all, Lydia did not find it particularly difficult. She most missed strong coffee in the morning and tea blends in the afternoon, yet after even a week, her body no longer thrummed with headaches in demand of those beverages. When they went out, she was proud to set aside silks and cotton for the family's fine Berkshire linen; one night, she even asked Benjamin if it would be hypocritical to make money by selling off her grandmother's Indian diamonds.

"After all, we wouldn't purchase those diamonds today, so as not to allow a Briton to profit off them." She almost forgot to substitute *we* for *your family*; it made her blush to include herself in the group. "If I sell them, I am making myself part of the problem."

"Except that you did not take them by force or trick." They were lying side by side in bed, naked after another fierce conjugal session. Benjamin slid his palm along the rim of her thighs, up her hip, and to the expanse of her rib cage just beneath her breasts. Lazily, because he had all the time in the world to touch her. "Besides, I have a hunch you are not selling your diamonds to spend the money on yourself."

Ireland was their main topic of conversation, yet it still felt a little like magic every time Benjamin read her mind so easily. Lydia caught herself smiling. She rolled onto her stomach, pulling away from his touch. "That is a dangerous line of reasoning. Take it a few steps further and you'll find yourself arguing that stealing from one man to buy bread for ten others is the moral thing to do."

Benjamin didn't rise to the bait; he only smiled back at her, as if they were in on the same joke. "'Stealing' is such an ugly word. Why not call it 'taxation' or 'rent rates' like the rest of our kind does?"

That kind of comment—lighthearted though it was—was perhaps the hardest adjustment for Lydia. She hadn't realized the extent of the Preston family's political beliefs. She considered herself a radical for trying to throw the British government from the shoulders of Ireland; the Prestons would remove the entire system of aristocracy and the capitalist economy if they could. The way Lord Preston—Papa, as he was trying to get her to call him, with the accent on the second syllable like the French—spoke at family dinners, Lydia sometimes believed he wanted a world with no money whatsoever. It was enough to make her want to shake him: how could anyone look at the terrible swath of human history and believe everyone would cooperate, if only resources were shared equally?

Yet the Preston household was a happy one. The servants acted almost like members of the family, save for sitting at the table and eating with them; during one dinner when Papa started a discussion on whether the rights of women needed to be codified into law, a passing maid stuck her head into the room to say, "If the Magna Carta is such a wonderful document because it wrote down the monarch's duty to his people, then you cannot question whether women deserve the same to declare our rights."

Papa and Max were the only family members who remained at the townhouse with them: Ellen had returned to Northfield Hall, where her two children were, taking seventeen-year-old Caroline with her; Sophia and John kept a separate address and were soon due somewhere in the northern counties to help Lady Windemere deliver twins. Max was barely there, coming in flashes of energy to change clothes between parliamentary debates or to steal a nap before heading off to inspect one of his charitable ventures. Papa, too, gave the townhouse a wide berth, spending more time at his chambers within the Society for the Propagation of Free Produce in Westminster.

Lydia wasn't sure if this was normal, or if they were trying to create privacy for her and Benjamin to get to know each other. Either way, she was grateful. Without them around, she and Benjamin could spread into the study and drawing rooms with their plans, eating luncheon off trays while they debated where to focus their energies first.

At the moment, they were in the dining room with drafts of a broadsheet spread before them. They had found a compromise on the question of forcing Parliament to think more closely about the Insurrection Act: they would spread an anonymous pamphlet at an upcoming ball with all the reasons why the Act violated the core tenets of British government.

They had each written a version, and now they were trying to choose which was better. Lydia felt Benjamin's was too tame; he accused hers of being too inflammatory.

"There's the question of the title, too," Benjamin said, when Lydia repeated for the third time that his draft gave too much credence to the threat of insurrectionists burning down the countryside. "What will we call it?"

"*The Irish Truth*," Lydia suggested.

Benjamin twisted his lips in dislike. "We need something less objectionable. Something they will pick up in the first place. *The Irish Question. The Irish Lament.*"

"*Lament* is too hopeless. We must be careful not to make people think there is no possible solution." Lydia drifted to the window, thinking.

"*The Irish Republican*," Benjamin suggested.

It could work. But it was too single minded. No unionist would pick it up out of curiosity. Lydia wanted something that would intrigue people so that they could win over new supporters. "*A Report on Ireland.*"

She turned to see his reaction and discovered him starry eyed, smiling at her as if she were one of the seven wonders of the world.

"You're doing it again," she said, but she couldn't help grinning back. The first few times she had caught him like this, she had wanted to run from the room, overwhelmed with guilt. He took such delight in her.

After a few weeks of this, though, Lydia discovered she took delight in him, too. And she was beginning to suspect that might be all right. She could delight in her husband *and* love Seamus, without betraying either of them.

That was what she told herself for now, anyway.

"I can't help it." Rounding the corner of the table, Benjamin caught her by the waist and drew her against him. Already, this spot, pressed into his body, felt like home to her. She linked her arms around his neck, expecting the kiss that came next.

"Do you like the name? Or is it just the way I was standing that called to you?"

"Both." He kissed her again, more deeply. Lydia began to forget the context of their conversation, his tongue sending her into a whirlwind of delicious nerves. "If we decide on *A Report on Ireland*," he said, drawing away for the briefest of moments, "may we remove upstairs for a half hour break?"

"Make it an hour," Lydia replied, "if you agree to using my conclusion paragraph."

This was how she knew he took the cause seriously: he hesitated, not even kissing her as he considered the proposition. "Three-quarters of an hour, and we revisit the question of the conclusion later this afternoon," he countered.

Lydia was about to agree, her fingers threading through his hair already, when Orla knocked at the door. "Pardon me, ma'am," she called, not opening it yet, "but my cousin has come to call."

Conor Devlin. Lydia withdrew from Benjamin before she even knew what she was doing. Her fingers rubbed across her lips, as if to remove his kisses. "I must speak with him." But her mind was too muddled to remember the excuses she had planned. "Orla is uncomfortable alone in his presence."

Benjamin frowned, the kindness that was always in his eyes deepening. "Why? Would you like me to tell him to stay away?"

"No, it is nothing like that. It's..." Lydia couldn't think of a lie that made any sense. "It's complicated, that is all. Orla wouldn't want to involve anyone else. Family matters can be very sensitive, you know."

He watched her, the confusion plain on his face.

Lydia turned away. "I'll only be a moment." Then she let herself out of the room and followed Orla downstairs.

Conor waited for them in the alleyway beside a stack of empty milk crates. He looked thinner than the last time she had seen him, his broad shoulders a little more hunched. Still, in that first glance, she saw Seamus, and her heart twisted.

"It's good to see you," she said, stepping close enough that they could murmur to each other without fear of being overheard. "How goes the petition?"

"I've been begging signatures from sunup 'til sundown. I have seven thousand or so by now, I reckon."

Seven thousand—more than Lydia could picture in her head, yet still not enough. "We'll need more than that. Have you anyone helping you yet?"

Conor eyed her. There was a new sulk to him, a reluctance, that Lydia wasn't accustomed to. "Have you got the money, then?"

When last they had met, just before the wedding, Conor had asked her for ten pounds to hire some of his friends to spend their days on the petition, too.

"That and more. We have a campaign planned, one to make sure the Insurrection Act is a top priority in everyone's mind. A pamphlet, funding for the Catholic Board, a night of theater dedicated to Irish stories..." Some of these were just ideas Lydia and Benjamin had thrown into the air without deciding whether to do them or not. She remembered them now as if adding one more effort on top of the others would earn her Conor's approval.

He frowned at her. "'We'?"

She had used that pronoun, hadn't she. Beside her, Orla hovered protectively, as if expecting Conor to provoke a fistfight, and Lydia considered for half a second roping her in on a lie. But there was no point. Conor was a smart man, and he would see for himself as soon as the pamphlet was published. "My husband and I."

"Ah." Now Conor looked just like Seamus had whenever the subject of the king arose. A vicious, furious scowl. "That precious husband of yours. How is the tosser? A worthier fellow than Seamus, then?"

His anger was sharper than a right hook. Lydia forced herself to remain in place, to stand tall and take it. After all, she deserved it. "You know I would do things differently, if I could go back in time."

"We don't need some Englishman telling us how to fight for our own liberty. He'll do nothing more than lead us in circles, as he is doing you, apparently. Are you going to give me the ten pounds or not?"

It was the way he spat the words. The way he implied with his mere tone that she was no longer worthy of his trust. Lydia imagined Seamus there, standing up for her, and it was enough to make her speak for herself. "No one is leading me in circles. I'm for the cause as much as you are."

"Oh, sure you are. Remind me, cailín, are you the one who left his home to take a fuck-all job in London in the name of revolution? Or are you the one who married a rich Englishman and will have rich English children and keep growing rich off the backs of my family?"

With each question, Conor stepped closer to her, his face getting redder with anger, until he ended his advance just inches from her face. Spittle from the *b* in *backs* landed on her cheek.

Lydia didn't retreat, not even an inch, and she didn't backhand him either. "I'm the one who married in order to get the money you need. To get signatures, to lobby Parliament, to hold a conference, or whatever it is you need to make this revolution happen. I'm the Englishwoman who whored herself out in marriage to help the cause."

They still spoke in murmurs, and they were far enough away from the kitchen entrance that Lydia didn't worry about being overheard. Still, when Benjamin interrupted them with a stern "Is something the matter here?" she jumped in fear.

She hoped beyond hope that he didn't know what she had just said.

Chapter Twelve

BENJAMIN HAD STEPPED INTO the alleyway too late to hear the words on his wife's lips, but one didn't need to hear in order to read the situation: her clenched fists, her tense shoulders; Orla hovering close as if ready to slap her cousin; and the cousin himself only inches from Lydia, far too near to an assault.

Benjamin forced himself to remain calm. A violent punch might soothe the protective fire surging through his veins, but it would only complicate things in the long run. He focused instead on inserting himself between Lydia and the cousin. It didn't take much; almost as soon as he spoke, the man backed away, head down, not even trying to prolong the fight by meeting Benjamin's eyes.

"You're Miss Maher's cousin." Benjamin tried hard to sound cool and unaffected, like he viewed the man as nothing more than a pest.

"That's right, sir."

"I understand you have a habit of making her uncomfortable with your visits. So much so that my wife feels the need to supervise them."

The man's obeisance flickered; he glanced at Lydia before responding. "If that's what Lady Lydia tells you, sir, then yes."

Benjamin felt his wife stiffen behind him. He wanted to turn around and wrap her in his arms. He didn't know what to make of the man's response. "It seems to me it is time this visit come to an end, then."

The cousin looked again at Lydia and then—as if following someone else's command—dragged his attention to Miss Maher. "I didn't get what I came here for. Cousin."

Benjamin turned to the maid. Over the past few weeks, she had been a regular presence in his life, enough so that he counted on her to be steady, good-humored, and decisive. Now, however, she was twisting a handkerchief between her hands, and she looked immediately at Lydia instead of meeting his gaze. "Ma'am..."

It was only then that it occurred to Benjamin that someone in the triangle was lying. And the way that everyone kept looking at Lydia, he suspected—with a ferocious flip of dread—that it was she who owned the secret.

Lydia withdrew a fold of paper from the pocket of her dress. As she handed it to the cousin, Benjamin saw it was bank notes—and the one on top was five pounds. "That should take care of it," Lydia said, her voice crisp as a fresh autumn apple. "Think on what I said, won't you?"

Benjamin wanted to seize the man and force an explanation from him as to what was going on. But he let him go, focusing instead on memorizing the shape of his body and the swagger of his walk in case they should ever meet again.

Then he turned to Lydia. "Perhaps you would care to explain to me what that was about."

LYDIA'S HEART WAS BEATING so fast that she was sure it would break free of her rib cage. She didn't know which was better: to keep the whole lie going, to tell a smaller lie, or to let loose her tongue and tell Benjamin the truth.

She bought herself time by taking him by the arm. "Not here in the alleyway, if you please."

They retreated indoors; the kitchen maids pretended not to notice anything as Lydia, Benjamin, and Orla paraded upstairs. "Do you need me, ma'am?" Orla asked at the first-story landing.

"No, thank you." Whatever Lydia decided to say, it was a conversation best kept between herself and Benjamin and no one else.

She decided on his apartment instead of hers. It was where they spent most of their time; her corner bedroom was more of a dressing room than a shared space. Benjamin followed. He made no objection to the delay, yet there was a resistance to his every move, as if to remind her he was waiting for an answer.

Alone in the bedroom, Lydia still didn't know what version of the truth to give. Benjamin stood on the rug, shoulders back, his brows and lips pulled into a bluffer's blank expression. It was bewildering to see him like this. Lydia was used to his emotions crossing his face the moment he felt them—and for the most part in these past few weeks, those emotions had been joy, excitement, and satisfaction.

She was the one lying to him. Yet she felt strangely betrayed by how he cut her off from his expression now, in the moment when she most needed to read him. She needed Benjamin as her ally, not another adversary.

With a deep breath, Lydia forced herself to say something. "I hardly know where to start."

"May I suggest beginning with why you paid Miss Maher's cousin five pounds?"

For a moment longer, Lydia weighed a lie: some family crisis that she was covering on behalf of Orla. Yet whereas that type of invention would have been necessary had Father or Alistair caught her with Conor Devlin, Benjamin could handle the truth. He might even applaud her. "He is gathering men who will sign the petition. How else did you think I would find them?"

He frowned, which was at least a new expression. "How often does he come calling?"

"Every few weeks or so. Not always for money. I was trying to tell him about the pamphlet just now, actually."

"Why was he so angry, then?" Kindness was leaking back into Benjamin's eyes—but so was confusion. "When I came outside, you and he were arguing."

"He didn't like the idea. He doesn't trust me, to tell the truth. I'm an Englishwoman. He probably suspects I'm laying a trap for him."

Benjamin ran a hand across his forehead in thought. Lydia had seen that exact gesture a hundred times these past weeks; it was comforting to see its return now. Until Benjamin said, "If he doesn't trust you, then why does he even speak to you? Did Miss Maher introduce you? Does she know what you are up to?"

"Oh yes, Orla knows."

"And it is on her word that her cousin takes orders from you?" He was incredulous. Lydia would be too. In the version of the story he was getting, there was no reason that Conor Devlin would ever believe she was a trustworthy ally.

Lydia didn't know how to explain it without telling the full truth. Yet she couldn't imagine how to even begin to confess about Seamus.

Benjamin didn't wait for her to reply. "How did you begin leading this movement, anyhow? Is this the first time you have had money to hand him? Is that why you needed your pin money so urgently?"

Perhaps because it was a distraction, Lydia seized on that last comment. "It is my pin money to do with as I want."

"I don't give a fig what you do with it. I am asking how you got involved with Miss Maher's cousin."

"She..." Lydia couldn't get the lie out. She should. It would be the best version of the story for the sake of her marriage. But she was too shaken by the argument with Conor and the lies she had already spun and the way Benjamin was looking at her with a mix of irritation and kindness and fear.

He could tell; she felt in her bones that even though there was no reason for him to know, her husband could sense that something threatening lurked beneath the surface of the story.

She didn't have the gumption to keep on lying. Nor the imagination to create a lie. So she told the truth. "I met him through his brother, Seamus Devlin. Orla had nothing to do with it. Seamus is the one who showed me the truth about Ireland. I started reading my father's correspondence, so Seamus introduced me to a few of his relatives, who are also active in the cause. That's how I know Conor Devlin."

And still Benjamin pushed. "Where is Seamus now? Back in Ireland?"

"No." She couldn't say the next words without tears. They surged to her eyes and her throat in red hot pain. "He is dead. Arrested for being out after sundown. He died on the transport ship to New South Wales."

The rest of it must surely be on her face, plain as a book for Benjamin to read. How she still loved Seamus. How she had given herself to Seamus, and would again, a hundred times over. Now Benjamin would turn away from her. Now he would decry her a liar, a slut, a woman unworthy of his name or protection or heart.

Lydia steeled herself to withstand whatever attack he launched at her. Yet she wasn't ready for him to choose ignorance.

"Why do you grieve him so?"

Said in a tender, plaintive voice. As if he wanted her to feel his sympathy, even as he demanded that she unpeel the truth further.

Lydia knew well enough that she was the villain in their marriage; she was the one who had deceived him, who had not been faithful to him in her heart, not even for a minute. Yet fury flashed through her that Benjamin could not draw the natural conclusions. That he was forcing her to say it as plainly as she could.

It was almost as if he were willfully not understanding her.

This time, Lydia made sure to look him in the eye. "Because I would have married him if I could have. And it's because of meeting me that he was out after sundown."

"Oh."

This time, Lydia could tell that Benjamin understood her.

IN THE PAST WEEKS, Benjamin had seen a half dozen emotions in his wife. Stiffness when she held herself in reserve. Sharp edges when she argued her point. Pink cheeks when she flirted with him. Smiles leaping from her lips after they coupled.

Perhaps he had fooled himself into believing he knew all her emotions already. But now he knew better, because he had never seen her whole body distill into one flame of passion before. Righteous passion. Whatever she felt right now, she felt it with her whole soul. And whatever it was, it wasn't an undying love for *him*.

No, if Lydia felt anything for him at all in this moment, Benjamin suspected it was pity. The pity of a woman letting down an unwanted suitor.

Benjamin whirled away from Lydia, turning his back so that his gaze could land on something else: the fire in the hearth, the patterns in the wallpaper, *anything*. "You loved this Seamus."

"Yes."

She didn't couch her answer to make it any softer. She didn't add *And now I love you*. She only said, "yes," and expected him to make do.

What a fool he was. What a fool he had always been. To believe that Lydia could love him. To believe that *anyone* could love him. He should have learned his lesson by now. He wasn't the type of man a woman loved.

Apparently, he was the type of man she married for convenience.

His voice spoke before he could stop it. "You should have told me."

"Yes, I should have." Her admission didn't make him feel any better. After a pause, Lydia added, "Would you still have married me, if you knew that I had loved before?"

The question hooked him back to his body. To reality. To his wife, waiting for reassurance that having a heart did not make her a bad person.

Benjamin forced a deep breath. The inhale steadied him; the exhale grounded him. He was being unfair. All Lydia had confessed to was loving a man before him. If that was a crime, then he himself was guilty of it eight times over.

"Of course I would have." Benjamin turned back to meet her eyes. "We didn't even meet each other until this year. It might even be unnatural if we had never loved before."

Lydia watched him as he said this. Her passion had drained away; now her shoulders crept towards her ears.

Just because she had loved before did not mean she did not love him now.

"I am guilty of the same," Benjamin added. "You are not the first woman I wanted to marry. That was Miss Amanda Fairchurch. I went to every ball, musicale, and salon that she planned to attend. She always danced with me, always spoke with me, always laughed at my witticisms. How I—" He paused, a little uncomfortable to say it now to Lydia. "How I loved her, and I thought she loved me back. Until she announced her engagement to the Marquess of Thorne, without so much as a word to me in advance as warning."

"Perhaps she had no say in the matter."

"No, I have long since reconciled myself to the fact that I was one of many suitors, and not one she ever considered seriously." That wasn't the point he was trying to make, anyhow. "As to the other matter...You were not my first lover, either. We mustn't waste any time feeling guilty for what came before each other."

Except now he remembered their wedding night. He had been so concerned about making her comfortable and about not hurting her. Meanwhile, she had known very well what was to come. She could have told him. She could have cared for his anxiety as much as he had hers.

Her hands twisted together. "I have felt so guilty. For not telling you."

A sign that she did care for him. "Now I know. We can put it behind us. After all, it is not as if we are pining after our past. I don't even have any mementos from..." If he ever knew the word he searched for, he lost it when Lydia's hands moved in a jerk to her ribs, below her breasts. Just as quickly, they fell away.

As if she had reached for something, then thought better of it.

He finished his thought: "Do you?"

Her chin tipped downwards, shadows crowding her face. "He was desperately poor and our love was forbidden. What mementos could he give me?"

And yet this man loomed in memory between them.

Only because Benjamin was letting it. He reached for forgiveness. He knew it was within himself somewhere. Sooner rather than later, he would think back on this moment and chastise himself for not having more charity for her feelings. For the moment, he pretended to have found it. "Knowing this about you doesn't change how much I love you, Lydia. Let us leave the past in the past."

Lydia blinked at him. Then she smiled. A smile that, to Benjamin's eyes, was genuine. "Are you sure you are a human man, and not an angel sent down from Heaven?"

"It is not so angelic if I am able to forgive you for something I hope you forgive in me, too. We both loved someone else before we met each other. That isn't worthy of melodrama, is it?" Benjamin held his breath, waiting for her reply. He knew what he wanted her to say. *I love you, too.*

"Hardly." Lydia still smiled. She stepped closer to him, even, and put a hand on his arm. "I thought I had to carry it as a secret, for the sake of our marriage. But now that I have told you, I feel such relief." Her fingers tightened around his forearm. "We're that much closer, aren't we?"

He should feel that. If he had found forgiveness already, Benjamin was sure he would. Hadn't he always dreamed of a wife with whom he could share the deepest, darkest shadows of his heart? The inverse had to hold. Lydia had trusted him with her secret. He should feel like her most treasured connection.

He shouldn't feel more alone than ever before.

"We're that much closer," he agreed. "Our love is that much stronger."

If only she would say the words.

Lydia's touch slid up his arm to cup his cheek. Her thumb brushed across his lips, a substitute for a kiss. "You're right, you know. We are incredibly lucky to have found each other. At least, I'm incredibly lucky to have found you."

Perhaps Benjamin was weak for needing to hear the words specifically. Perhaps she was as good as saying it in her soft, tender tone.

Each time she *didn't* say it, all Benjamin heard was *I don't love you.*

He didn't have the courage to ask for it again. So he did what his wife had done all these weeks: he let her believe him the happiest of men. "We had better return to our pamphlet if we want to honor your Seamus's memory."

If only the reward—Lydia's grin, luminescent from deep within her—was enough to dislodge the dagger in his heart.

CHAPTER THIRTEEN

T HEY FINISHED THE PAMPHLET later that week. Lydia won on its name, *A Report on Ireland*. Benjamin won on content, with his paragraph proposing that a moderate solution was preferable to no solution at all. Lydia consoled herself, knowing it was only four sentences (though one of those sentences stretched across three lines with all its semicolons and clauses), and that it was on the back of the pamphlet, which many people would neglect to read. Besides, Benjamin knew more about the *ton* than she did, and his family had more experience winning change in and out of Parliament than she and Seamus combined.

It was easy enough for Lydia to trust Benjamin, now that he knew the truth. All week, she had been floating on a river of relief. Lydia had assumed she would hold onto the secret of Seamus for the rest of her life. Never had she imagined telling Benjamin; never had she pictured how that might reshape their relationship. Yet now that she had told him, she wondered why she hadn't from the start. Benjamin, so kind and understanding, didn't hold it against her.

And knowing that he knew—it was like gulping for air after being underwater for too long.

Every part of her life felt different. More comfortable. More breathable. More like it was *hers*, and not some other woman's life to which she aspired. Lydia hadn't realized how much the specter of Seamus—and the secret of him—had hovered over her until she confessed to Benjamin. Now, she didn't feel like her lips were sewn shut to keep from saying the wrong thing. She woke in the mornings refreshed, because she hadn't spent the whole night tortured by anxiety. Her appetite even improved, though she hadn't known that it had suffered.

And now, when she looked at Benjamin, she didn't feel that maelstrom of guilt. He knew that she loved Seamus, that she had always loved Seamus, and that everything they did to free Ireland tied back to Seamus. Lydia didn't have to lie anymore, not with falsehoods nor by omission. Benjamin knew who she was, and he loved her for it.

That was the one sliver of guilt that remained with her. Every day, he still told her he loved her. Even though he knew she wouldn't—*couldn't*—say it back. Lydia gave him what she could: how grateful she was for him, how much she admired him, how lucky she felt to have found him. All true—profoundly true, in a way that sometimes staggered her with awe. Benjamin was everything she had hoped for in a husband and more, the type of partner she hadn't dared dream of. If she couldn't marry Seamus, she would choose Benjamin a hundred times over.

But she didn't *love* him. Not the way she had loved Seamus, so deeply and urgently that her every thought tied back to him. And not the way that Benjamin loved her.

Lydia refused to lie again to Benjamin. So she didn't say what he wanted her to say. She hoped, instead, that her honesty was enough.

They decided that she should be the one to take the pamphlet to the printer. Benjamin had suggested hiring Conor or Orla to do it, but Lydia feared that if anyone started investigating the pamphlet, whoever took it to the printer would be prosecuted. Equally, it didn't make sense for Benjamin to do the errand because if anyone happened to recognize him, they would immediately assume he was at the printers' for political purposes. If Lydia were discovered, the *ton* would conclude she was consulting about printed invitations or dance cards for an upcoming party.

"You'll be careful anyhow, won't you?" Benjamin followed her into her apartment, where Orla waited to help her into her drabbest day gown, a brown linen otherwise kept for at-home days. "I would prefer if you weren't venturing down to Fleet Street unaccompanied."

"I shall be careful, I promise. Before you know it, I shall be home again." And a fortnight following, their pamphlet would be printed into a hundred duplicates, ready to be dispersed to the most influential people in the empire.

The idea of it thrilled Lydia.

She wasn't sure if Benjamin felt the same excitement. With every step that took them closer to printing, he lost some of his enthusiasm. Just now, he leaned against the door, pale, his lips screwed together and his gaze lost somewhere in the carpet.

Lydia waited for Orla to finish tying her into the gown, then dismissed the maid so she could have Benjamin alone. She cupped her palms around his elbows. "Nothing bad shall happen. Our language is not seditious. Even if we are found out, the worst consequence is that we shall have to declare publicly our support for the cause. That would not be so terrible, would it?"

The corners of his lips twitched upwards. "I daresay you wish we could declare ourselves publicly already."

They had discussed this, too, ad nauseum. Lydia understood all the arguments for biding their time. The Prestons were an influential family—but a radical one. The more that Lydia and Benjamin could win people over to their cause before aligning the Prestons with it, the more chance they had of building a coalition that could win change in Parliament.

Lydia was used to pretending she agreed with the status quo. But now that she knew how refreshing it was to confess her truth to Benjamin, she was eager to declare it to the rest of the world. She was beginning to imagine what it would be like to enter every room with the confidence to tell people she disagreed with them.

She suspected she was going to like it.

"We'll wait until the moment is right." For now, Lydia was waiting for some of the enthusiasm to return to Benjamin. He hadn't responded to her touch; he was stiff, holding himself instead of her.

There had been more moments like this since her confession. Benjamin didn't say anything about it, and so neither did Lydia. She supposed it was the natural male reaction to discovering she had not been pure. That first night, Lydia had come to him, and they had coupled, but it had been dark, furtive—desperate. Afterwards, the room had been quiet, though Lydia knew neither of them were asleep, and she had resolved to wait for Benjamin to approach her again.

If she gave him enough time, he would stop fretting over Seamus.

And if Benjamin never came to her again, Lydia supposed she should be grateful. At least that way, she wouldn't be guilty of betraying Seamus's memory again.

"What will you do while I'm at the printer's?"

Benjamin's shoulders lifted in a shrug, dislodging Lydia's hands from his elbows. "Mope around missing you, I suppose."

The type of thing he would have said on any day of their marriage. Except there was something absent in the way he delivered it. It felt bitter, instead of a tender joke.

Lydia turned away, gathering her bag with the pamphlet and money, then tying on her bonnet. It was useful not to be looking directly at Benjamin as she asked, "Will you really miss me? Or are you still trying to forgive me?"

At least that jolted him from his post against the wall. He stalked to the little hearth beside her dressing table. "I already forgave you. I told you."

"Yes, you did." Lydia wanted to argue that if he had really forgiven her, she wouldn't feel as if he were a hundred miles away. Perhaps she was wrong, though. Perhaps it wasn't that he hadn't forgiven her; perhaps the strain was because he wasn't committed to Irish independence the way she was, or perhaps he was worried about something else entirely.

Orla interrupted them to announce that a hackney coach awaited Lydia on the street.

Whatever Lydia might find to say was a larger conversation than they had time for at the moment. She contented herself by concluding, "If you say it is so, then I must believe you. I'll see you for supper."

Benjamin called after her, "See you at supper." But he didn't ask for a kiss goodbye or even walk her to the street.

No matter what he said, Lydia didn't believe him. He hadn't forgiven her. And the relief she had been feeling all week shattered into a new kind of dread.

FROM THE THRESHOLD OF her room, Benjamin listened to the sound of her leaving. Her footsteps through the foyer. Mr. Smart's hoarse voice saying something in indistinct words. The door opening, then shutting. At last, the muffled sound of hooves and carriage wheels turning.

He waited, counting silently the moments it would take for the carriage to turn the corner towards the square, and then counting again for it to cross Broad Street. He reminded himself of all the reasons he shouldn't do this. Lydia deserved her privacy. He might find out more than he wanted to know. He was an honest man, and this was a dishonest act.

Benjamin's body acted despite all that. Even as his brain whispered *Orla will catch you*, he shut and locked Lydia's door. His fingers were full of energy, as if his consciousness had relocated there from his mind. They ran across her dressing table, circled porcelain pots of cream, pricked her hairbrushes. They opened drawers, rifled between handkerchiefs, untwisted ribbons. They seized on everything. They decided nothing.

He didn't know what he was looking for. He didn't know for certain that there was anything to look for. He just needed to look.

He had tried to put it all out of his mind. To stop speculating. This idea that Lydia still loved Seamus was in his head. The specter of all his own previous hurts rearing up to haunt him.

Except she still hadn't said she loved *him*, Benjamin. She touched him; she told him she was glad he was her husband; she said everything but *I love you*.

And Benjamin was still too afraid to ask for it.

So here he was. Looking through her apartment in search of something. He told himself he wanted proof that she *didn't* still think of Seamus. If he found a journal, he wanted it to be filled with her thoughts on their marriage and him and how he made her world whole again.

Yet his heart told him that if he found a journal, he would be holding a love letter dedicated to one Irish revolutionary, with no mention of a husband at all.

There was no sign of anything in her dressing table, unless one of the ribbons or amber necklaces had been a gift from the man. But Lydia had said it herself; Seamus had been penniless. Benjamin opened her armoire, where ten gowns hung in order of elegance. Simple spring wool on the left; laced and embroidered linen on the right. Lydia had left anything more—her silks, her cottons, the bejeweled and dazzling—behind when she married him.

Benjamin told his fingers to pause. To take that as a sign of her respect for him. Except the question of linen instead of cotton wasn't really *his*. It was his family's, his parents' legacy that Benjamin carried on. Lydia respected the concept the way she respected the tradition of moving into his house and accepting the name Mrs. Benjamin Preston.

It didn't mean she loved him.

Benjamin whirled away from her armoire, trying to order himself out of the room. It felt like poison to have doubt spearing through his heart. He did not want to interrogate every belonging of Lydia's in search of affirmation. He did not want to wonder whether she laced her dresses with green ribbons because of her love for Ireland or her love for Seamus. He wanted to go back to the version of him that didn't know a thing about Seamus. That didn't see every shadow crossing her face, that didn't question her every touch.

He wanted to believe again that their marriage was the perfect match of two like souls.

He crossed to the escritoire, which sat beside the room's narrow window. Aunt Charlotte had gifted it to them when they set up their London household, a beautiful relic from his mother's childhood home with a pattern of lighter wood inlaid against a dark frame. In Lydia's care, it was organized for functionality: a blotter across most of its face, with a pen and inkwell awaiting her touch. Opening the top drawer, he discovered the tools of letter writing, including more pens, sand, and cleaning sponge. The following drawer contained her kit of Preston-watermarked paper. Benjamin opened the final, lowest drawer, expecting to find her wax and seal.

Instead, it was empty. Empty save one old, worn letter. The type of letter that had clearly been read a hundred times. The type of letter that one shouldn't read without permission.

Benjamin's fingers lifted it from its resting place. The paper was folded in half along its width and thrice down its length; it yielded under his grip as if begging to be opened. The writing was a little faded, a little brown, but the script was confident. Each letter took up exactly as much space as it was supposed to.

Even before he read it, Benjamin knew what it was.

Dearest Emer,

You are in my thoughts, always, and now you are in my pen, on my paper. Soon this paper will be yours, as I am, so that I may live in your hands and thoughts as well as your heart. What a miracle is this, and what a miracle are you!

You, my warrior queen. You stun your enemies with your beauty; you lull them into safety with your gentle voice; you turn them to fire at themselves with your sweet words. I sleep the night through knowing you fight at my side, yet I gape at how much stronger you are than me: unbending in your convictions, no matter the sacrifice. Pledging your heart and life to Ireland even when it means surrendering your family, your friends, your very name.

Emer, my love for you and your unflinching vision for our country knows no end.

Keep me always in your heart,

Cúchullainn

Just the previous week, Lydia had told Benjamin the story of the warrior Cúchullainn and his queen, Emer. Characters every Irish peasant knew from childhood. The warrior feted for his strength and cunning. The maiden with the six gifts of womanhood: beauty, a gentle voice, sweet words, wisdom, skill at needlework, and chastity. When Cúchullainn fell in love with Emer at first sight, she set him a series of impossible trials. After years apart, they finally married and stood in Irish legend as an example of matrimony.

Even he couldn't fool himself into believing this was anything other than a love letter from Seamus.

It was a moment of a thousand reactions. Bewilderment—that Seamus would see in Lydia a woman who would lie and coerce to get her way, even if that way was Irish independence. Betrayal—that Lydia had let him believe she didn't have anything from Seamus, when she had this letter. Heartbreak—that he had found proof after all that Lydia still kept Seamus alive in her thoughts.

But most of all, shame. Shame that he had been so stupid. Shame that even after she confessed to him, Benjamin had convinced himself *he* was in the wrong, that the poison in his heart came from his own past and not from Lydia. Shame that he had ever believed Lydia when she told him she wanted to marry him.

It had never been about him. She hadn't married him because he made her days brighter or because they could converse for hours with ease. It was not Benjamin that Lydia found attractive; it was his blind willingness to follow her lead. Not even one whole day after their marriage, she had gotten him to commit his life's work to Ireland—and to hand over all the money he could to her cause. Like a puppet, he danced at her command.

You stun your enemies with your beauty; you lull them into safety with your gentle voice; you turn them to fire at themselves with your sweet words.

Benjamin had been an enemy. One Lydia stunned with her beauty, softened with her conversation, felled with her promises of love and affection and commitment.

But now he knew better.

The only question was: what would he do about it?

Chapter Fourteen

IT WAS THE WAITING that put the dry patches on her skin. Waiting for word that the pamphlets had been printed. Waiting for the night of the duke's birthday ball to finally arrive.

Waiting for Benjamin to say something more to her than a cordial cliché.

Every morning, Lydia woke and applied Orla's cold cream; every evening, she washed her forehead and cheeks with a lotion from *The Mirror of Graces*; yet still her skin erupted in objection. They were splotches, uneven in size and geography, united in being ugly, red, and scaly. The first one, in the shape of France, arose on her forehead. Then two parentheses framed her nose, little curved islands like the shape of Britain. Now there was an archipelago stretching down her chin and onto her neck.

She had been plagued by this sort of invasion before, ever since her menses had started at the age of eleven. Usually, Orla's cure worked after a day or so. Even when the spells had lasted longer, Lydia had rarely cared; the patches were a little irritating, but mostly they were offensive to anyone looking at her, and so long as Mother was off in England instead of exclaiming in horror, Lydia wasn't concerned with what anyone thought when looking at her.

But this rash of patches was lasting longer—four days already. Lydia scrubbed at her face, desperate to do something about it.

"It's the stress of it all," Orla said, handing her a clean, hot washrag. "You've taken on too much. Why, between the marrying and the moving houses and being in London and everything else, anyone's body would be crying out for a rest."

Lydia laid the steaming towel across her face, tipping her head backward to balance on the ridge of the chair. It was so hot it felt like it would boil her skin off—but that might be an improvement to showing up to the Duke of Berkwell's birthday ball looking like some kind of maladapted dragon.

It was the moment they had been planning for. Their first opportunity to see how much they could sway the peers friendliest to Ireland. Lydia had one hundred copies of their pamphlet, *A Report on Ireland*, ready to be snuck into the assembly rooms and littered through the retiring room, the card tables, even the narrow outdoor gardens to interrupt lovers' trysts.

Lydia didn't want to hide her face on the very night they were igniting the revolution.

"It could be the linens, too," Orla said, removing the hot towel from Lydia's face. "Your skin has never met these Berkshire cloths before. I'm not one to have an opinion, but the Irish linen seems much finer for a lady's complexion such as yours."

"My skin will have to get used to it, then. I won't ask the Prestons to import a good simply for my own vanity." Sitting up, Lydia examined her skin once more in the mirror. Her whole face was red from the heat of the towel, but the patches remained. She slathered cream—so cold it made her shiver—across the map of rebellions again. "If it isn't any better tonight, we'll have to use powder to hide it."

In the end, even powder didn't help. Instead of hiding the patches, it clung to them like snow on mountain peaks. Orla wiped Lydia's face clean of everything, fixed her hair one last time, and proclaimed that she would have to go to the party with the rash on display or not go at all.

Lydia went. Still, she cringed when Benjamin knocked at her door, ready to collect her. He was dressed in his best evening suit, with formal breeches that clung to the shape of his thighs and stockings that curved down his calves. His hair—which had grown longer since their wedding—framed his broad forehead in a loose wave; Lydia suppressed the urge to run her fingers through it.

He looked at her for all of two seconds before smiling. "You look beautiful."

The scripted line of a good husband. Lydia had pretended long enough to recognize that it was Benjamin's turn to act the part.

She wanted to grab his shoulders and shake him out of it. Even if he hated her, even if he could never forgive her, Lydia preferred an honest Benjamin to a fake one.

Instead, she responded with an equally false "Thank you," and followed him to the carriage. They made it all the way into the Duke of Berkwell's ballroom without another word, and then Benjamin disappeared, leaving Lydia to her family. Mother pulled Lydia into her arms—as if embracing her—to hiss, "You could have at least worn a veil. Really, child."

Lydia's fingers flew to her face before she could stop herself. "I tried to get rid of it."

Adelaide, as always, stepped in to protect her. "It's so dark in here that no one can see anyhow."

Lydia's family was in full splendor, showing off even more wealth and power than they actually had while in the midst of a duke's palace. Mother had been talking about her ballgown for months: a silk dress embroidered by a dozen seamstresses in Calcutta with beetle wings that glimmered with iridescent rainbows in every gleam of candlelight. Father—weaving along the far side of the room in search of brandy or cards or both—boasted a matching waistcoat. Even Adelaide, who mostly wore muted colors in deference to the younger debutantes, was done up in a frothy buttercup organza kept atop her silk undergown with diamond-headed pins.

A surprising rush of relief flooded Lydia as she took them all in. Had she not married Benjamin, she would still be a part of Mother's flock, trumped up in something just as expensive. Except what Mother considered exquisite, Lydia had always found ostentatious. It was only now, free from the deciding hand of her parents, that she realized how trapped she had felt. How liberated she was as Mrs.

Preston, wearing a lovely but simple linen dress and nothing more than carved amber for ornamentation.

And instead of spending the ball searching for a husband or ingratiating herself to people more powerful than she, Lydia could forge her way into conversations about Ireland.

If only Benjamin would forgive her enough to stay by her side.

"I'll consider a veil next time," she said to her mother. Then she took Adelaide by the hand. "Come help fix my dress in the retiring room?"

Even though it was early in the party, the retiring room was already busy with mothers instructing debutantes on their dance cards, friends stealing a moment for gossip, maids fixing torn dresses, and more than a few women waiting for a chance to pee in the chamber pots. Lydia eyed the maids; Conor Devlin had gotten a few sympathetic friends hired into the household for the party to help distribute the leaflets. She wondered which of the women in the duke's burgundy livery was there under false pretenses: the tiny girl scurrying after Lady Fairfax's request for a fan, the Creole woman mending a seam for Miss Hunt, or the flame-haired girl minding the pots.

It didn't much matter. Lydia and Adelaide needed do no more than sit on the plush velvet settee before Lydia discovered a stack of the pamphlets on the side table. She handed one to Adelaide, feigning surprise. "Whatever do you think this is?"

They had decided to keep it anonymous. A broadsheet folded in two, each of its four faces featured an argument against the Insurrection Act. The first article spoke from the economic perspective; the next discussed why Catholics were no threat to the English church; the third shared the story of an innocent Irishman condemned to transportation for running out to find a midwife in the middle of the night; and Benjamin's final argument quoted Montesquieu, Rousseau, and England's own Locke to remind the British that the question of Ireland's freedom was one of man's rights, not a political debate.

Adelaide cut Lydia a shrewd, knowing look as soon as she saw the masthead reading *A Report on Ireland*. "Do you have something to do with this?"

Lydia didn't like to lie to her sister. She lifted her shoulders in a shrug, as if to say she didn't know. "It has some interesting ideas, don't you think?"

Before Adelaide could respond, their friend Lady Claudia swooped in. "Oh, isn't that just the most scandalous thing you've ever seen? Supposedly the duke is hiring the Bow Street Runners to discover who brought those in. To his birthday party, no less!"

Lady Claudia was in almost as dazzling a dress as Mother: deep red silk with a web of pearls in the shape of a Celtic cross across the stretch of her bodice. Her hair—an unremarkable shade of brown—was twisted into a dozen springy ringlets, and a string of sapphires clung to her neck.

She pressed a kiss to each of their cheeks in greeting. Her eyes lingered on Lydia a little longer. "I've been dying to see you, Lady Lydia. You're looking...how is marriage treating you?"

Lydia didn't know if the hesitation in Claudia's expression came from discovering the red rash or from Claudia's concerns in her own marriage. Either way, Lydia smiled. "Well. Mr. Preston and I are very well suited to each other." Or they had been, anyway, before Benjamin had discovered the truth. She added, "How is Lord Chatteris?"

"He is at a hunting party in Scotland." For the briefest of moments, sorrow flashed through Claudia's eyes. Then she took the seat beside Adelaide, diving into gossip again. "And when will you be rescuing Lady Adelaide from her tower and inviting her to move into the Preston townhouse?"

Lydia had, in fact, already offered Adelaide a room in Soho. "Our mother insists that Adelaide remain as her companion through the end of the season."

"Much to my chagrin." Then Adelaide lowered her voice. "Although, if I may be honest, I'm not sure I can live without tea and sugar for any extended period of time, as much as I admire the principle."

"I got used to it more quickly than I expected."

"Choosing between the devil and the devil's temptations," Claudia said knowingly. "Well, let us change the subject before we find ourselves amidst a sisters' dispute. Lady Thorne was just telling me these pamphlets are all over the party, and the duke is none too happy about it. Can you imagine, trying to turn his birthday celebration into some sort of political forum?"

"It's not as if it was void of politics without these." Lydia tried not to sound too defensive. "What do you think the men discuss in the card room?"

"Whores and horses." Claudia peered at Lydia. "Really, dear, I've never met a peer who wouldn't rather discuss his own concerns than get into a fusty quibble about some parliamentary measure."

Adelaide said, "In Lydia's defense, the Prestons are a different breed. I imagine Lord Preston and Mr. Preston do expect to have political conversation here tonight."

"When one holds all the real and economic power, nothing one does is apolitical," Lydia added. "Either way, I don't think these pamphlets are scandalous. They are intriguing. Have you read one?"

Claudia smiled, humoring her now. "I couldn't possibly read in all this excitement."

"Well, you should take one home to read tomorrow. Perhaps there are a few points you'll find you agree with."

There was a reason they had been friends all this time. Claudia tucked a folded pamphlet into her bodice. "I shall do exactly that. After all, I love anything to do with Ireland. Tell me, did you negotiate regular trips home as part of your marriage settlement?"

"Not in writing, but I have so captivated Mr. Preston with my descriptions of the countryside that he is as anxious to travel there as I am." At least, he had been. They had discussed it a few times already: a trip in the summertime, once everyone else quit London, to visit Dublin and Balise House.

Lydia hoped it would still come true. It would be expensive—perhaps more money than they should rightly spend on luxuries—but she wanted to see Benjamin's reactions to the luscious green hills, the magical look of morning dew on the fields, the sense that one had woken in Heaven instead of on Earth.

Claudia sighed. "Lord Chatteris has promised to take me back as well, but only after I have provided him with a healthy son."

Lydia couldn't help glancing down at her friend's decidedly unswollen womb. "It seems particularly difficult to fulfill that promise if he is always away hunting in Scotland."

"That is only one of a dozen reasons why it is particularly difficult." Again, there was a flash of true sorrow with this statement, and then Claudia turned away from it. "Shall we return to the ballroom and see if any other scandals have erupted yet?"

They walked as a threesome, Lydia and Adelaide linked into each of Lady Claudia's arms, until the crowd of the corridor forced them to break into a line. Lydia had forgotten entirely about her face by now, her heart speeding as she strained for clues as to how the overdressed men and women felt about the pamphlets. Her heart raced at every word that drifted her way: *bold, unbelievable, crucial.* She heard only snippets, caught from midair without context, yet Lydia's stomach stirred with excitement from the certainty that at least half the words were in reaction to her and Benjamin's work.

They had discussed—ad nauseum—what kind of reception they could hope for the pamphlets to receive at the duke's ball. Lydia knew not everyone would welcome the anonymous interruption;

nor would even a tenth of the party change their views on Ireland because of it. Yet, wreathed by heated spring air and the smell of champagne, Lydia's veins surged with hope. She looked at each passerby as a potential new ally. She wanted to run to every guest one by one, seize them by the shoulders, and ask what they thought now that they had read about Ireland from a truer perspective.

She wished Benjamin hadn't peeled away so quickly. It was his arm, not Claudia's, she wanted to be holding as she deciphered the faces of their set. He would find her for a dance, Lydia assured herself, and she could tell him then how much she wanted him at her side.

The hired maids had done a good job: by the time Lydia, Adelaide, and Claudia returned to the main ballroom, the pamphlets were well and truly distributed. Lydia spotted a handful by the bowl of mild ratafia punch for ladies; fans of pamphlets sat waiting on the benches where wallflowers retreated during dances; and, most rewarding, a dozen pamphlets speckled the clumps of guests, with more than one head bent over the paper to read.

"The pamphlet is causing quite the stir, to be sure." Lydia tried not to sound triumphant.

Claudia replied, "Perhaps the duke distributed it himself to show off how many candles he can afford in his chandeliers. Otherwise, how could anyone read a word?"

"Poppycock is what it is," a nearby viscount proclaimed in a voice loud with drink.

His companion agreed equally loudly. "If a ball is going to purvey any literature, it ought to be a gossip rag or naughty limericks."

A female voice entered the conversation now: "Gentlemen, you mistake its purpose. It is not here to entertain. The duke merely ran out of napkins and is offering this rubbish to help us wipe away our sweat."

Adelaide angled herself to stand beside Lydia. "You haven't had anything to drink since you got here. Shall we fetch some punch?"

"Thank you, but I'm sure it is full of imported fruits and cane sugar." Still, Lydia no longer felt she was sailing on energy. "Perhaps we can find some cooler air by the garden doors."

Claudia looped her arm through Lydia's again as they moved. "Some people wouldn't know how to have an original thought if it hit them in the face. You mustn't let either the pamphlet or what people think of it bother you. One person's opinion is exactly as worthless as the next person's."

Lydia knew her friend meant well. Except she missed the point entirely. Here they stood in a ballroom full of the empire's most powerful people. These were the very men who shaped laws, who could—in Benjamin's dreamy perspective—vote to give Ireland every inch of freedom it deserved. And these were the women who shared their houses, bore their children, and shaped their social circles. If any group of people needed to be swayed for peaceful change, it was this one.

And instead of even considering new ideas, they complained about a lack of gossip.

By the garden doors it was no better. The air was cooler—by a slim margin—but almost as soon as they arrived, one of Lady Claudia's elderly relations by marriage assaulted them with, "If the duke thinks I am going to spare a single tear for those Irish barbarians, he might as well not invite me to his next party."

Lydia didn't know the woman. She didn't have a right to respond, by courtesy's rule. Yet she couldn't stop herself: "I am sure you are welcome to leave this very moment, ma'am."

"Lydia!" Adelaide gasped. Lady Claudia turned to apologize to her relation.

Lydia couldn't bring herself to feel guilty. Anger roared through her, more welcome than dismay. She didn't understand why these people who had everything needed to dismiss the topic with such vitriol. All she asked was for them to recognize Irishmen as human beings with the same rights as Englishmen, yet they reacted as if she had held a knife to their throats and threatened their children.

If they wouldn't even consider a few new ideas, Lydia didn't see how she could ever hope to wrest Ireland from their claws.

Adelaide and Lady Claudia were turning to her; Lydia saw the reprimands sparring with concern in their eyes. She didn't want either, not unless they could pledge to her they were on her side. "I need air," she said, breaking away, and let herself through the door into the garden.

The fury was not becoming, but she welcomed it anyway. It cut through the worry about her patchy face and the concerns about what she could or could not eat and reminded her of who she was at her core: an Irish-raised girl who cared most about winning Ireland its freedom. Everything else in her life was just trappings, ornaments she wouldn't mourn if they fell away.

Everything except one: Benjamin. That was the one emotion piercing through her veil of anger as she hurried through the duke's manicured gardens in search of privacy. She wanted to be alone, except she wanted—yearned for—Benjamin to be with her. For him to forgive her, and for him to hold her.

Lydia didn't know how to feel about that at all.

B ENJAMIN HAD ALWAYS FOUND it odd that society expected husbands and wives to spend the duration of balls as far apart as possible. Perhaps, when they were newlyweds, they might be forgiven for dancing one set together. For the most part, however, they were expected to arrive together and then divide, almost to the point of ignoring each other.

He had always imagined that, once he snagged himself a wife, he would eschew that expectation entirely in favor of soaking up as much of her company as he could. Yet here at Robert's birthday ball, he was grateful for the custom.

It had been a week since he had discovered the letter from Seamus Devlin in Lydia's escritoire. A whole week—and Benjamin still hadn't decided what to do. In the moment, he had returned it to its hiding place, fingers shaking, and fled from the room as if he had never been there. When Lydia returned from the printers', she was so happy that she wrapped her arms around his neck and kissed his cheek, right in front of Papa and Max as everyone gathered for supper.

More of her games, Benjamin supposed. Her sweet words and gentle voice to keep the enemy lulled.

He didn't say anything then. They got through supper, and then the rest of that evening, and then the following day, and so on, until here they were at the ball.

And Benjamin still didn't know what he was going to do.

After depositing Lydia with her family, he ventured to the duke's card room. Papa wasn't much of a gambler, but he was more likely to spend a ball deep in conversation with the players than watching the dancing. Benjamin found Max there, too, winning a low-stakes game of faro. "Should I include your game in my letter to Ellen this week?" Benjamin teased after exchanging greetings.

"My accounting of it will be much more entertaining, I'm sure," Max drawled. "Besides, I thought we were in league together, now that you're a married man, too."

"Blood is thicker than water." Benjamin took the seat beside Papa. The duke had set up the card room in the residence's parlor, which was spacious enough to hold three large card tables, a billiards table, and an assortment of chairs for spectators. The air churned with tobacco smoke; the various blends were going to give Benjamin a headache if he stayed in there for too long. He spotted white pamphlets on each of the side tables, arranged in respectful piles like the programs at a musicale.

"What are those?" he asked.

"A political screed on why Ireland should be an independent country," Papa replied, not quite meeting Benjamin's eyes.

He suspected, then. Max probably did, too; they lived in the same household, after all, and couldn't have missed Benjamin and Lydia's hushed discussions.

Already he was nostalgic for that time when he had believed Lydia was fueled by a pure, empathetic desire for justice. When he had thought of them as two white knights united in purpose as well as in their hearts.

When instead, she had picked up this fight in the name of her dead lover, whom she would never forget.

Keep me always in your heart.

"Does it make any interesting points?" Benjamin asked. The cause was bigger than Lydia, bigger even than a man whose memory could not be vanquished. The cause was a nation being subjugated to British rule, an entire class being excluded and punished for their religion. If he focused on the cause, he could get through the night.

Without looking up from his cards, Max replied, "The usual. The Irish economy is not benefitted by a population living in constant fear of arrest; the Irish Catholics are poorly treated when Roman domination is no longer a threat to the British Crown; the rights of man should extend to the Irish as well as the English."

"Conveniently, it forgets that France will invade us via the Irish shores the very first moment we take our attention away from Dublin." This from Robert, who had entered the room in all his birthday splendor without Benjamin noticing. He looked tired, rather than celebratory, and sank into the chair next to Benjamin with a sigh. "It is well and good to see the world through ideals, until you must also reckon with reality."

"Then you don't endorse these pamphlets?" Benjamin asked.

Robert poured himself a glass of brandy. "I endorse neither their ideas nor their presence at my party. This is why one needs a wife, I suppose, to keep a closer eye on who may or may not disperse papers at a ball. But let's talk of something more pleasant. How is Lady Lydia, Preston? As divine as you found her before the marriage?"

Benjamin didn't want to lie. Neither did he want to confess he had married a woman who would never love him back. There weren't words, really, for how he felt about Lydia, the agony of loving her and grieving her all at the same time.

"Precisely," he replied to Robert. "Though, now that you mention it, I had better excuse myself to go make sure she found herself a glass of punch."

Weaving back into the ballroom, Benjamin noticed the pamphlet clutched in a few hands, as well as littering the floor here and there. He bent to pick up one copy that was twisted and wet, right in the crowd's path; the last thing he wanted was for anyone to slip and fall against the duke's parquet floor.

"You know there are footmen to do that."

The words slipped behind Benjamin's neck and into his ears like a drip of cold water. He stood, the wet pamphlet in his hand, to discover Amanda Fairchurch standing before him.

She wasn't Amanda Fairchurch anymore, of course. She was the Marchioness of Thorne, a wife of five years and the mother of two children. And she dazzled: blue silk gown, gold lace trim, diamonds on her ears and neck and wrists. Her brown eyes—to which Benjamin had composed sonnets he had never been brave enough to share—were like dark black pools in the dim candlelight.

How he had loved her. From the very first moment he saw her six years ago, Benjamin had been unable to tear his thoughts away from her. For a blissful month, he had run around London believing her to be his soulmate. Believing her to be as in love with him as he was with her.

And then she had announced her engagement to the marquess. At a ball, not unlike this one, without a word of warning or apology or even regret to Benjamin.

"You're looking well, Mr. Preston," she said. "Are you enjoying His Grace's ball?"

"Thank you." With the tenderness of poking an old wound, Benjamin measured his own emotions. He had last seen Amanda this past autumn at an opera benefitting a new orphanage. Even then, all these years later—all these *loves* later, with his heart wallpapered over with a half dozen new desires and losses—the sight of her had stabbed him. For the rest of the evening, he could think of nothing but her: what could have been, what he still wished might have gone differently; whether she was happy; whether *he* was happy; even a new, bitter anger that she had let him believe she loved him back.

Now, he wasn't sure he felt anything. Except his old friend shame, wearing a new disguise: where Lydia and her first love were true to each other even after death, Benjamin hadn't even been able to inspire honesty from Amanda.

"I have not yet filled my dance card." Amanda offered up her wrist, from which an elegant piece of cardstock dangled. "I was on my way to the card room to see if I could muster up a few more partners."

Benjamin had always been charmed by this self-deprecating way of hers, and how her lips turned up in the slightest smile as she acknowledged her own ridiculousness. He waited for the tug of familiarity to plunge him back into something: heartbreak, puppy love, even anger. But he felt the same as if encountering an acquaintance, one with whom he no longer had anything in common.

"I wish I could oblige, Lady Thorne, but I am on assignment to fetch my wife a refreshment."

"Ah yes. I heard you married." Amanda dropped her wrist back to her side. "I have only seen Lady Lydia from afar. She is striking. So very tall."

It was strange to hear Lydia abstracted into just a few adjectives. He felt the need to defend her from such a summation, if only to prove himself a tender husband. "Her character is as striking as her person. She is a woman of great kindness, strategy, and intelligence. I am dazzled by her."

"Oh my. I'm not sure I've ever heard 'strategy' used as a compliment before." Amanda's words curdled as they left her lips. "Does that mean she has already told you how to spend your ten thousand pounds?"

Whatever faint fondness Benjamin still felt towards Amanda evaporated. Taking her in one last time, he didn't even like the soft shape of her lips or the diamonds she wore in such a desperate display of superiority. Of all people, she had no right to cast aspersions on Lydia or his marriage or anything he chose to do with his life.

Even if it was true that, in the end, his inheritance was why Lydia had married him.

"Please excuse me," he said. "I find it gauche to discuss money."

Turning on his heel, Benjamin forged through the crowd. The wet pamphlet clung to his palm; he stopped a footman and scraped it off onto the man's awaiting silver tray.

If he was being honest with himself, seeing Amanda again, a part of him had hoped he would realize *she* was the woman he truly loved, and every woman who came after her—Lydia included—was merely a substitute.

But it wasn't true. Benjamin felt only distaste for Amanda. It wasn't even as strong as hate or disgust. He simply didn't like her anymore. She was not an interesting person, nor was she kind, nor was she curious about him.

Which meant he loved Lydia. These feelings that overwhelmed him were not placeholders for his feelings for Amanda. Even though

Lydia used him only as a pawn, Benjamin had fallen in love with her and her alone.

If there was one consolation from his encounter with Amanda, it was this: he had, eventually, somehow, stopped loving her. Perhaps that meant that one day, if he found a way to break free from her spell, he could stop loving Lydia, too.

CHAPTER FIFTEEN

They didn't get home until after two in the morning. Poor Mr. Smart napped in an armchair in the parlor, waiting for their carriage to arrive; Orla was awake as well to help Lydia out of her gown. She cast Lydia a questioning look but didn't ask a thing about the pamphlets. "Your rash is looking better, my lady."

"That's just the poor lighting, I'm sure."

Orla lifted the dress over Lydia's head. "My cousin stopped by earlier. We had a long talk. The Ribbonmen are trying to convince him to join their lodge."

The Ribbonmen. The very bogeymen that Parliament thought it needed to protect itself from with the Insurrection Act. The men who took it upon themselves to purchase weapons and prepare for violence without any plan for how to govern. And who didn't admit women into their ranks. If Conor joined the Ribbonmen, he would leave Lydia alone with all her plans and no one in Ireland to execute them. "Is he tempted?"

"Truth be told, I couldn't tell. He asked that you call on him at Shepherd's Inn in Whitechapel soon. He'll be there tomorrow all day, or in the evenings all the rest of the week." Lips pursing, Orla unlaced Lydia's corset. "Did you want to change into a nightgown, my lady, or stay in your shift, since it is such a warm night?"

Lydia had been staying in her shift of late, rather than changing into her frilly, less comfortable nightdresses. There was no point in dressing like a wife if Benjamin wouldn't come to her. Lydia had been biding her time, waiting night after night for him to at last shuffle off his concerns about Seamus.

She didn't want to wait anymore. The shock of the ball rattled through her so that she didn't feel an ounce of the exhaustion she should have. She wanted to parse it all with Benjamin. And she wanted to burn off some of this energy.

Lydia wanted Benjamin, plain and simple.

"I'll change into my lace." The lace had been spun and woven in Honiton, just a hundred miles from Northfield Hall. It was not a gown designed to be slept in. Unless Benjamin was violently ill that very moment, Lydia expected he would have no trouble understanding her intentions.

Orla helped her into the nightgown, unpinned her hair, and handed her a hot washcloth for her face.

"No need to wake me in the morning, Orla," Lydia said by way of goodnight. "Take a nice lie in yourself, too."

Protected in her wrapper, Lydia tiptoed barefoot down the woven carpet running down the corridor. She knocked once, then let herself into Benjamin's room. "Do you mind if I come in?"

He was alone, his evening clothes replaced with an old, yellowed nightshirt and stockings drooping down to his ankles.

Strange, how she felt a flood of relief from the mere sight of him.

"I'd have thought you were already asleep. Did you enjoy the dancing?" Benjamin moved to the fire, which was banked for the night, and poked at the coals.

"The dancing?" Lydia had forced herself to participate in the ball as if she were a normal heiress to a barony; she had danced three sets, though she couldn't even remember her partners. "Tonight was a disaster. I hardly had time to notice the dancing."

He looked at her now. For the first time, she realized. His eyes dragged across her face as if they were fingers. "A disaster?"

"People mocked the pamphlet. We did not achieve anything. We did not change anyone's mind."

Benjamin prodded at the coals. "Lydia, you and I both knew we weren't going to change minds tonight. This was about claiming attention. Now the gossip rags will discuss it—the scandal of sharing political pamphlets in favor of Ireland at the duke's birthday party! Now it will become something that all of London discusses. Not just the Irish revolutionaries, and not just the members of Parliament."

"I heard the duke was offended. The Duke of Berkwell! If we can't count on him to be concerned for Ireland's rights, there is no point in trying to change anyone else's mind."

Still, Benjamin stood away from her instead of coming close and wrapping his arms around her. "It has not come to a vote yet. You cannot declare the outcome of the battle before it has actually happened."

"How can you be so calm?" All night, she had heard nothing but derision for the idea of *discussing* Ireland, much less granting its freedom. And Benjamin acted as if it had been just another party. "Every day that the Insurrection Act stands, men are arrested who have done nothing wrong. Men are sent away from their homes and families for doing nothing more than swearing loyalty to each other instead of the Crown. Don't you feel that? Don't you feel how urgent this is?"

"Of course it is urgent. But no solution is going to happen overnight. We must trust that seeing this campaign through each step will work, not give up now, when we are just beginning."

Tears threatened her again. Lydia turned away, pressing the heels of her hands into her eyes to keep Benjamin from seeing them.

She hadn't felt this desperate before. Even when Seamus died, Lydia hadn't felt so completely without hope. She'd had a plan: she would marry well, get her own money, and make the revolution happen.

Well, here she was on the other side of that plan. And for the first time—was she really so naïve that now was the first time she realized this?—Lydia wasn't sure it would work.

"Conor Devlin told Orla tonight that he is considering joining the Ribbonmen."

From behind her—still over there, not beside her, not touching her—Benjamin said, "We must do our best to persuade him otherwise. Violence won't win Ireland any favors. If anything, it will only make Parliament pass more stringent restrictions than the Insurrection Act."

"If Parliament is unwilling to negotiate when we come from a peaceful position *and* unwilling to negotiate when we come from violence, then it is unwilling to negotiate. At some point, we must stop trying to win Parliament's favor one way or another."

Those were Seamus's words, parroted through her mouth. Lydia clung to them as her new hope, the one flickering flame that might keep her from plunging into blackness. Anger felt better than despair, anyway.

"I see." From behind her came the sound of Benjamin replacing the poker in its stand. Iron against iron. "And how long has this been your plan? Were you ever going to give the pamphlets a chance to work, or was it just another of your—how did he say it—'sweet words' to trick me into helping you?"

Ice couldn't have chilled Lydia's blood faster. She hadn't looked at the letter in weeks. It was put away in a drawer where she wouldn't be tempted to open it.

There was no reason Benjamin would have found it.

"I have no idea what you mean," she lied.

"Do you not, warrior queen?" Now, at last, he came closer. But not to comfort her. Benjamin paced around her. His voice was soft, almost a whisper, yet each word landed on Lydia's skin. "You stun your enemies with your beauty. You lull them with your gentle voice. You turn them on themselves with your sweet words."

Seamus's words had been tender. From Benjamin, they were terrible. A panic swirled, taking her breath away, as Lydia's mind raced for a way to stop him from saying anything more.

"You played me for a fool. Let me believe you married me because you loved me. Convinced me that Ireland was worthy of my time and my inheritance by virtue of the rights of man alone. You even had me humiliate my friend by infiltrating his ball with subversive pamphlets. And all this time it had nothing to do with me or even Ireland, did it?" Benjamin landed in front of her, chin raised to see her eye to eye.

His were darker than the night itself.

"This is about Seamus. This is about proving to him, even in death, that you are the Emer to his Cúchullainn."

"No." Even if he was right, he was wrong. "I didn't try to fool you. I told you even when we were courting that I would use your money for Ireland. The only thing I didn't tell you about was Seamus. And I'm glad I didn't. It is clear you wouldn't have married me if you knew."

"How monstrous of me to prefer a wife who hasn't promised her heart to a dead man."

There was nothing but fury in him. Not a scrap of compassion nor forgiveness nor kindness. Nothing that made him Benjamin. Nothing that made him fair. It lit Lydia's own anger. "Have I been cold to you? Have I withheld my person or my conversation? Have

I not served you in every duty expected of me?" Lydia tore open her wrapper, cold air rushing in to prick alive the skin beneath her lace. "I came here tonight to throw myself at you because I wanted you. Do not accuse me of selling you false goods. I am doing everything I can to be the best wife I can be."

He didn't even look at her body. "Why do you keep that letter, then? And why did you lie when I asked if you had any keepsakes from him?"

They were past the point of pretending she didn't know what he meant. Lydia tied her robe tight around her torso again. "I don't know."

Benjamin shifted; more cold air filled between them. "If you want to be my wife, then burn the letter and never think of him again. I'll not accept anything less."

Burn the letter. The one and only thing she had of Seamus. Seamus's words. Seamus's handwriting. Seamus's paper. How many times had Lydia pressed it to her heart, imagining that the letter had once sat in Seamus's breast pocket, against his own heart? How many times had she lifted it to her nose, hoping against hope that she could smell his tobacco and peat scent again?

Benjamin might as well ask her to remove her own heart from its cage.

Lydia took stock of her husband. She didn't like this Benjamin. Yet she had created him. With her own planning and scheming. Just as he accused her.

She hadn't meant to fool him. But somehow, she had.

Guilt weighed like ten thousand transport ships atop her shoulders. Still, she couldn't burn that letter.

And he shouldn't ask that of her.

"If you want to be my husband," she replied, "don't be cruel."

Afraid of what he would say next, she whirled around and fled the room.

Chapter Sixteen

T HE WHOLE CITY FELT a little sleepy, as if everyone was still waking up from the duke's ball. There were no votes that day, only preparation for debates and resolutions to come later that week. As Benjamin made his way to join Papa in Westminster, he saw hardworking clerks, shopkeepers, and street peddlers, and no one else. A warning: anyone with enough money and good sense had stayed home.

A different Benjamin would have stayed home, too. The Benjamin he had always dreamed of becoming. The doting husband. The one who was desperately in love, who held his wife close in his arms, who never said anything wretched and who could never make her cry.

He was not that Benjamin. And so he left the house before the clocks even chimed nine, ceding the whole of Soho to Lydia.

No matter that she had lied to him. No matter that she still had that letter and would probably always love Seamus Devlin instead of him. Even if she *had* set out to fool him from the very beginning.

When he remembered how he had let anger get the best of him—circling her, like a wolf stalking a lamb!—how he had hurled accusations at her—how he had threatened her!

Don't be cruel.

Benjamin felt physically ill with shame. All his hurt and fury had turned into venom in his veins, turning him into a man even he didn't recognize. And the worst of it was he hadn't any idea how to make things right. Not when the situation remained the same. Not when Lydia clung to that letter instead of him.

So he came to Papa's offices, leased from the Society for the Propagation of Free Produce, where Papa spent most of his days in London to manage his political affairs. Benjamin ordinarily hated this part of being a Preston: building alliances, writing speeches, and corresponding with the public. People from all parts of the empire wanted Papa to take up the mantle for them: the African and Asiatic Society, who needed money for the poor and ill; the Jewish community, who had been slandered by Mr. Lockhart in the House of Commons as oath-breakers; even a widow in Cornwall who hoped he could help her purchase her farm so that she and her children wouldn't be turned out at the end of the year.

That morning, Benjamin took up the correspondence as penance. As if assisting others would erase the harm he had done.

He made it through ten letters, about seven more than he could usually manage. "How can you possibly help all these people?"

Papa looked up from his desk, where he was working on a draft of a speech. Though his fingers were stained with ink, his eyes didn't carry any hint of exhaustion. "I can't. I do what I can for as many of them as possible, without losing sight of what I think will make the biggest impact for the most people in this empire."

"Ending slavery."

Placing his pen carefully in its cradle, Papa steepled his fingers. "At first, transforming Northfield Hall was enough for me. It took all of my energy, anyhow. Mine and your mother's. There was so much to change, physically, but also so much persuasion to be done, with ourselves, with our tenants, even with the people we welcomed into the estate. We barely even came to London because we had so much to do at home. But now it is—well, there is always something to be improved, of course, but now it is settled. And I have the energy to look elsewhere. To remember what else I dream of for this world." He nodded at Benjamin. "It will be the same for you. What consumes you now will change because you will work at it, and it will change, and your position of influence will change; in a decade, you will be consumed by something else; in the following one, something else; and then one day you will be here, reflecting with your son on all the things you have done. Some more successfully than others, but still, you will have done them."

An optimistic answer. Filled with Papa's own assumptions about why Benjamin was in a foul mood and what he would do with his life and how alike they were.

When Benjamin looked down at the letters in his hands, he didn't feel optimistic. The needs of each and every one swirled around him, tugging at his conscience and there was no calculus for which initiative would have the most impact on the most people.

And why should the number of people matter, when to the widow in Cornwall, her home was her home and she didn't know what to do if she didn't have a roof over the head of her family?

And—weighing down each and every one of these thoughts—the irrationality of depending on *him* to make any difference. All he had was his name, a little bit of money, and Papa's legacy. Benjamin couldn't even handle his wife with care; how could he help a whole class of strangers?

It was one thing for Papa to lead the charge. He had spent decades examining the empire's political and economic foundations. And Ellen had been born with a fire in her, an unwavering faith that putting one foot in front of the other would eventually lead to change. Pair that with Max's political talent, and they would forge a new country whether anyone wanted it or not.

Benjamin had always thought that one day, his instinct for leadership would kick in, like his voice lowering or a beard thickening on his jaw. But perhaps the truth was that he had none. He didn't even have a vision for how to help Ireland, despite Lydia placing the cause in front of him like a roast pig on a silver platter. He only followed her passion, borrowing ideas from Papa's past campaigns, without any of his own ideas.

Perhaps the truth was that Benjamin wasn't fit to lead his own life, much less help anyone else in theirs.

"How long do you think a tour of the empire would take?"

Papa's face shrank into a puzzled frown. "Three years at least. More, if you want to allow yourself time to explore beyond the cities."

Three years without seeing Lydia. The idea of being apart from her ignited an ache in his heart; yet remaining near her seemed impossible, not when he treated her the way he had the night before. "I would have to give custom to the shipping companies and importers I have derided my whole life."

"You would also see with your own eyes and settle for your own heart whether it is important to continue fighting against them."

Benjamin had no real interest in witnessing the horrors of sugar plantations in the West Indies or the cotton plantations growing beyond the Indus River. He believed what he had heard from Papa and the people who came to Northfield Hall; he had read reports and seen pictures. But the trip would take him away from Lydia and give him something new and pressing to think about instead.

Perhaps by the time he returned, when he looked at her, he would see only a friend, not the woman who had grabbed his heart with her hands and broke it in two.

Perhaps by then, he wouldn't be cruel.

Papa asked, "Is Lady Lydia interested in seeing the empire, too?"

Benjamin knew his father was asking more than just that question. Papa shared the townhouse with them; he and Max both must surely have noticed the cooling between Benjamin and Lydia.

But Benjamin wasn't ready to discuss it with his family. He wasn't sure he would ever be ready to tell them the truth. He still wanted to protect Lydia. And he didn't want to admit that they had been right.

It had been too good to be true that such a smart, vibrant woman would want to marry him.

"No, she would stay here. At Northfield Hall, I suppose."

For a long time, Papa said nothing. Then, he replied: "Ellen would be delighted to have her company, particularly when Max is in town."

It became a picture in Benjamin's head: Lydia at Northfield Hall, organizing the Irish revolution over supper with Ellen and the little ones. A future so very different from the one he had always imagined. The one where he was at that table and Lydia looked to him for encouragement.

He rose, shifting the correspondence back onto his father's desk. "I have plenty to think about."

The trip might be necessary to heal his heart. It might even be better for the long term to put him and Lydia on equal emotional footing.

But in that moment leaving his father's office, Benjamin could admit to himself that even if it was the right thing to do, it wasn't what he wanted.

L YDIA'S SLEEP WASN'T RESTFUL. When she awoke to discover that Benjamin had left without so much as a message to her via Orla, she searched for the release of relief. If he was gone, then she didn't need to face him. So she should feel the tension in her shoulders rush away; the headache pressing behind her temples could disappear. Yet it didn't. She felt just as wretched as she had all night.

Dressing in a simple summer gown with a more durable spencer thrown over it, Lydia resolved to leave aside the question of Benjamin. He deserved a better wife than she, one who didn't lie or plot or otherwise spend her days thinking about everything except him. However, what was done was done. He had chosen her as much as she had chosen him; somehow, that must absolve Lydia of this guilt weighing her down. In any case, he was gone, without word of when he would return. Lydia was free to spend the day as she saw fit.

Still, she felt sick to her stomach, leaving the townhouse without any further resolution with Benjamin. She penned a note, in case he returned before her:

To my husband,

I am off to visit our friends at Shepherd's Inn. We are engaged to attend Lady Gresham's musicale this

*evening. I hope we can speak privately at home before
that.*

Lydia

It wasn't much of a note. Lydia wasn't much of a writer. Still, as long as Benjamin received it, and as long as he understood she wanted to fix things between them, it would have to do.

She took a hired coach—hailed from the street by Mr. Smart—to Shepherd's Inn, where Conor Devlin had said he was staying. Vaguely, Lydia knew there were parts of London, just as there were parts of Dublin, just as there were parts of any city, that were more dangerous for a woman like her to enter. She had never much contemplated that before; now, she resisted the urge to pull shut the gingham curtains hanging in the coach's windows as the surroundings changed from wide, stately homes to crumbling stone and old wood. It was louder here, with the cries of peddlers and beggars and rushing pedestrians and impatient coachmen and overworked horses mingling in the air.

Watching a woman cough the contents of her stomach onto the street and a man walk right through that puddle, Lydia didn't know how anyone could live in a neighborhood such as this. And yet people did. These people did, every day, without hope of escaping to Mayfair or Soho like Lydia would within the hour.

Lydia shut her eyes, not wanting to consider it. She had one purpose: to find Conor Devlin. She didn't have room to think about anything else.

The Shepherd's Inn sat on the corner of two thoroughfares. As Lydia exited her coach, she felt male eyes land on her: those of an orphan boy in the street, of two older men negotiating a deal on the sidewalk, of a drunk leaning beside the inn's entrance, of three men crowded over tankards in the pub's window. She turned back to her hired driver. "I shall be back within the half hour."

"You want I should go in with you?" he asked. He was a foreigner, his words slanted with some Slavic accent, and he eyed the whole neighborhood as he added, "You can't trust an Englishman farther than you can throw him."

Seamus and Conor had said this sort of thing all the time in Lydia's presence, yet now, from this stranger, Lydia felt a disorienting urge to defend her countrymen. "Thank you, but I am meeting a trusted acquaintance."

Chin held high, she entered the inn. Conor sat in the back corner at a wooden table with three other men, all a similar age. Conor said something that made all three of them laugh. His head thrown back, a smile on his lips, he looked almost exactly like her memory of Seamus.

That didn't warm Lydia the way it sometimes did, nor did it sting her eyes with tears. She thought only of Benjamin: *It isn't actually about Ireland at all, is it?*

She didn't have time to dwell on the accusation. Conor, seeing her, rose and caught her elbow like some sort of overeager guard. "You came alone? I thought you would bring Mr. Preston, or at least Orla. It isn't safe here for a lady like you."

"I'm not alone. I'm with you." Letting him lead her to the table, Lydia extricated herself from his grasp and sat on the opposite bench from him, beside a man who was short and wiry and sported a mop of red hair atop his head. "How do you do. I am Lady Lydia."

"Declan Fox, ma'am."

Conor introduced her to his other fellows, two more men with thick Irish accents. They looked at her with a mix of curiosity and wariness. Lydia wondered how many of them—if any—were already sworn Ribbonmen.

"How did the pamphlets go down, then?" Conor asked. "Orla said you printed a hundred or more."

Lydia decided optimism served the men better than despair. "They were the talk of the ball. I shouldn't be surprised if you read about it in Fashionable World on Monday."

Conor nodded. "Is it time for the petition, then?"

"Have you gathered more signatures?"

"Twelve thousand." Conor gestured towards Declan and their other companions. "We've all been asking for signatures. But we're moving into neighborhoods we don't know so well, where we aren't much welcome..."

Twelve thousand was no small number. Yet in March, the Manchester weavers had tried to carry a petition to London only to be arrested, beaten, and ignored.

Lydia pushed away dismay. There was no point in bewailing the current state of affairs. There was only moving forward. "Let's push to fifteen thousand. That should make the point. Send me a note when you've completed it, and Mr. Preston and I will see to submitting it to the House of Commons." She hesitated, inhaling a breath as she considered how best to introduce the next topic. "I trust you have not joined the Ribbonmen yourself?"

Declan replied for Conor: "If he has, he would be sworn to secrecy about it, wouldn't he?"

"We're all here because we want to see the petition through," Conor said. "The question of the Ribbonmen is different. They protect our families back home, you see."

Lydia did see. The Ribbonmen had formed in the first place to protect the Catholics from rowdy mobs of Protestant Orangemen. Only now, they seemed to expect anyone who was Catholic to support them with unquestioning loyalty. Lydia had even heard reports that they threatened to burn a family's crops if the family didn't pay them dues.

But she didn't know if those reports were true or spread by the British to discourage dissent.

"My issue with the Ribbonmen is the same one Seamus always had. They have no strategy. If they would only plan towards a specific campaign, then we could effect change. Instead, they only engage in sporadic acts here and there, frightening the countryside and fomenting rumors. The result is the Insurrection Act."

"You do not condone violence, my lady?" Declan asked.

"On the contrary. I imagine violence will be necessary. I only object to using it without a plan for what and how to win."

The air between them all vibrated with a new energy, one that grew stronger as her words settled and they all looked from one to the other. This was the opposite of dismay. This was a vision—hazy though it might be—of a future in which they at last seized control.

And then a hand clamped down on her shoulder.

Her body reacted in two halves: the frightened half of her screamed and tensed, ready to fight for every inch of her freedom; the intuitive half of her sensed from his touch that the hand belonged to Benjamin and that she wasn't in any danger at all. Around them, the pub went silent, waiting to see what would happen between the lady and the gentleman.

"Don't be frightened," Benjamin said. "I arrived home just after you left. I don't like the idea of you in Whitechapel alone." His hand still on her shoulder—like a protector or proprietor, Lydia wasn't sure—Benjamin moved his attention to Conor.

Conor leaned back, arms relaxed. "She is safe with us."

"Still, I prefer to be at her side."

The air crackled with words unspoken. Lydia knew why Conor resented Benjamin: he was yet another Englishman who had never set foot in Ireland, inserting himself into the conversation about Ireland's fate. She didn't know where the threat in Benjamin's voice came from. Did he resent Conor just for being a commoner in their presence, despite all the egalitarianism the Prestons supposedly stood for? Or was this something baser—did he feel threatened by Conor because he knew Lydia loved Seamus?

Or was this just how Benjamin was now: angry and untrusting?

Whatever lay beneath his words, she didn't like it. She stood to put herself between Benjamin and the fire in Conor's eyes. "We were just finishing, anyhow. Will you take me home, please, Mr. Preston?"

"As you like." He offered her his arm, and they strode out of the pub like the out-of-place gentility that they were.

Lydia waited for the privacy inside the hired coach to reproach him. "You needn't have followed me. It makes me look weak, and I wasn't in any danger at all."

He started to say something, a spark of anger in his eye. Then, as Lydia watched, waiting to hear what his reply would be, Benjamin stopped himself. He shut his mouth, his words disappearing somewhere deep inside. And the spark disappeared from him, too; he leaned back against the carriage wall and looked out the window, more a statue than a man.

Fresh guilt swirled inside her. Only a few weeks ago, Benjamin had said whatever was on his heart, the instant he felt it. Lydia hadn't realized what a gift it was. She had just thought that was how he was and how he always would be.

Last night, she hadn't liked him consumed with anger. Yet she liked even less this version of him, silent and unfeeling.

If they were ever going to move past the question of Seamus, they had to talk about it. Even if it meant they lost their tempers.

"About what we discussed last night."

Benjamin didn't move even the tiniest muscle in his jaw.

Lydia wasn't sure how to unfurl their argument, so she started with the apology she hadn't quite gotten out. "I never meant to fool you. Or to lie. I never meant to lie. You asked me to say that I loved you. On our wedding night." She didn't mean to sound petulant. Yet there it was: an edge of defensive steel to her words. "I never planned on saying things I didn't feel. But you begged me to. It was the heat of the moment. I didn't think you meant it any more than I did."

"I only say things I mean."

It was the starch in his tone, as if it were so easy to be a true and morally upright human being, that made Lydia argue back. "But how could you? You asked to marry me after knowing me for a few weeks, and you said right then you *loved* me. Even if you think you meant it, you couldn't. You didn't know me. You still don't. We haven't known each other long enough."

"Love isn't knowledge. It's a feeling."

Lydia had lusted for Seamus from the instant she saw him, but she hadn't pretended to herself that it was love. "So you contend you love me no matter what, simply because in those first few exchanges you found me pretty and interesting? What if I refused to give up tea? What if I supported the Insurrection Act? Is there nothing you could discover about me that would make you not love me?"

"Apparently, I love you even though you have confessed your heart belongs to another." He shot this back at her in hot, angry syllables. Then he took a deep, uneven breath. His next words were cold and stilted: "Believe me, madam, I am willing myself to stop loving you."

Guilt resurfaced above her frustration. Whether or not his feelings were love, Benjamin had been good to her—and true to her—in more ways than she could ever return.

Lydia fell back against the carriage bench. There was no point in arguing semantics.

"I have always known I would have to marry. Adelaide didn't, but she doesn't mind my parents as much as I do. I couldn't stomach the idea of living with them or Alistair for the rest of my life. My only option was to marry. And even when Seamus...I always knew I would have to marry an Englishman."

Benjamin turned away at Seamus's name, his gaze on the dirty carriage windowpane instead of her.

"My mother wanted me to marry as well as possible. My father wanted me to marry as rich as possible. I only ever wanted to find a husband I could respect. A husband with whom I could be friends." Her mouth felt dry saying all of this. "That was the most I hoped for. And I knew from the moment I met you that we could be friends. I didn't expect...I didn't imagine..."

Lydia almost stopped then. She had given him her anger, now her guilt. Did she really need to admit to him the unnamed feeling tugging at her? It wasn't the unending obsession she had felt for

Seamus. Nor was it the surprising lust that had overwhelmed her on their wedding night. It wasn't even simple, pure friendship.

It was something deep. Something frightening. Lydia didn't want to share it with Benjamin only to have him bat it away.

But after everything she had put him through, Benjamin deserved to know she felt it.

"I never imagined that I could treasure my husband as much as I treasure you. It never occurred to me to hope for it. I am so lucky that you married me, Benjamin. I feel that with all my heart."

Benjamin's eyes were fixed on his hands now, his whole body leaning away from her. "Could you ever love me as you loved him?"

Oh, if he could ask anything of her but that. "I'm not sure a person can have two true loves."

"Then—" Sorrow spilled through his voice. He cleared his throat. "Then I hope for nothing more than friendship. And respect. As you said. That is all anyone can ask for from their spouse."

They were her own words. Yet hearing them from him, while he remained so far away on the other side of the carriage, Lydia couldn't help knowing they rang hollow, like a long and empty future stretching before her.

Chapter Seventeen

T HE PROBLEM WITH THE petitions was that they were pointless. As pointless as remaining in a marriage with a woman whose true love was someone else. Parliament received countless petitions from the public, and never had it changed the outcome of a vote. It didn't matter if Mrs. Trim placed the vase of roses on the left casement window or the right; Ireland's fate didn't rely on providing Papa and Max their favorite honey cakes on a wooden tray handmade by Ellen. Whether or not Papa and Max agreed to present the petitions to their Houses of Parliament, Ireland would remain yoked to Britain.

Just as whether or not Benjamin stayed in London, Lydia would remain true to Seamus. Instead of him.

He went along with her plan anyway. It was easier than changing course, since Benjamin didn't have any better ideas, or declaring the cause of Irish independence futile. He had promised Lydia to end the Insurrection Act, and he meant to keep that vow.

Still, as she carried in the sheaves of paper to the perfectly appointed drawing room, he felt nothing but yawning apathy.

Lydia set her load of papers down on the oak table. "Here they are. Two petitions, with fifteen thousand signatures on the one for the House of Commons and five thousand for the House of Lords."

Any citizen of Great Britain had the right to submit petitions to the House of Commons, the House of Lords, and even the Prince Regent himself. After giving Conor Devlin the funds to hire a dozen men to spend their full days finding signatures for the petition, Benjamin and Lydia had done hardly anything except debate whether to submit it to the House of Commons or the House of Lords. The committee that would vote on the Insurrection Act sat in the former, and so Lydia had always intended to submit the petition to a member of that chamber. Yet Benjamin knew that the House of Lords held debates on the Irish Question as well, and besides, their members had more prestige and power overall. If the House of Lords received the petition, it might have more impact on the government's overall Irish policy, not just on the single vote about the Insurrection Act.

When they embarked upon the debate for the hundredth time, Benjamin suggested they simply submit the same petition to both Houses.

As if it would make a difference either way.

And so here they were, waiting for Papa to accept the one to the House of Lords and Max to accept the one to the House of Commons.

"Are you anxious?" Lydia asked, eyeing him even as she moved away from him, towards the roses in the window.

Benjamin was beyond any feeling except despair. "Why should I be anxious? They'll hardly say no."

"It is a momentous occasion. Sometimes that is enough to make one anxious." Lifting a blossom to her nose, Lydia said into the flower, "It's all right to admit to such feelings, you know. I am your wife."

For this past week and a half, she had been trying to be friends with him. Soliciting his opinion on extraneous matters. Asking Cook to make all his favorites for supper. Inviting him to join her at musicales or the theater or assemblies.

Benjamin did his best to be civil. In the company of others, he even managed to return her compliments, and he seemed to be fooling the rest of the world into believing he was still besotted.

Internally, however, he kept himself in check. He knew better than to believe her attentions. She was not flirting with him. She was throwing him a bone, the cat tolerating a foolish dog. She wanted a husband who partnered with her, not one who pined for her; the friendship she offered was the limit of the love he would ever receive from her.

The second he forgot that would be the second that his heart broke all over again.

Max arrived then, striding with his usual overly purposeful energy and flopping onto the sofa. "Ah, good, honey cakes. Just the ticket."

"There's peppermint tea, too," Lydia said, replacing the rose in its vase. "I've heard that is your favorite."

"It is my favorite non-tea tea. Which makes me suspect this is not a simple family afternoon tea and instead that one or both of you seek something from me."

Lydia pouted her lips playfully. "Why can't I simply be a good hostess?"

"There is no good answer to that," Benjamin warned, trying to join in the jovial spirit, to keep pretending that everything in the London townhouse was as it seemed. "You might as well stuff your mouth with a honey cake."

It was through that stuffed mouth that Max announced, when Papa entered the room, "Be warned, Preston: it is a trap! These two want something from us."

Papa smiled, as one had to do with Max. "Ah yes, I see the honey cakes, and—why, is that a pot of apple blossom tea, brewed just for me? If these are the conditions of a trap, I am amenable."

As he sank onto the sofa beside Max—who had to straighten up and sit properly with Papa there—Benjamin and Lydia took the two chairs opposite. Gracefully, Lydia served the various teas and prepared a plate of honey cakes for Papa and Benjamin. Then she looked his way, a cue to begin.

They had agreed that Benjamin should be the one to broach the topic. As much as Papa and Max might extoll independent thought in women, they still had a predisposition to assign more value to what a man had to say. And so Benjamin was the one who had to lead the speech:

"It is important to both Lady Lydia and I to devote our time and effort to those who need our support. In particular, we are passionate about finding more just ways to govern Ireland. The Insurrection Act, which is coming up for debate in the House of Commons, is yet another of the Gagging Acts that usurps the natural rights of the average citizen in favor of a government that can arrest and sentence people for crimes no bigger than staying out after sundown. We have created petitions with thousands of signatures from Irish and English alike requesting that Parliament consider striking down the Act instead of renewing it. We ask that you accept these petitions and take them to the debates to share them with your fellow parliamentarians."

Lydia retrieved the petitions and set the thick stacks of paper between the tea pots and the cake tray. "Twenty thousand people signed these, and we can get more signatures if you think it is necessary."

Papa and Max both leaned forward, each reading the petition that topped their respective stacks. Benjamin watched Lydia instead of them; she sat very erect, summoning the full height of her spine and neck, her attention wholly devoted to the men before her. Until her eyes darted over to meet his. Her lips parted, as if to say something, and then she closed them and looked away.

She was anxious. It struck Benjamin for the first time. He had been so focused on batting away his own feelings that he hadn't even noticed hers.

This time, he tried looking at the petitions through Lydia's eyes. Those two stacks of paper, each spanning the length between her wrist and elbow, were the fruit of months of hard work. At some point, Lydia had decided she needed to petition Parliament. And now, she had twenty thousand people standing with her.

Anxiety wasn't the right emotion for her. She should be brimming over with pride, not sitting stiff as if awaiting judgment.

"This is a worthy petition," Max said, picking up another honey cake. "I am happy to enter it into the debate. It won't have much of an effect, though."

And just like that, Benjamin didn't feel despair anymore. Indignation lit through him. He could punch Max for dismissing Lydia's work so summarily. After only a moment's consideration!

Max waxed on: "Peel doesn't care about what the Irish people *want*. He doesn't consider them capable of having their own rational thoughts. This might sway one or two peers with Irish landholdings, but not enough to change the vote."

Benjamin watched Lydia's nostrils flare. Yet she sounded perfectly composed when she asked, "What do you propose we do instead?"

"It's time for Benny to find his own seat in the House of Commons. Get on committees and start making policies yourself." Max chomped into the cake, crumbs spraying from his mouth as he said, "I don't know why you haven't started looking for a borough already."

"He is still young," Papa replied, not waiting for Benjamin to compose his own response. "He needs more experience before he runs for that sort of thing."

"He's hardly much younger than I was when I first ran for election."

As if he weren't in the room. As if he weren't capable of determining his own future for himself. "*He* is right here, and he doesn't appreciate you diverting attention from the petitions."

Papa launched into a soothing, conciliatory tone that was a direct, poor imitation of Mama. "Max isn't trying to divert attention. The question is whether you care more about the short-term outcome or the long-term."

"Actually, the question is not about the outcome at all." And as Benjamin said this, he realized it was true. It was the principle stolen from him in his desperation over not earning Lydia's love. Yet it was the very principle that for the whole of his life had fueled him. Saying it again, believing it again, felt like breathing again. "It is about doing *something*. It is about proving to each other that we do care. Twenty thousand people care. At the moment, I don't care whether that matters to Parliament. I care about showing those twenty thousand people that they are not alone."

Papa looked to Max as if this proved a point. Benjamin added, "If being hopeful is a mark of inexperience and naïveté, then so be it.

I'm sure I wouldn't find life very worthwhile if I woke every morning thinking my efforts would amount to nothing."

These past few weeks, that was exactly what he had been doing. It was time to stop that. He was done with moping. From now on, Benjamin was going to do whatever he could to help Ireland, without worrying about the outcome.

And he was going to do whatever he could to win Lydia, even if he would never be her true love.

Perhaps settling for second best would be enough.

LYDIA WATCHED LORD PRESTON and Max carry away the petitions with a twist of her stomach. Since the past November, when magistrates in County Louth started making noise about needing the Insurrection Act renewed, her energies had been devoted to this. First: make a plan. Second: find a husband to fund the plan. Third: carry out the plan.

And now the plan was executed. The petitions—two, in the end—were submitted. Lord Preston and Max would do them justice. All that was left was to wait and see if the plan was enough to yank Parliament away from its intended course. Or if it would plod on with blinders on, determined to serve its own interests instead of Ireland's.

All that was left was Lydia and Benjamin, alone in the drawing room, silent.

"They will do right by the petitions." Benjamin shifted as he said this, lifting the teapot and pouring more peppermint tisane into her cup. "For all that bluster, they'll make sure to speak for Ireland with the petitions."

Lydia accepted the tea. She didn't remember drinking any to begin with, and she didn't particularly want any now. But this was the most care Benjamin had shown her in weeks. It felt like months. It felt like an eternity.

She wasn't about to turn up her nose at it. "What if Max is right? What if it isn't enough?"

"Then there is nothing we *could* have done. We can only fight the battles available to us."

Easy enough to say. Harder to hold in moments like this. Lydia forced a sip of tea. These were her favorite cups, a relic of the late Lady Preston, with hand-painted inscriptions along the inside. Each drink revealed one more line:

And let us not grow weary of doing good, for in due season we will reap, if we do not give up

"Whatever happens with the vote, it won't bring him back."

It took a moment for Lydia to realize Benjamin meant Seamus. His voice had dropped, true, but there was none of the fury or hurt she expected. If anything, when she dared look up at him, she saw compassion in his eyes.

Her husband's eyes. The man who was not Seamus, comforting her about Seamus.

Lydia tested how far he would let this conversation go. "If we win the vote, though, it would prevent someone else from losing their brother or son or...husband."

Benjamin looked away. But he did not turn from her. He remained at her side, lopsided on the sofa so they could face each other. "By way of convictions without juries, perhaps. Yet until Ireland is actually free of British rule, the government will find ways to rid itself of agitators, with or without the Insurrection Act. If they hadn't been able to arrest him for being out after sundown, they would have found some other reason to take...him, so long as they thought he was plotting something."

That Benjamin couldn't say his name made Lydia's heart swell. With guilt or tenderness, she couldn't quite tell.

She wished she hadn't made such a muddle of things. What she wanted now was for Benjamin to wrap his arms around her and kiss her head and tell her that everything would work out if they only kept at it.

"You look terribly sad," Benjamin said. His hand reached out, but it only landed on the cushion between them. "I wish you would feel terribly proud. You organized twenty thousand people to speak up for what they know to be right. That amounts to something. It has given *me* renewed hope. Imagine what it is doing for all the mothers and sisters and wives who didn't think there was any chance of change."

It seemed like an eternity since they had last touched. Lydia placed her fingers in his. Warm and solid. She didn't want to let go. "You must take some of the credit. And Conor and Declan Fox and all the men who collected the signatures."

Benjamin curled his thumb over the top of her hand. "None of us would have done anything without you."

And she wouldn't have done anything without Seamus. Lydia tried to miss him, to wish it was he holding her hand. But the London townhouse was too out of place for him. If he were alive, she would have found an excuse to stay in Ireland. She would be running about the countryside, meeting him in whatever abandoned barn they could find.

If Seamus were still alive, she would be following his plan, instead of forging her own.

"Do you think you'll ever forgive me?" She heard her voice come out as a whisper. That wasn't very brave of her. With more strength, she added, "I mean truly forgive me. So that this can all be in the past, and we can be husband and wife again."

Benjamin looked down at their hands. Lydia realized she was chilled to the bone, so much so that her fingernails were purpling. "I didn't think I could," Benjamin replied, adding his second hand over hers. "But if I can try for Ireland, I can try for you, too."

When his smile came, it was still a little sad. Lydia didn't mind. Hope sometimes felt like that.

CHAPTER EIGHTEEN

T HE HOUSE OF COMMONS called for the vote the very next week; Max sent a note by messenger boy when the debate began. Benjamin held it in his hand for a moment, weighing the paper and observing a few grains of sand stuck to the letters, before he found the courage to go find Lydia.

This was the culmination of so much for both of them. All the work they had done together on the pamphlets and then the petitions—the writing, the planning, the socializing, the lobbying—would be decided by this vote. Whatever happened today, tomorrow would begin a new phase of their marriage. One not determined by wheels that Lydia had put into motion before they even met, but by goals they decided together.

Benjamin wasn't sure what that future would look like. Forgiving Lydia, once she asked for it, had not been hard. Forgetting everything proved harder. He still felt rejected when she looked away, disappearing into some private thought. He still wondered how often she read that letter. He still couldn't do more than hold her hand without wondering if she wished he were Seamus instead.

And in some ways it was worse now. Before, Benjamin had been too hopeless to feel anything but despair when in the same room as Lydia. Now that they were trying to move forward, he noticed every little movement of hers again. The tilt of her head. The twist of her shoulders. The sway of her hips.

His body yearned for her. His heart was still afraid of her. And so he existed in purgatory, close to her but not close enough.

Perhaps this vote would put Seamus behind them. He knew Lydia wished it; he was the one standing between them and whatever their future could be. It wouldn't be love, but neither would it be apathy. Friendship. Tenderness. Holding hands during the good and the bad.

Not quite what Benjamin wanted, but better than loneliness.

He found her at the escritoire in her bedroom. Her hair was mussed, no doubt from her fingers raking through it with hard thinking, and when she turned to greet him, he saw a smear of ink tracing a line from her left ear down her neck.

How he wanted to follow that line down the rest of her body.

"The debate has begun," he said, waving Max's note in the air to keep from giving into that physical pull. "They are voting today."

The smile on Lydia's lips froze. In the next instant, she was out of her chair, pulling a spencer from her clothes rack, a bonnet from the dresser, and gloves from her pocket. "I'm ready."

"Are you sure you don't want to call for Orla to dress you properly?"

"There is hardly any time. The longer we wait, the less likely it is there will be seats in the gallery." Lydia frowned as she brushed past him into the corridor. "You don't care whether I am the most elegant lady of the *ton*, do you?"

"No, but I thought you might want to clear off that ink stain." More importantly, he wished to soothe her nerves. To give her time to set her expectations for the vote. To remind her they could only bear witness, nothing more.

She didn't slow down. "What ink stain?" But by then, she had reached the bottom of the stairs, and she called out, "Mr. Smart, a carriage, if you please."

Benjamin had already asked for one, and so as he joined Lydia in the front hall, a hired coach pulled up to the townhouse. He had to rush to fetch his hat, gloves, and cane in order to keep up with Lydia.

"I don't want to miss a second of the debate," she said as he handed her into the carriage. "If we lose, I plan to write a pamphlet refuting each of the winning arguments."

Years ago, on Benjamin's first visit to the strangers' gallery, he had envisioned a room full of passion and insults and genius insights uttered in perfect syllables. He suspected Lydia would be even more disappointed than he to discover it was not that different from observing a room of peers sharing a cigar, with some of them speaking too loudly and others too softly and none of them making enough sense to warrant the passage of a law.

He should keep her expectations low. Yet Benjamin couldn't help asking, "And if we win?"

"Then I shall still write the pamphlet, only with much more condescension."

She grinned. Her excitement was almost physical, a third party rattling around the carriage. Benjamin wondered if she attached the outcome to their marriage at all, too, or if her thoughts were only on Ireland. On Ireland and on avenging Seamus.

That was the type of thought that kept him from kissing her right then and there.

"We know the ten votes we can count on, with fifteen I'm not sure of." Lydia listed them off, beginning with Max. They had spent the last week socializing at musicales and the theater and assemblies, seeking out any member of the Commons who might be sympathetic to the cause.

But even twenty-five votes would never be enough to win in the House.

"I sat down this morning to write a letter to *The Times*," Lydia said. "A plea to the general public to consider the Act from a place of reason, not fear."

They had known only that the House would debate the Act sometime soon, not the day or week specifically.

"It's too late now to do anything else, I suppose." Fear began to lurk into the corners of her words. Benjamin watched as she looked through the window, her lips twitching as she almost spoke. Then she put on a smile. "I'm glad you are here with me. I don't know if I could manage this on my own."

He wondered what she had decided not to say. Yet he knew he should focus on what she did say. "I'm glad to be with you, too."

Beneath her bonnet, her hair still frizzed from where her fingers had unconsciously teased it. And that ink remained like a birthmark along the length of her neck.

He couldn't let her walk into Westminster Hall like that.

Crossing to her bench, Benjamin leaned forward. "You have something there," he said by way of explanation. Then, withdrawing his handkerchief from his waistcoat, he wet the skin below her ear with his tongue.

Lydia gasped. An exhale he knew so well from those blissful weeks when he had thought her in love with him. Without touching her, he could feel the quiver of her thighs; if he wound his fingers beneath her gown, her quim would be hot and wet. Even though she didn't love him.

Meeting her eyes—he'd forgotten, somehow, how beautifully complex their color was—he raised the handkerchief to the spot he had just licked. He dragged it downwards in little scrubs. Lydia was trying to hold her breath, but it hit his cheek in hot puffs as his handkerchief reached that soft part of her neck that always made her melt. He looked down, watching his work now, until her neck was clean.

"You see?" He held up the handkerchief, now brown with ink, as proof. "It is all gone now."

"Benjamin..." Her hands linked behind his neck, holding him there. Not that he was actually leaning away. Lydia licked her lips—those perfect, rosebud lips—and he knew she was going to kiss him.

He wanted her to kiss him.

He missed her kissing him.

Her lips were only a breath away when the carriage stopped. The hired driver thumped on the roof to announce they had arrived. And Benjamin returned to his good senses.

He stepped into New Palace Yard unkissed.

L YDIA WAS FAR TOO flushed to be in public. As she followed Benjamin out of the carriage, her legs quivered, too excited to hold her weight.

She couldn't believe Benjamin hadn't let her kiss him.

She couldn't believe he had *licked* her and then left her, as if the interaction were no more arousing than cleaning a child's skinned knee.

He almost fooled her into thinking the sizzle in the air only existed for her. She might have thought he really had become immune to her. Except she could see his arousal on display, pressed against the white linen of his breeches.

All week, she had been trying to create a moment like this. Complimenting him at breakfast. Brushing her arm against his at supper. Sitting too close to him on the settee in the evening, pretending to lean towards the firelight to read when really she wanted him to feel the press of her thigh against his.

He hadn't succumbed to her flirtation. He had smiled at her compliments, laughed at her jokes, and fled to different chairs.

This was the first time he got anywhere close to kissing her.

They crossed the square in a flurry. Benjamin led the way through the lobby and upstairs to the stranger's gallery, where he presented an invitation from Max to the doorman. Lydia's heart was still thumping from the almost-kiss; she tried to get herself in order as they entered the gallery.

The gallery was a series of narrow benches—as uncomfortable as church pews—stretching above either side of the chamber. For a debate about the rights of citizens within the empire, it was sparsely attended: a handful of reporters sat in the front rows, heads bent over their notebooks as they rushed to note down every word said; a representative of the Irish Catholic Board stretched across a back row; the rest of the visitors were unknown to Lydia and watching with varying degrees of attention.

She and Benjamin found a seat in a middle row. They had a view of Lord Castlereagh as well as the members of Parliament to his left. Leaning forward, Lydia spotted Max's broad shoulders.

The debate was well underway. Lydia struggled to pick up what the current speaker—a stooped old man whose wig was askew—was saying, except that every now and then he raised his voice to spit out *"violent men."* She tried to focus. Benjamin sat so close beside her. She could feel every inch of his bicep against her arm; his thighs were as tense as steel next to hers. She looped her arm beneath his elbow, the way any loving wife might, and watched as his breeches tented again.

He wanted her. And, God forgive her, she wanted him too. She was so wet with desire that she worried it would soak through the seat of her gown.

It was so selfish a reaction to be feeling now, of all times. But it was also such a relief compared to the anxiety that had propelled her through the week. For once, her limbs were light, her skin like fire, instead of feeling like she was trying desperately to get through a fierce ocean current.

The speaker on the floor yielded his time. Lydia tried to focus as Lord Castlereagh called up the next man to speak. Her marriage could wait; for now, she owed Ireland her attention.

Max took the floor. Lydia had grown accustomed to seeing him around the house in his more casual linen suits and constant energy. But here he wore a formal outfit of the finest wool, his hair covered in an expensive white wig. He looked more like a figure in a portrait than her dynamic brother-in-law.

She leaned forward to hear his words, though he spoke loudly enough that even the back row of the gallery must have been able to understand without straining.

"I have previously submitted to this committee a petition to reconsider the Insurrection Act as unnecessary, unjust, and cruel. This document was written by the people of Ireland and signed by fifteen thousand of the same, entrusting this body with the responsibility to act in their best interest.

"I do not object to the arguments that the countryside of Ireland is a dangerous place. However, as I have heard more from the Irish themselves, including the fifteen thousand men and women who signed the petition, it strikes me that any government who must restrict the movements of its people, the speech of its people, or the freedoms of its people in order to maintain its power does not deserve that power at all. If the common men of Ireland are turning to arms, it must be because they feel the situation merits arms. Arresting and transporting them will only increase their aggravation with us. Let us instead offer more freedoms to the Catholics and a stronger economy to the farmers."

It was no rallying cry for Irish freedom. Lydia hadn't really hoped for that; she had engaged with Max enough over the dinner table to know that he viewed the Irish situation as an unfortunate circumstance over which he would not exert much personal energy. Still, her heart felt a little more tattered at his speech, especially when it was met with only a murmur of agreement from the rest of the house.

She slid her hand into Benjamin's. Without thinking, really. His fingers curled around hers in response. Lydia braced herself, expecting him to pull away after the moment of comfort, but there he remained with their arms entwined from elbow to palm.

How she yearned for his entire body to wrap against hers in the exact same way.

Sir Robert Peel, the Chief Secretary for Ireland, took the floor next. He spoke loudly, like a cannon expelling its shot with only horrendous things to say:

"I refer here to the discussion which took place on a former night, in which many members stated their opinions on this measure, and pleaded, though reluctantly, its justification. A right honorable baronet allowed its necessity, though he recommended previous and more extensive examination. The declarations of other honorable gentlemen were to the same effect, with the same qualification. Against this general concurrence of opinion, there were only three members from Ireland that opposed it—the member for Queen's county, the member for Tipperary, and the member for Colchester. The two last could not be supposed to be so well acquainted with the country, as, they have not resided in Ireland much of late. The honorable baronet has said, that the Insurrection Act was an evil, and I am disposed to allow it in its fullest extent; but, unhappily, now there is only a choice of evils. Is it better to extend to government the means of preserving tranquility, even by a severe measure, or to allow the country to be converted into a scene of confusion by withholding the present act?"

Benjamin's fingers tightened around Lydia's with every word. Worse than what Peel was saying was the fact that others agreed with him. House members stomped or grunted or even yelled "aye!" in support as he made each point. The reporters bent over their notebooks, fingers flying in even more of a frenzy than when Max had spoken. Only the members of the Catholic Board looked as ill as Lydia felt, their faces pale as Peel finished.

Lydia had known better than to believe that Parliament would ever grant Ireland its political independence, not when keeping it within their control was so important to them. But there was a part of her that had thought there was a chance Parliament wouldn't be so cruel. That the men who ruled the United Kingdom were men of sense, not superstition; that they were men of compassion, not fear; at the very least that they cared so little for Ireland that they would want to ease the burden of hunting down and transporting men out after curfew.

Yet unfolding before her was the truth. All her months of hard work—organizing the petition, disseminating the pamphlet, even coaxing a room full of powerful women at tea into discussing it—evaporating into thin air. All her planning to marry well and use her influence going to hell. Even her promise to Seamus that she *could* help and that she *would* help; even that was disappearing, all in the space of this pointless parliamentary debate.

Everyone already knew how they were going to vote. And Lydia knew how the vote would go.

When Sir Robert Peel finally finished, the room rattled with noise. Most of it was in favor of his words. Beside her, Benjamin cupped his free hand to his lips to shout, "For shame!"

Lydia wanted to scream, too. Except hers would be in agony. It would split the ears of everyone around them. It would cause men's ears to bleed.

And it still wouldn't do any good.

Benjamin slid an arm around her waist. "Are you sure you want to stay?"

She had thought she would serve Ireland by bearing witness to this. But suddenly, Lydia didn't want to be in that gallery. She couldn't stand to watch Ireland get locked in cuffs.

Better to focus on a fight she could win.

"Take me away," she said, clinging to Benjamin's hand. Her husband's hand.

"I'll call the carriage," Benjamin said when they were in the corridor, drawing away from her.

"No, wait. Let's go somewhere quiet for a moment." Never having been to Westminster Hall before, Lydia didn't quite know where to lead him. She turned left to get out of sight of the doorman, then took the next corridor leading away from there.

At last, Lydia found what she was looking for: an empty room with a door. It was more of a closet, really, with no windows and nothing hanging on the plastered walls. But for her purposes, it would do.

She turned to Benjamin. She set free all the sensations she tried most days to keep at bay. Just looking at him lit her nerves on fire. All she could think of was how she wanted to curl her fingers through his hair, drag her lips across his jaw, and pull the clothes from every inch of his body until there was not a single element of the earth between them.

Lydia was tired of pushing these temptations away to focus on her plans. To give Benjamin space. To wait for her marriage to heal itself.

It was time to let temptation lead the way.

Benjamin frowned at her, as if she were a puzzle to figure out. But he was hard again, his erection so large that she thought the buttons of his breeches might come undone. There was a part of him that still wanted her. That still loved her.

Lydia could still win him. She was sure of it.

"I never apologized properly to you. May I now?"

"I have forgiven you, Lydia. I swear. You needn't apologize."

"But I want to. Please let me." Tugging him by the hand, she pulled him into the room, then shut the door. It was dark now, with only a few strands of light sneaking in from the corridor. "I'm sorry I wasn't honest with you from the very beginning. I'm sorry I can't give you my whole heart. I hope one day I am enough for you. I understand if I'm not. But in the interest of being honest, there is something I need you to know." Lydia stepped forward, using her sense of touch to find him in the dark. She found his nose first, then his lips. When she kissed him, she inhaled him, a scent of berry wine and oat cakes that was now as comforting to her as arms wrapped around her.

"I need you to know—" she whispered, "that when I kiss you, I'm thinking of no one but you."

The sound he let out was half gasp, half growl. Lydia traced her lips along the line of his jaw, relishing in the prickle of his shaved cheek against the soft skin of her lips.

"When I yearn for touch, I yearn for you."

Her fingers followed the lines of his waistcoat until they reached his throat. She undid his cravat with blind tugs. Beneath her touch, he moaned. Lydia kissed the base of his neck, her tongue singeing his skin in return for his lick in the carriage.

"When I think of you, Benjamin," she said, her fingers falling again, down this time to the rim of his breeches, "I want you. Please, may I have you?"

She waited, hands hovering over his buttons, until he replied, "Yes." Then she fell to her knees. Freeing his erection from its fabric trap filled her with such a sense of victory that her quim was immediately drenched all over again. She grasped it in her palm first, relishing in Benjamin's gasp of pleasure.

Then she took it in her mouth. Tasted her husband with the full length of her tongue. Felt him give in to her. There was nothing in the world except for this spectacular point of connection. Lydia sucked him in and out, up and down, over and over. Each time he moaned, her quim quivered. His fingers twitched against her shoulder, and she felt them like a drumbeat against her own desire. He couldn't deny her now.

She thought he would erupt in her mouth. But before he finished, he grasped her by the underarms. "I want to be inside you," he hissed. And the next thing she knew, Lydia was the one against the wall, her weight suspended by Benjamin's body. "Please?"

"Yes," she agreed, and he speared into her. If she hadn't already been so aroused, it would have been disappointing how quickly he came. But she was ready, aching for him after so many nights without him. When his fast thrusts ended, she dissolved with him into an endless pool of pleasure.

"Benjamin," she sighed, and her lips almost continued with *I love you*.

But Lydia stopped herself. She didn't really mean it. Loving his cock inside her was different than loving him. Admiring him was different than loving him. Counting him her best friend was different than loving him.

She couldn't love Benjamin. Could she?

He set her back on her feet. They separated for a moment or so, putting themselves to rights. Benjamin was the one to take her hand again, just before opening the door. "Are you ready to return?"

"Yes," she lied. But in the end, they needn't have returned at all. While Lydia had been off winning back her husband, the House of Commons had voted: the Insurrection Act would continue for another year.

CHAPTER NINETEEN

I T WASN'T A PERSONAL tragedy. It was a loss for Ireland, six million souls who were subject to Parliament's whims. A betrayal of the twenty thousand men and women who had just that month signed their names to the petition begging relief from the Act. A bald announcement that the government cared more about protecting its own power than caring for its subjects. Leaving Westminster Hall, Benjamin half expected riots on the streets, or at least jeers from the laborers watching as the parade of gleaming carriages returned to Mayfair.

Instead, London acted as if nothing had happened.

"We should have arranged for our Irish fellows to wait outside the Hall with rotten tomatoes to pelt," he said. They sat together on the carriage bench, hands entwined, jostling over the cobblestones. Lydia was pale, every muscle of her body tense, whereas Benjamin still felt languid and calm after their lovemaking.

He knew that, for her, it wasn't that. Lust-slaying, perhaps. Existence-affirming. Maybe nothing more than a necessary distraction.

Yet she claimed to think only of him when kissing him. She promised that he was the one she wanted.

That had been enough to unlock the desire he had been so long suppressing. It might be enough for Benjamin to be happy with her, even knowing that if Seamus were alive, she would be running off for trysts with him instead of making do with Benjamin.

"Tomatoes wouldn't make a difference," Lydia responded, her chin tucked and turned away from him.

"No, but it might make us all feel better."

"We should have made a plan for what comes next." She opened her mouth on a thought, then shut it. The way she used to censor herself when they were in her mother's presence.

"There's nothing we can do about the Act except persuade Parliament not to renew it next year." Benjamin paused, waiting to see if she would say whatever was on her mind. When she didn't—her whole face still turned away from him—he continued. "We'll write that pamphlet, like you said. We can go to Ireland ourselves and find stories of men who are unjustly apprehended due to the Act. In a whole year, there is so much more we can do to win this fight."

"And while we are focused on revoking the Act, what other fights will we neglect?" With these words, she looked at him at last. Yet Benjamin sensed they still weren't the thoughts swirling around her head unvoiced.

There were emotions in her eyes, murkier than the frustration or fury he had expected. Benjamin didn't know what to say to them.

"You are my leader in this. I pledged myself to you and your cause. Only tell me what you need from me."

She squeezed his hand and looked out the window again. "Let's go to Shepherd's Inn and sort out a plan."

By the time they got to Whitechapel, it was nearly dark; Conor and Declan and a half dozen more men were there already, talking in hushed voices in a corner. Benjamin hired the private room in the back, which was hardly big enough for five men to meet, much less the ten of them. Benjamin and Lydia stood by the hearth, facing a group of expressions mixed with caution and hope.

"We failed." Lydia somehow looked taller than ever, even as she opened with so stark a statement. "*I* failed. I wanted to win Ireland a few meager freedoms—freedoms that every citizen of Great Britain takes for granted—while playing by the rules. However, this afternoon Parliament voted to extend the Insurrection Act for another year, which means our countrymen are not even allowed to leave their houses after sundown. I failed."

A murmur rippled through the men, a few of them cursing, a few of them grunting. Conor spoke up for the lot of them. "What now, then?"

"Now, we move our focus from the Insurrection Act to the greater problem. We apply all our energy to removing the British Crown from Ireland entirely."

She said it very simply, as if it were as obvious as explaining that one plus one was two. By the time Benjamin caught up to the weight of her words, she was already continuing:

"We must make it clear to Parliament that we will not accept this kind of government. It will take some forward planning. We must rally men here and in Ireland alike. We must detail what our alternative will look like. This will not be a quick plan, yet we will put all our energy towards it so that in the span of a year, we will be prepared to extract Ireland from the clutch of Britain."

The men listened to her with avid attention, straight-backed like soldiers taking orders from a general.

Which was exactly what Lydia was fashioning herself into.

Benjamin shifted forward, inserting himself into her line of vision. With a half smile—trying to deflate the situation—he asked, "Is this a declaration of war? Are you planning to invade Liverpool?"

Lydia let her gaze fall down the slope of her nose to reach him. "The government exists in contract with its people. This government forced that contract on us, and now it isn't even honoring its own terms. That leaves us with no recourse but to find a new government."

Find a new government—as though governments were available for the picking. "If everyone with a grievance against the government started taking up arms and declaring new leaders, we would be in a constant state of civil war. The empire is imperfect and unjust, but we must work within it, or else abandon our lives to constant chaos."

"We tried to work with Parliament." Lydia's tone softened, but only a little. "We failed. The people of Ireland don't have the time to wait for malfeasant Englishmen to see reason."

For a moment, all Benjamin could do was stare at her. She had thrown around rhetoric like this before. But it was one thing to say it in the privacy of the bedroom, where there could be no consequences.

It was another entirely to say it in the midst of revolutionaries.

"Violence cannot be the answer," he said, his voice hoarse.

Lydia put a hand on his arm—gently, like a caress. "You said I am your leader in this. You promised you would do anything for Ireland."

He thought he already *had* done everything for Ireland. She had torn his heart out, ripped it into shreds, and forced it back inside him, and still, he supported Ireland's freedom.

"I can't be party to violence."

How small the room felt with the men crowded inside and Lydia towering over him. He willed her to ignore the men, ignore the anger that must be igniting her words, and to focus on him. On the reality of what they could do, if only she had the patience.

She smiled instead. The small, beatific smile of a medieval saint. "Then you needn't be. You have done enough. If this isn't your fight, then don't fight it."

The dismissal stung. They had trod this territory once before, and the argument had ended with silence. With Benjamin believing she heard him, she cared for him, when instead she had only been letting him think what he wanted.

He should leave right then and there. Turn on his heel, march to the docks, and book himself passage on the next ship out of England.

He did not want to battle the ghost of Seamus; he knew he would lose.

But he had promised Lydia he would try to forgive her. He had promised himself he would try to save this marriage. And this was no longer just a personal question.

"Lydia." He said her name without any formality, hoping it would shake loose her good sense. "Please consider this. It is not wise to act from desperation. That is a place of weakness. You must act from a place of strength if you want to succeed."

Her chin lifted again. "And how is one to have any strength if the government insists on stealing it all away?"

"If you don't resort to violence, you may always rely on a moral strength." They were the words of the pacifist philosophers Benjamin had read with his tutors and the pamphlets handed out by the Peace Society. Yet they came out sounding like something a preacher might say. Immediately, Benjamin tried to think how to rephrase it.

Lydia looked to her audience of Irishmen. "How can standing by to let men lose their families and their lives be the morally strong thing to do?"

"Must those be the only two options? Stand back or attack? Can't there be another solution?"

She lowered her voice, as if to shelter her words from the rest of the room. "You heard for yourself how little interest even your father and Max have in the topic. If not even the great Preston family is interested, do you really think we can convince enough peers to care?"

"We barely gave it any time. By next year, we could win over at least a dozen more members of the House of Commons to see things our way. Change cannot happen overnight. It must be given time to brew."

"Do you really think it is *time* that has created change?" How she looked down at him now, her eyes narrowing in incredulity. "The French tried to earn more power from their monarchy by working with it first. The only way they achieved any true change was revolution. The United States tried diplomacy first. The only way they earned independence was war. It wasn't because your father supported Wilberforce that the slave trade ended; it required the bloody war in Haiti. We are fools if we think we can earn Ireland any freedom by asking for it with a 'please and thank you.'"

"I am not being naïve when I beg you to reconsider." Benjamin wished they were at home, where he could place a whole stack of philosophy books in her arms to prove his point. "Read the Cathars, the Jains, the Hindus. They lived through harrowing times, worse than ours. They believed the ultimate sin was to compromise one's soul by going to war or using violence to win change. There are other options. Please, consider another option first."

His voice broke when he said "please." The word was unsustainable. The conversation was unsustainable. There was no compromise here: no matter what happened, one of them would fail the other.

Lydia drew him away now, to the corner of the room furthest from the other men. "You may have the luxury of calculating the most moral solution for any given problem. I do not. Whatever happens to my soul in the afterlife, I cannot live this life without taking action."

As if his touch might make a difference to her, Benjamin gathered up her hands in his. "Lydia, whatever your plan is, do you really want to have the deaths of fellow humans on your conscience?"

She opened her mouth then shut it, as if to censor her words. Then she spoke anyway. "I already do. If it weren't for me, Seamus would be alive. I carry that on my soul every day."

And there it was. The ghost Benjamin would never vanquish. He let loose her hands.

Her voice dropped to a whisper. "This is the best way for me to make it right about Seamus, don't you see? I have to honor his memory by trying to make sure it never happens to anyone else."

"Yes, I see." After everything, Seamus still ruled her thoughts and actions and heart. "And what of our marriage? What role does a loving husband play in your plans for revolution?"

Benjamin didn't wait for her answer. He knew what it would be. She did not want his love. She did not really want a husband. From him, she wanted money and protection and nothing else.

"Make whatever plans you must. I shall leave you with the necessary funds. As for me, I shall be on the next ship to Calcutta. It is time I took a tour of the empire."

L YDIA WATCHED BENJAMIN GO. His declaration settled around her like a fur cloak too hot and heavy to be borne. He couldn't mean it. He was trying to stop her.

A Preston wouldn't go to Calcutta.

Benjamin wouldn't leave her.

A part of her wanted to run after him. To explain herself. He made the whole mess so black and white, when all she felt was a spectrum of grays. Love for Seamus, guilt about Seamus; love for Benjamin, guilt about Benjamin; love for Ireland, guilt about Ireland. She was trying to find a balance, to somehow make right all the things she had done wrong by all the people she cared about.

She didn't have time to run after him. Conor and Declan and all the men who had worked tirelessly on the petition still stood only a few feet away. Waiting for her to take charge. Waiting for her to lead them in the movement of a lifetime.

Benjamin would have to wait.

Turning back to the men, Lydia tried to marshal the fury ignited by Parliament and the indignation fanned by Benjamin's moral superiority. She didn't know the first thing about revolution. She hadn't the faintest idea what their next step was. But even as Benjamin had thrown philosophy at her, a new future glimmered in her imagination: an actual Irish government, one with men who represented the tenant farmers and the shopkeepers. One which spoke in Irish. One which only levied taxes to pay for things that Ireland needed. One which didn't arrest and murder its own citizens.

Eight Irishmen was hardly an army. But it was a start.

"We have much to do," she began, mind racing as she tried to think how best to transmogrify their small group into a revolution. "Each of us must lead a different initiative. Conor, I'll need you to be my military strategist. Declan, have you any contact with the Ribbonists?"

"Aye. We all do." Declan folded his arms across his chest. "There's a reason I'm not a part of them, and it's not because I trust an Englishwoman to do the job better."

Lydia realized a half moment too late that the "Englishwoman" he referred to was her.

"Seamus always said we were going to do it the bloodless way," Conor said. "Else we'll just have another '98 on our consciences."

Bloodless—except Seamus was dead, his blood spilling across the ocean floor.

Lydia resented Conor for invoking his name. "If we don't act, we have the fate of six million people subject to unfair and cruel government on our consciences."

Declan still scowled. "I lost my father and all five of his brothers to '98."

"They burned our house without checking if we were inside," Conor said. For the first time since Lydia had known him, danger sparked behind his words. "War isn't about who wins on the battlefield. It's about whose soul gets destroyed more. And in war between Britain and Ireland, they'll crush ours, every time. If that's what you're wanting, then it's time you find someone else to do your bidding."

Shock froze her. She had never tried to issue orders to Conor. She had never seen him as a servant executing tasks on her behalf. *He* had come to *her*, pleading with her to intervene for Seamus, then asking her to pick up where Seamus had left off. *We need a leader*, he had said, *and I'm not the man for the job. Seamus trusted you. That means I trust you, too.*

Never mind that Lydia hadn't any idea what to do. Never mind that Lydia's heart was so full of grief she could barely think straight. Conor had asked her to take Seamus's place, so she had.

Apparently, now he was asking her to step down.

Now, after she had already married herself off in the name of the cause. After she had broken a good man's heart. After she had driven Benjamin away for the sake of revolution.

"You'd have done better to listen to your husband," Declan said, though not unkindly. "We'll consider another option or none at all."

Lydia surveyed the men before her. Far from home, down and out, living off her coin in hopes of winning a small victory for Ireland.

She had thought she was leading them. But apparently, she was only their benefactor, and now they expected her to shut up and step back.

At a loss, she could only ask, "Well, then. What do you propose we do now?"

It was Declan who answered for the group: "We make ourselves a thorn in Sir Robert Peel's side. And that's where you come in."

Chapter Twenty

On his quest to find a ship leaving for the East Indies, Benjamin wound up with an unlikely group: his sister Sophia, John, and Robert. In an unlikely place, too; they were drinking the worst ale Benjamin had ever tasted from some dockyard pub. There was no food to be had, which meant they were all four of them more than a little drunk already.

"That's the trouble with idealists," Sophia was saying, her words still precise even after three healthy tankards. "They expect so much of you."

Benjamin hadn't shared any real details with the group. He wasn't idiot enough to do that. As far as they knew, he was nursing an injured heart after an explosive argument with Lydia over how best to fight for Ireland's freedom. They needn't know his wife was actively plotting something violent. Something insidious.

You have the luxury of calculating the morally right thing to do.

He didn't like the accusation she had thrown his way. A failing of his character, simply because he wasn't personally affected by the issue. Or because he saw the issue of Ireland's freedom as just one piece in a great, ever-expanding mosaic that added up to all the human error in the world.

He couldn't help the fact that he wouldn't be arrested for being out overnight or that he had never known gnawing hunger from lack of food or that he could take up whatever occupation he desired. But Lydia was right: that meant it left him luxury. Luxury to stop thinking about a problem when it became too painful. Luxury to put a blanket over himself when he heard stories of people freezing in the cold.

Perhaps it was why he couldn't commit to any cause. Even now. Even after promising his whole heart, mind, and bankroll to earning Ireland's freedom, he wanted to turn away. Already, he was thinking about what else he could do with his money; on the ride to the pub, he had been mulling over the problem of street urchins and how best to ensure every child had food in their belly each day.

When it came to causes, his heart was fickle. Benjamin couldn't think of a single issue over which he would even consider violence.

Was that because he followed a stronger moral code? Or because he didn't care enough?

Robert was agreeing with Sophia. "Even when they tell you they don't expect you to choose the same as them, they look at you with such disappointment when you don't." He widened his eyes, imitating a hangdog expression he must surely have received from his cousin once or twice.

"Imagine earning nothing but that for your entire childhood," Sophia said with a laugh.

"Your family loves you," John replied, wrapping an arm around her shoulder. "You are exaggerating."

"She is indeed," Benjamin agreed. Their parents had tried to instill in all of them a sense of responsibility for the people around them, but they had been forgiving about it. He remembered Sophia roping him into a protest against the family's ban on buying cotton; together, they had purchased some calico fabric from town that Sophia fashioned into matching handkerchiefs. Papa had been the one to notice first. He hadn't been angry. Benjamin didn't even remember receiving disappointment. Papa had pulled out an illustrated book on the American South, one that showed the harsh truths of slavery, and asked if they wanted to empower the people treating their fellow humans so poorly.

Sophia—always defiant, always determined to forge her own ideas—had begun a years-long argument that small economic protests had no impact on labor exploitation.

Those pictures had made Benjamin cry, though. In a way that had embarrassed him even at the age of eight. And he had promised Papa not only that he would never buy cotton again, but also that he would do whatever it took to end slavery.

Now here he was seventeen years later, without having done much of anything to follow through on that promise.

Not caring that it was a non sequitur, he asked the group, "If you knew you could outlaw slavery and free all the slaves in the world, but it meant fighting a war where two hundred thousand men died, would you wage the war?"

"Without question," answered Robert.

"Even though the deaths of those men would be on your conscience?"

The duke heaved a sigh over his tankard. "Excuse my moment of idealism, but I already feel the lives of those enslaved on my conscience. Particularly the ones my family were responsible for."

"What if the outcome weren't guaranteed?" Benjamin pushed. "What if you could wage the war, but you didn't know if you'd win?"

It was Sophia who answered this time, surprising him. "If there is a chance of achieving what you want, even if the cost may be high, I believe you should do it."

"During a birth," John added, "there are times when it is impossible to deliver both the baby and the mother alive. As the accoucheur, I must kill one to save the other. It is..." He sighed, rather than find the right word. "But it is necessary. Violence, sometimes, is necessary."

Benjamin hadn't expected them to have such clear answers. His mind was full of his pacifist philosophers: that change earned by violence isn't change at all, that one must retain the moral ground or else become one's enemy, even that Jesus turned the other cheek.

But perhaps that was naïve. Perhaps Lydia was right: change could only be seized from those in power, by any means necessary.

Benjamin had committed to supporting the Irish fight for freedom the same as he had vowed to be Lydia's husband for as long as they both should live. This was his chance to prove to himself once and for all that he could see a fight through. That he could support a cause with the same fervor as his parents.

His fight might look different than theirs, but he would stick with it just the same.

As for his marriage, he would hope for the courage to stick with that, too.

Night had fallen by the time Lydia left Shepherd's Inn, though it was still only early evening. It felt right that shadows should encroach, creeping from the tops of the buildings down to her skirts, and that a cold chill should sink into her skin. It was the union of the physical world with her spirit. Dark. Frigid. Unredeemable.

She hired a hack to take her home. It stank of stale sweat and urine, as if the previous occupant had used it as their privy instead of a carriage. This, too, felt like her just reward. All this time, Lydia had convinced herself she was the virtuous one. The only member of her family to see the wrongs of their life; the strong one who could push through her grief to take Seamus's place; the sacrificial one to marry without hope of love, in the name of Ireland. It was virtue, she had thought, to dedicate her life to a cause greater than herself. Grace, she had told herself, to find the wherewithal to care for Benjamin instead of wallowing in the memory of Seamus.

Unwanted, was what it was. Useless. All she had accomplished was getting Seamus killed, breaking Benjamin's heart, and dashing the hopes of twenty thousand petitioners.

The carriage deposited her at the townhouse without her even realizing she had provided the address. Lydia stood on the street for a time, staring up at the façade, trying to understand how she was meant to enter with her head held high. She had done nothing to earn the esteem of the Prestons. She was a liar. A manipulator. She had played them all for fools.

Perhaps if she had chosen some other family, some other husband. One who laughed in the face of Ireland's suffering or who lavished his money on champagne and syllabub while the rest of the country went hungry. Then she might be able to reclaim her spot with no more than a "Please *do* excuse me."

But Lydia had targeted the worthiest family in London. She was no better than a thief who saw a house full of silver and decided it was his for the taking.

If only it were as simple as returning bags full of silver with her head hanging low.

Before she could start up the stairs, Mr. Smart opened the door. "Do you need assistance, Lady Lydia?"

She shook her head. "Is Mr. Preston at home?"

"Not presently." After a pause, Mr. Smart added, "He mentioned something about the Duke of Berkwell."

Lydia didn't have a specific plan. She only knew that if Benjamin weren't at home, then she didn't want to face the townhouse at all. But she had to go somewhere.

So she found herself at the Duke of Berkwell's, disembarking from yet another hired coach to knock at the imposing oak door. It was dreadfully gauche to show up outside of calling hours, yet Lydia lifted the brass knocker anyhow. Her mind was blank except for one thought: to find Benjamin.

The duke's household bestowed upon her a pity she didn't deserve, informing her that Benjamin had indeed shown up and he and the duke had removed themselves from the premises. The duke's coachman delivered Lydia to the pub where he had deposited them, for the price of a crown and the promise that Lydia would not wander unescorted through the neighborhood.

Benjamin was easy to spot. A stranger might notice the duke first, in his perfectly black jacket and bleached cravat, or even Sophia and John, who sat arm in arm across the bench. Lydia saw only Benjamin. There were his lopsided ears, and his brown hair flopping in a wave down his neck. His shoulders were caving in towards each other, as if to protect his heart from some great blow.

From her, then. Lydia could hardly remember what she had said to him at Shepherd's Inn except that it had made him flee. At the time, the words had coursed through her with great, righteous virtue.

They had been her knives, and she had swung them at Benjamin as if he were her enemy. When all he had been trying to do was save her from herself.

If she were truly a good person, Lydia would turn around and leave the pub before he saw her. She would march herself to the docks and book passage on some ship and leave poor Benjamin to live his life.

But Lydia did not know how to make such a sacrifice. She took up the seat beside him instead, without even asking for permission. "There you are."

He smelled of ale. Not the pleasant, yeasty aroma that came with the Northfield Hall home brew, but a sour smell. His eyes were a little wide and his cheeks red. Still, he smiled when he saw her. "There *you* are." Then, giving his head a shake, "How did you get here? What are you doing here? How did you know where to find me?"

So kind and forgiving, even after all this time. Lydia deserved to be greeted with *How dare you* and *You have no right*. She wrapped her hand around his elbow, tugging herself close so that she could feel the safety of his form. "I owe you an apology."

"No, you were right. I was making it too much about principles. I always do that. I make it so much about the principles that I can find a principle to keep from doing anything."

As the duke and Sophia and John all slid away into their own private huddle, Benjamin's hand snaked around her waist. Lydia didn't have the resolve to stop him from holding her. Not when it was what she wanted. "I *did* play you for the fool. I didn't want to, and I didn't entirely mean to, but I knew I was doing it and I did it. It was the right thing to do, I told myself. But it wasn't at all. You don't deserve me. I'm guilty of so many things. I hate myself most for the way I treated you. I hope you know that."

Benjamin stilled. His palm hovered between her rib cage and her hip, uncommitted to any next action.

"It wasn't just about Seamus, whatever you think. I truly do care about Ireland. And I thought if I dedicated my life to something greater than me, then my life would be valuable. Instead, I've only hurt people. If I had only kept to myself, Seamus wouldn't have been caught. And you...you would be married to a wife who loves you with her whole heart. Which is what you deserve."

Saying it all out loud made it true. Lydia felt it crystallizing on her tongue and shattering the air with a million jagged edges. At least it made her chest lighter, flinging these truths out. Admitting not just to herself but to the world how terribly, humanly flawed she was.

Benjamin stared at her in horror.

Lydia couldn't bear to see it. "Don't leave London on my account. Send me to the East Indies or the West Indies or America. You stay here with your family and your life. If one of us must go, it should be me."

It would be the start of her penance to live in exile, where she knew no one and had no mission to attach herself to like some kind of martyr. She would have to live as Lydia, neither a lady nor a warrior queen nor a saint. A human, whose existence was of no great consequence one way or another.

She waited for Benjamin to agree. Instead, his arm finished tracing its way around her waist. His other one, too, captured her, hauling her against his chest in a rough, tight hug. His lips buried in her hair. "You are valuable for being you. That's it. You don't have to do anything more."

There was nothing like his embrace. Lydia melted into it, even though she didn't deserve it. The smell of him, the feel of him, the warmth of him, the safety of him. Benjamin, who wasn't Seamus. Benjamin, who was her husband. Benjamin.

"What is this all about, then?" he asked, his lips still brushing against her ears. "Last I saw you, you were marshalling an army. What happened?"

She wouldn't have been able to confess it aloud to anyone else. "You were right, and I was wrong. So very wrong."

"I'm not so sure about that." Leaning backward, Benjamin slid a finger along her jaw, lifting her chin so she had no choice but to meet his gaze. "I've spent the last couple of hours coming around to your way of thinking. Which goes to show it isn't as simple as either-or. There is more to choosing a way forward than right or wrong. There's the when and the how and the why to consider, too. Won't you tell me what happened after I left?"

His arms still held her steady against him, which gave Lydia enough strength to admit to it all: how not even Conor had wanted a revolution, how they'd come up with their own plan, how they only needed her for funding and connections. "If I disappeared tomorrow, they would hardly notice. That's how useful I've been."

Benjamin squeezed her close. "Come now, it doesn't matter what any single one of us contributes. What matters is the cause. Right?"

A simple concept. Yet one that, somewhere along the way, Lydia had lost sight of. Hearing it aloud, steeped in compassion, set her head back on her shoulders.

Conor and Declan and the other men were the ones who lived as Catholics in Ireland. Theirs were the necks that might end up in nooses. Lydia had thought she was their leader, but she and Benjamin were in their service. For if they did not manage their own revolution—however it might look—they would never truly be in power.

Benjamin rested his head against hers. Temple to temple, he said, "I say we follow their plan and see where it leads. What say you?"

A part of her swirled words upwards. It wanted to gush at him how grateful she was for him, how much she admired him, how much she needed him.

The word *love* hovered there again. Lydia didn't know what to do with it. So she pushed down the entire instinct and answered him only, "Aye. I say aye."

Chapter Twenty-One

CLOUDS CROWDED THE SUMMER evening sky as Lydia and Benjamin arrived at her parents' ball. Not enough to threaten rain, but a thick layer that blocked out the stars and the moon. If this were the sky in Ireland, the men wouldn't be able to see beyond their own hands as they snuck across fields and through woods.

But this was the center of the empire. Darkness would not conquer here. The city sparkled: carriage lanterns, streetlamps, Grecian torches, and the glow of a thousand candles from inside the leased assembly hall. Lydia could make out every detail of the embroidery on Benjamin's waistcoat even from inside their hired coach.

She focused on those details—a maze of emerald Celtic knots, the kind where she couldn't tell where one ended and the next began—rather than on the nerves rioting through her stomach. The plan was in place. It would happen whether she was anxious or not. So she might as well relax.

The first sign that everything was going as planned was when Conor himself opened their carriage door. He wore the full Devereaux livery, down to the polished silver buckles on his formal shoes. Lydia searched for comfort that he was where he intended to be. Still, her nerves only jangled.

Inside, she spotted more familiar faces among the footmen taking cloaks, offering champagne, and guiding guests towards the ballroom. That was good. It meant that so far, nothing had gone awry in the Irishmen's plan.

Why, then, did her fingers tremble as if she were about to meet her maker?

Her parents waited by the threshold to the ballroom, glittering in diamonds and gilt thread as they greeted each guest. Lydia clung more tightly to Benjamin's elbow. This was not the first time she had ever lied to her parents. But it was the first time she had invited so much chaos into their home. Even though she believed in the plan and in the cause behind it, the little girl in her cowered, afraid to be caught out by Mother and Father.

They didn't notice a thing, of course. Mother pressed a kiss to Lydia's cheek, whispering into her ear, "Is that the best you could do? Where are the jewels I sent over?"

Indeed, Mother had tried to lend Lydia a whole case full of jewelry for the ball. But Lydia couldn't pretend to be a dutiful daughter. So she wore her deep green evening gown and an amber necklace.

"I didn't want to distract from you," she lied.

She and Benjamin danced the opening set—again, as planned. It was a minuet, far too sedate to distract Lydia's thoughts from racing ahead to the rest of the night. She was supposed to seek someone else for the next set, to behave as if it were a regular ball and not one that would go down in history. Benjamin tugged her closer to him instead.

"Perhaps we should take a turn around the room, or step outside for fresh air."

What she really wanted was to run home with him and forget everything in the cocoon of the Preston townhouse. But tonight wasn't about her or what she wanted or even what she needed. Tonight was about Ireland.

Tonight and every night, until Ireland could call itself free.

"A turn around the room would be welcome."

Arm in arm, they milled along the perimeter of the dance floor. The room was too crowded for it to become a promenade; every few steps, they were hailed by an acquaintance or relative to stop and make the noise of polite chatter. Benjamin, somehow, behaved as if he had no idea what the evening had in store. He complimented the ladies, made jokes with the men, and in general seemed his usual charming self.

Lydia wished it were a normal evening. One in which she could stand at Benjamin's arm and admire him, not worry about whether anyone would notice the nervous tremble of her fingers. But each little interaction, each new group they encountered, each call of a dance set brought them closer and closer to the moment of the plan unfolding. Lydia couldn't tear her thoughts away from it, not even when she knew she should.

"Worry won't help anyone," Benjamin murmured when they were still an hour away. "We must remain calm."

"There are a million things that could go wrong. And if they do…"

"If they do, then everyone involved knows the risk they are taking tonight." Drawing her into a corner, away from eavesdroppers, Benjamin drew her gloved hand to his lips. "Including us. After tonight, we might be ostracized. We might even be locked up in the Tower of London. It will be worth it, won't it?"

His words were all exactly right. He even tinted them with the right emotions: conviction, courage, and compassion.

"Do you say that because you believe it, or because you feel it is the right thing to say?"

Benjamin let loose her hand. "Does the distinction matter, if my actions are the same either way?"

A moral argument again. Lydia didn't know which philosophers to marshal into her response. She didn't have a chance, either: before she could respond, Adelaide and Claudia found them. "Lady Lydia, we have barely seen you all night!" Claudia chastised, laughter on her lips. "You don't mind if we steal her away, do you, Mr. Preston?"

Benjamin shook his head, silent.

Lydia let Adelaide loop their arms together. But she didn't leave her husband before replying: "Yes, the distinction matters. To me, it matters."

"I hope we didn't disrupt a marital dispute," Claudia said. "Only did you hear about the wicked plan afoot tonight?"

Lydia's heart stuttered. If *Claudia* knew about the plan, then there was no hope of success.

"It's not much of a plan," Adelaide amended. "And not that wicked. Dishonest, yes, but I don't think it's wicked."

"What is it?" Lydia asked, too panicked for her sister's words to make any sense.

Claudia grinned. "We are announcing at supper that Lord Chatteris has been kind enough to sponsor both Lady Adelaide and myself on a tour of the continent."

Relief flooded Lydia. "Oh. And what is so wicked about that?"

"He hasn't said any such thing. But as he himself is still in Edinburgh, by the time he hears about it, we will be well on our way to Paris and not a thing he can do about it."

It was a good plan. One that, any other night, would fill Lydia with joy. Her sister and Claudia both deserved an escape from their fates, and the best part was they were plotting this themselves.

But tonight, it was all Lydia could do to find a smile for them. "You'll write me a letter a week, I expect. And be safe. I shouldn't like to hear of anyone's disease or misfortune from afar."

Adelaide kissed her cheek. "I promise. We shall be careful, healthy, and very happy. And you shall do the same?"

On a lie, Lydia replied: "Of course."

They found a drink—French champagne, not the worst of all possible imports—to toast each other. Lydia still stood with them, pretending it was a night like any other, when the clock chimed twelve o'clock.

Father took the dais beside the violinists, demanding everyone's attention. "Lady Devereaux and I thank you for joining us this evening to celebrate so auspicious an occasion. Though I must spend much of my year away from London, my heart and thoughts remain here always. I am honored that so many of you, my dearest friends, are here tonight. Now, if you please, Lady Devereaux has outdone herself yet again. Let us eat."

This was the cue that Conor had been waiting for. As soon as Father finished his speech, the footmen all put down their trays, whisked off their livery jackets, and revealed green cloaks they wore underneath with hoods to pull over their faces. Conor and Declan stepped forward, reciting in unison, "Halt! By order of the Insurrection Act, declared by Sir Robert Peel, any man outside of his home after curfew is committing a felony! We hereby arrest you for trial without a jury of your peers!"

As one, the footmen—and there were six dozen of them, materializing from all parts of the assembly hall—started seizing the lords and gentlemen nearest them. Lydia watched, heart pounding, as Conor wrapped his bulky hands around Father's wrists. On the opposite side of the ballroom, a footman grabbed Lord Preston, too. Shrieks filled the air, some from the ladies but most of them from the men. Their faces twisted with surprise, confusion, and outrage.

They couldn't actually be arrested. Anyone in the peerage existed with near-total immunity to the law, subject only to Parliament's censure. None of the Irishmen had the authority to take anyone to gaol, anyway. The next step of the plan was to march them all to the center of the room, force them to listen to a speech so that the night's events would make it into the newspapers the next day, and then let them go, the footmen disappearing into the night.

No one had said anything about a gun. And so when a pistol shot rang through the air—chipping off a part of the plaster ceiling—Lydia screamed. She wasn't the only one, either. It seemed the whole assembly hall was nothing but a scream. On the other side of the room, a lady in a towering feather headdress fainted.

Benjamin found her, his two arms snaking around her waist. "Are you harmed?" he asked, but she could only decipher the words because his lips brushed against her ears. She clung to him as she shook her head, looking around for the shooter.

"Unhand them!" someone shouted. "Unhand them, or I'll shoot to kill!"

It was the threat that parted the crowd enough for Lydia to see the gunman. Her brother, Alistair, standing on the dais where just moments ago there had been a string quartet. His gold waistcoat glinted in the candlelight, but his jacket bunched at his shoulders as he raised his two arms. In each hand he held a mother-of-pearl handled pistol.

One of those guns had already spent its shot. The other was still loaded. As she watched, Alistair lowered his arm to point it at Conor, who stood a few yards away from him still holding Father by the wrists. His hood had fallen, revealing his face to everyone. That face that looked just like Seamus's.

The room fell silent as everyone—Irishmen and peers alike—waited to see what Alistair would do.

"Unhand him," Alistair said again.

The key to the plan was that the footmen would tie the hands of every peer before the speech, then flee. That way, the peers would be busy freeing each other, leaving the Irishmen a chance to get away.

If Conor let go of Father now, even if Alistair didn't shoot him, he would be the one tied up and carried off to gaol. Lydia knew what would happen then: an execution.

Conor didn't unhand Father.

And Alistair cocked his pistol.

Horror coiled at the base of Lydia's throat. She needed to say something, do anything, to stop this moment from happening. She couldn't watch her own brother shoot Conor dead.

But before she could even let out a scream, Benjamin released her. In the span of a breath, he launched himself between Alistair and Conor. "You don't want to do that, brother." He raised his hands, as if calming a wild dog. "Let's not spill any blood tonight."

"I mean to see every single one of these men hanged."

"In due process," Benjamin coaxed. "Let them be pursued by law, not by you."

"He will unhand my father or I *will* shoot him."

In a rush of words, Conor began the speech that was supposed to come later, when they had everyone rounded up and listening.

"The Insurrection Act violates the rights of Irish citizens just as these arrests violate your rights."

"This is a stunt!" Benjamin cried. "He means Lord Devereaux no harm. We only want to make a statement. Won't you put down your pistol?"

"We?" Alistair's exclamation was drowned out as Conor continued, confidence thickening the timbre of his voice:

"Shame on the government that must maintain its power by robbing its people of their natural rights!"

"Stop that!" Alistair cried.

"The Insurrection Act has no place in Ireland. We demand that you revoke the Insurrection Act!"

"I said, stop!"

Alistair shot his pistol.

Lydia couldn't watch. Her body reacted involuntarily, hands flinging to her eyes, chin ducking to her chest, knees dropping to the ground as she tried to protect herself from what happened next. Everything was muffled from the gunshot. Someone's skirt brushed against her elbows as they rushed forward. Someone else, rushing the opposite direction, stepped on her hem, tugging her off balance.

If this was revolution, she couldn't stomach it. She couldn't believe she had ever advocated for anyone picking up a gun. Now Lydia knew why Seamus had turned away from the Ribbonmen. Why she would never be able to ask for battle again. Hell.

Looking away wouldn't help anyone.

Lydia forced herself to open her eyes. She rose to her feet first, ignoring the quiver in her knees, and then dropped her hands and—at last—lifted her head to see what had befallen Conor.

But it wasn't Conor lying prone on the dais at all.

It was Benjamin. On his back, one leg folded beneath him. His left hand clutched the opposite side of his chest. And there was blood—on his fingers, on the crisp white of his linen shirt, on the parquet floor beneath him.

Lydia, at last, screamed.

CHAPTER
TWENTY-TWO

THE STRANGEST PART WAS that he didn't feel anything. Not the fall to the ground and certainly not the gunshot, which he knew was there from the blood on his hand. Benjamin didn't even feel Lydia as she claimed him, pushing Conor and Lord Devereaux and Papa away so that she could cradle him in her lap. He could only see her, like an angel, as she tugged his head onto her thighs and wadded her green skirt over the hole in his chest.

And he heard her: "I love you, Benjamin Preston. I'm not going to let you leave me."

He knew better than to believe her. Except, he couldn't help but believe her.

Things progressed beyond his comprehension from then on. There was the darkness of the night; the smell of horses from the back of a carriage; a bed with all its curtains pulled closed. He slept for a long time. He flashed between hot and cold. His body ached. His shoulder seared. He didn't know anymore if he was awake or if he still slept, caught in a terrible dream like an arm in a stained sling.

All through it, though, he knew Lydia was there. Hovering. Waiting. Her hand tucked in his, even when he wasn't sure whether he had hands attached to arms attached to shoulders anymore.

She didn't leave him.

When Benjamin woke for good, he could feel again. The pain in his shoulder was immense, like a knife was stuck in it, tearing apart his skin and muscle and tendons. He was too uncomfortable to stay lying down in the same position, yet trying to sit up was like getting shot all over again.

"What do you need?" Lydia appeared in his field of vision, leaning over from the side of the bed. Her fingers, long and cool, pressed against his forehead. "You mustn't strain yourself."

"Sit up," he managed to say, and Lydia hooked her arms around his waist to help prop him up against a mountain of pillows.

Now Benjamin had a view of her even when she didn't lean in. She sat in a stuffed armchair with a light summer blanket across her lap. Her hair was braided, yet still she had managed to fuzz it up so it sat in a halo around her face.

She evaluated him with a thorough, discerning glance. "Are you thirsty? You should drink some water now that you are awake."

Before he could even reply, she disappeared somewhere beyond the bed curtains. When she returned, she held a crystal glass of water.

"Here, you must drink."

The truth was that he was parched. Benjamin drank greedily, even though he wanted to push aside the cup and bask in Lydia.

"Thank you." He returned the glass to her. "Tell me what has happened. Did Conor get arrested? Did the speech make it into the broadsheets? Have you slept at all? Can't you open these curtains? I feel as if I am in a casket."

"Thank goodness you aren't." Lydia drew back the velvet drapes and tied them to the bedposts. Then she returned to her chair, her hands folded on her lap. "It is two days since the ball. It certainly did make it into all the newspapers. Not quite as we wanted, I'm afraid. Mostly, the reports have been 'LORD DEVEREAUX SHOOTS MR. PRESTON.' Still, below the headline, the articles paint you as a noble defender of Irish virtue. Well, most of them. *The Morning Post* seems to think you had it coming for interrupting Alistair's heroic stand against Irish invaders."

"We were never going to win over *The Morning Post*. What of Conor and the rest of them? Did they manage to leave?"

Her expression clouded. "Most of them did. Conor and Declan were both stopped. They're at Newgate now. At least they will go to trial at assizes. If we can get enough Irishmen on the jury, perhaps they will be acquitted."

Benjamin's stomach twisted at the idea that they might hang.

"Conor reminds me that they knew the risk before they entered the assembly hall, and that he will gladly pay the price if it means fighting for Ireland." Lydia's eyes landed on him, shining. "As you were willing to pay the ultimate price. Your life for Conor's. Your life for the cause."

When Benjamin had seen Alistair's pistol aimed at Conor's head, his body had leapt to action before his brain could catch up. He didn't know if his instinct had been to protect a man from death or to protect a brother in arms. "I'm not sure I would pick up a gun in Ireland's name, though."

"No, you only announced to a room full of important people that you supported its independence."

"I suppose we won't get many invitations after this." Gingerly, Benjamin reached towards her. She was on his wounded side, and so he could only extend his arm so far. His hand rested on the edge of the mattress, waiting for her to take it.

Lydia rose again, refilling the glass of water and pressing that to his palm instead. "The Prince Regent has requested an audience once you are healed. Your father and Max discuss nothing else, trying to decide whether he plans to order your execution or offer you a commendation."

Benjamin had met the Prince twice, though he didn't think he had made much of an impression either time. He tried now to picture a private audience; his imagination cut him off. "Perhaps I had better take my time healing, then."

"John says the bullet went straight through your shoulder, so you've two wounds to heal in addition to whatever damage was done internally. You must remain in bed until he says you are no longer in danger of infection."

"There are worse things than remaining in bed."

Lydia's cheeks flamed red. "I don't think anything of that sort would help you recover."

Benjamin had meant it as a statement of fact. Yet his body reacted to her suggestion with a great surge.

He remembered what she had said in the ballroom. But telling a man you loved him as he lay bleeding to death was a very different thing from meaning it.

He had promised himself not to fall into this trap again. He could not keep accepting fractions of affection from Lydia, not even when it came in the form of her body rocking beneath his. That way lay madness. He wanted Lydia's whole heart and nothing less.

"You're one to talk," he replied. "You look as if you haven't slept this whole time. You should go rest in your own room, without worrying about me."

Her fingers flew to her hair. "I didn't want to leave you alone. In case..."

In case he died. It was all too likely after a gunshot.

Benjamin lifted his arm, even though it felt like a thousand blades piercing through his shoulder. "I'm healing now. You must look after yourself, too."

"I am. I've slept, I swear."

"In a bed," Benjamin insisted.

Lydia's head dipped down, her cheeks pinkening again. "Actually, I slept next to you for a few hours last night." The confession was barely out before she lifted her chin. "Perhaps you would like me to join you in there again?"

There would be a sweetness in having her beside him. Benjamin's hopes lifted at the thought of it, imagining her warmth stretching next to him. They could tuck against each other, the way they had in those heady nights at the start of their marriage. They could pretend the rest of the world didn't exist.

Except Benjamin still wouldn't be Seamus. And Lydia still wouldn't love him. Not the way he wanted her to.

"I would sleep better without you." The words were hard to say. Even worse was watching Lydia's face shutter at them. There had been a shine to her eyes before; now she looked as icy and remote as the Alps.

Folding the blanket that had been on her lap, she stood and draped it over the back of her chair. She didn't quite look at him as she said, "I'll let you rest, then."

Even though he was the one asking her to leave, each step she took towards the door was like being shot all over again. They punctuated the truth that he had to start believing, no matter that he didn't want to: that she was not his. Never had been and never would be.

When he was better, he would take a tour of Ireland instead of Calcutta. Lydia could make herself a home in Dublin; he would spend a year or two traveling to each and every little town. To learn the country—and to learn how to live with a wife who didn't love him.

For now, he needed to keep away from her, or go mad.

Eyes shut, Benjamin waited, preparing himself to hear the door open and for the last of her footsteps to disappear into the corridor. It seemed like it was taking forever, but that must only be an illusion, his heartbreak so acute that it could slow time into seconds that lasted for hours.

Yet what he heard next was not the mechanics of the door. It was Lydia. "If I burn the letter, do you think we could go back to the way we were?"

Benjamin opened his eyes. She stood at the threshold, one hand curled around the knob. The rest of her body was turned towards him. The orange glow of the fire in his hearth reflected in her eyes.

"I thought there was only one kind of love. I imagined my heart had died with Seamus, that it was there with him in the cold ocean. But then I married you. I never knew a person like you existed. I knew there were good people, people with conviction, people who treated everyone with kindness. I expected you to be that. I didn't expect you to be my best friend. I didn't expect to want to spend my whole day with you. It took watching you get shot—thinking I might lose you, too—for me to realize this feeling I have for you is love. I love you, Benjamin. I'm saying it because I mean it, not because it sounds like the right thing to say. I love you, and I'm so sorry that I ever doubted that I could. I'm so sorry I made you think I couldn't love you. Because I do, and I have for a long time now, only I was too stupid and guilty to know it. And my question is, do you think you could ever forget it all? If I burn the letter, do you think we could go back to the way it was before you knew anything about Seamus?"

Benjamin's mouth was dry, his throat aching again. He had never known an ache to feel so sweet. Still, his voice broke when he tried to reply: "No."

Lydia wilted against the door. "Oh."

He raised his good arm to stop her, to beg more time. "I should never have asked you to burn the letter. It is a part of you. I don't want to pretend I don't know anything about Seamus. How can I love you if I don't even know you?"

She understood this time. She crossed the room again, pausing at the far end of the bed. Her arm wrapped around the bedpost, too far away for him to reach. "I'm not saying I have stopped loving him. That younger part of me still exists. But I've had to live on without him, and I'm a different person now, for better or worse. I'll always remember him with love, but that doesn't stop me from loving you. From being in love with you."

Benjamin was still waiting for her to take his hand. "Say it again."

Lydia smiled, her lips curling shyly under that solemn nose he adored so much. "I love you, Benjamin Franklin Preston."

There was a part of his brain still ringing the alarm. She could say it all she wanted without meaning it.

But his heart believed her. It didn't feel like hope this time. It didn't feel like betting his future on a narrative he was spinning out of straw.

It felt like Lydia, his wife, loved him.

"I love you too," he said, grinning.

"You're not just saying that because you are my husband and you feel like you should?" Lydia's fingers stroked the bedpost instead of him. "The distinction matters."

Benjamin knew that better than anyone. "The distinction is everything. And I love you, whether or not I am your husband. Whether or not you love me back."

At last, she took his hand. She had to climb onto the mattress to reach it, one knee after the other, her skirts flinging away so he saw the bare skin of her legs. Her fingers were warm against his. Next thing he knew, she was stretched out on her stomach beside him, propped on her elbows. She arced her head over him. "Tell me if I hurt you."

There were a hundred ways she could hurt him. A kiss on the lips was not one of them. Her mouth was soft and light as a feather. He slipped his good hand behind her neck to keep her there. After all they had been through, he wanted a kiss that was more than a little brush.

Benjamin deepened the kiss hungrily. With his tongue in her mouth, his fingers in her braid, his knee against hers. But he wasn't the only one claiming this moment between them. Lydia was just as greedy. She framed his jaw in her two palms, the better to kiss him. She slid her left leg between his knees, bridging her hot groin over his hip.

"I don't want to hurt you," she said again, their lips hardly parting.

"You won't." Benjamin barely felt his injured shoulder anymore. She was his wife, and she loved him; he no longer knew the concept of pain.

"I should let you rest." Yet Lydia kicked down the bedsheets so they pooled at his feet. Her fingers slid beneath the hem of his nightshirt. They glided across his skin like fire across coals as she guided the shirt up over his hips.

"This will help me heal, I'm sure of it," Benjamin promised, lifting his buttocks so she could free the nightshirt from under it. "The doctors don't mention it for fear of offending your delicate ears, but it is a tried-and-true remedy throughout the centuries."

Lydia kissed him again. Her hand landed on the mattress just beside his wounded shoulder. Pain seared through him, even through the opium of desire.

"Not like that," he gasped.

Immediately, Lydia stopped. Benjamin threw his good hand against her hip to keep her from dismounting entirely.

"Don't stop. Only let's be smart about it." He took a few breaths, waiting for the unpleasant throbbing to stop. Lydia remained above him, knees splayed out on either side of his hips. Her hair was almost entirely out of its braid now, her lips red and swollen from their kisses. Her breasts heaved against her bodice in gulps of breath.

"Tell me what you need," Lydia said.

"Avoid my shoulder." Benjamin bucked his hips, just a little. His cock was already standing free and ready, and the motion rubbed it against the inside of her thigh in a way that blanked his mind.

But it also rocked his shoulder enough for the pain to interrupt his elation.

"You'll have to do most of the work, I'm afraid."

Lydia's lips curved into that shy smile again. "I can do that. What else?"

Since they were having the conversation, Benjamin decided he might as well add, "Take off your dress."

She grinned now, an evil, mischievous grin that stole all the power away from him. Slowly—cruelly—she inched her gown up her body and over her head. Beneath it, she wore a short corset and a chemise that hung from her shoulders all the way past her hips. Her breasts were already escaping, the pink upper arcs of her nipples peeking out from above the corset, and the insides of her legs were bare against his.

But the rest of her might as well have still been fully clothed. "You want me like this, husband?" she teased.

"I want you naked," he growled, using all his willpower not to thrust himself inside her already.

Lydia ran a finger along the rim of her bodice, as if considering the point. "I'm afraid it might be too much for you. I should hate for you to be overcome and faint."

"Please, my love."

Her smile turned tender again. "As you wish." She made quick work of the corset, then pulled the remaining shift over her head. At last, Benjamin had his wife naked above him. He could relish the small, firm shape of her breasts; the column of her torso; the thatch of wiry hair hiding the most sensitive part of her. His cock twitched at the sight.

"I love you," he said again, not quite on purpose.

"I love you, too." Lydia lifted from her knees, poised above his cock. "Are you ready?"

"Yes."

She slid onto him with exquisite slowness. Benjamin felt every millisecond as its own tantalizing, sweet agony. When at last she took him fully inside her, he could no longer string together coherent thoughts. Her body was all that existed, hot and wet and squeezing him ever tighter.

"I love you," she said, twining her fingers through his.

"I love you," she said, kissing the inside of his wrist.

"I love you," she said, rocking her hips.

"I love you," she cried, as he burst into the delicious flames of an orgasm.

And she said it one more time, lying beside him with her arm wrapped around his waist, when they fell asleep together as husband and wife.

CHAPTER
TWENTY-THREE

I T WAS THREE WEEKS later that Lydia alerted the Prince Regent's household that Benjamin was well enough to make a visit. They set an appointment for Thursday afternoon, that slice of day when the sun was almost down yet the Prince Regent was just waking. Lydia wore her topaz gown with amber-studded netting; she added her grandmother's pearl-and-diamond necklace out of deference to their royal host. Since Benjamin's arm was still in a sling, he opted for an opera cape whose wool billowed out behind him as they followed the page through the palace to the receiving room.

Those three weeks they had done nothing but discuss how best to use the audience with the Prince. Well, nothing besides that and making love between changing Benjamin's bandages. The Prince Regent was known to be many things: selfish, gluttonous, vain, lewd, a wastrel, even perhaps vapid. But he was also the divine leader of the United Kingdom. If they were granted an audience with him, they intended to use it as best they could.

Especially since he himself had been the victim of laws against Catholics, seeing his own marriage to the Catholic Maria Fitzherbert declared illegal.

"We mustn't expect too much," Benjamin cautioned over and over again. "He will see the matter as Alistair did."

Yet he wanted an audience with Benjamin. If the Prince wanted to censure him for defending Conor Devlin, then he would have Benjamin arrested. He wouldn't invite him to Carlton House for tea.

Lydia didn't expect the Prince Regent to do anything as grand as granting Conor and Declan clemency. If she had the chance, though, she was certainly going to ask for it.

"I am so glad you are mending and at such rapid speed," the Prince said upon entering the room. Footmen rushed forward to serve them tea from an opulent silver service. Lydia hadn't been so close to Chinese tea in months; it wafted at her with a bitterer smell than she remembered.

Benjamin took the cup offered him. "Thank you, Your Highness."

"I was most upset to hear about the incident. It is disappointing, either way one looks at it."

Lydia could feel Benjamin, like her, stiffening in his seat.

"What upsets me the most is that my government is being criticized unfairly. The Act of Union was for the betterment of Ireland. I do not understand why that is so hard for the Irish to comprehend."

Words bubbled up Lydia's throat, pressing against her shut lips. The Prince would not listen to her opinion, even if she dared voice it. And she knew better than to voice it, at least until they were sure the Prince was not about to condemn them for life.

Which was why Benjamin surprised her with his reply: "It is my understanding that while the Act of Union was intended to benefit the entire country, in actuality, it has only benefitted the Dublin elites, and the rest of the country feels left behind."

"The Catholics, you mean." The Prince Regent sipped his tea in a noisy slurp. "The King disappointed them greatly in the Act. Long live the King, but I am keen to prove to all of Ireland that they are as dear to me as the rest of the United Kingdom."

His eyes rested on Lydia, who hadn't yet picked up her teacup. She did so now, murmuring, "That is admirable, Your Highness."

"You have spent most of your life in Ireland, Lady Lydia. Yet it was your own brother who shot Mr. Preston. What is your view on the matter?"

This, Lydia knew, might be her only opportunity to use the appointment for good. Her mouth dry, she aimed for a response that was both true and incomplete. "The Irishmen meant no harm, sir. They had no guns themselves, nor were they threatening anyone's life or property. I am proud of Mr. Preston for defending them, and I beg for mercy for those who were arrested."

Despite the formality of the room and the weight of the Prince's gaze, Benjamin reached over to take her hand. His touch, shrouded by two layers of kidskin gloves though it was, soothed her nerves. Even as she waited to see what the Prince Regent would make of her stance.

"It seems to me it was a matter of theater gone wrong, not a criminal act," the Prince said. "The Duke of Berkwell assures me it was Devereaux, not the Irishmen, who introduced a gun. He also said you displayed great forbearance and grace, Mr. Preston. He showed me several Irish newspapers praising you as well."

It depended on the newspaper, of course. The Irish peers tended to take Alistair's view that any protest of any sort threatened violence and therefore needed to be stamped out like a stray ember from an open hearth. But the Prince was correct: the more moderate Dublin papers—and certainly the Catholic ones—were lionizing Benjamin for taking the bullet on behalf of an Irishman.

"I only acted as my conscience dictated," Benjamin said. "I ask for no praise."

"The monarchy has for decades tried to install leaders in Ireland who will shepherd the country to the same greatness as England, yet too many of my Irish lords spend their time in London. You intrigue me, Mr. Preston, as a man who would take the charge seriously instead of treating it as a feather in your cap."

Her husband stared at the Prince, white-faced and openmouthed. Squeezing his hand, Lydia replied for him. "Mr. Preston is the most dutiful man I know, Your Highness."

"We shall have to arrange a ceremony, of course, and everything else required, but I should like to award you the barony of Athenry, in County Galway. Tell me you will accept."

Lydia's head spun. Never in a thousand years had she dreamed that her husband—real or imagined—would be an Irish peer. That she could be mistress of a country seat, with all the influence that entailed. It was nothing close to revolution, but it was power, and it was within their grasp.

Benjamin's hand was stiff in hers. She looked at him, expecting to see the same surprise in his eyes.

Instead, he looked horrified. "Surely I am too young, sir, and you would prefer a man with experience."

Lydia heard the shadows of Papa and Max in Benjamin's words. For all they tried to protect Benjamin, this was the result: he didn't believe himself capable.

She reached out for his hand. "You are too humble. What other man in London knows as much about Ireland as you? What other man can represent His Majesty with the proper feeling for the difficulties of the people?"

"Lord Devereaux informed me you organized the little piece of theater that interrupted his party," the Prince Regent said, his voice sharpening into a blade. "That shows me you have plenty of abilities that need to be put to good use."

One did not need to be a mind reader to understand that the Prince was threatening consequences if they did not accept. Yet still Benjamin hesitated. He even dared look away from the Prince long enough to ask her, "I know the love you feel for Ireland. Do you object to becoming the Baroness Athenry?"

Strangely, Lydia could hear the words he left out. *I know the love you feel for Ireland*; by accepting this peerage, Benjamin would join the very ruling class they were trying to throw out of Ireland. If they were part of the problem, could they be part of the solution?

The truth was that there was no good answer. Lydia had been born into the Protestant Ascendancy, just as Benjamin had been born to the Prestons, just as Seamus and Conor had been born Irish Catholics. No matter how much they wanted to fight arm in arm with the Devlins, Lydia and Benjamin would always be different: more English, more powerful, more immune.

They could only do their best with the tools available to them. And an Irish peerage—even one that didn't come with a place in Parliament—was an excellent tool to wield.

It was Benjamin who had to answer. It was Benjamin who had to decide, once and for all, if this was a cause worth choosing for the rest of his life.

Lydia squeezed his hand, gently, and let the choice rest with him. "We could show our love for Ireland very well by living there. Yet it will consume our energy. Will that be a fulfilling life for you?"

Benjamin held onto her fingers as he listened to the silence, his brown eyes steady but clouded. Until he smiled. Kissing the back of her hand, he turned to the Prince Regent and said, "It would be the honor of our lifetime, Your Highness."

EPILOGUE
1820 – THREE YEARS LATER

THE JOURNEY—BOTH LITERAL AND metaphorical—had been long. Benjamin's stomach still ached from crossing the Irish Sea the day before last, and now his legs and back were sore from so long on a hired horse. Yet here they were, cresting the hill to discover after these three years exactly what the barony of Athenry encompassed.

Benjamin knew everything there was to know about his holdings on paper. He was responsible for a modest piece of Ireland, only about three hundred acres, on which were scores of tenant farmers, a few landowners, and an adjacent medieval town of about one thousand citizens. Over the last three years, he had read every history book he could find about Ireland in general and County Galway in particular; after Conor and Declan had been pardoned by the Prince Regent, Benjamin had hired Declan to teach him the Irish language;

305

he subscribed to the Dublin newspapers and began corresponding with his land steward as soon as he was officially granted the title.

But until now, he had not yet been to Ireland. He had not yet seen this land and the people for whom he bore such responsibility.

He pulled his horse to a stop as they neared the top of the hill and dismounted. The carriage in which Lydia and Orla rode paused, too. Benjamin handed his reins to the groom beside the driver, then opened the door for Lydia. "Lady Athenry, would you care to join me for the view?"

His wife smiled at him. A grin so familiar he should be immune to it by now. And yet it delighted him, sparking a firecracker of joy within his breast. She put her hand in his to climb down from the carriage, and he didn't let go once she was on the dirt road.

"I'm a little afraid it will be disappointing after all these years," Lydia admitted as they walked together to the top of the hill. "I've been building up in my head that it will be the most beautiful place in the world."

"Not unlike how I built up in my head that my wife would be the most beautiful woman in the world." Benjamin teased, but it was true, too: Lydia had married not only him but all his expectations for a wife.

How glad he was that she had broken down each and every one of those expectations. And then surpassed them.

"And what am I, if not that?" Lydia replied, summoning her full height to stare down at him in a mock-glare.

"The most beautiful woman in the world—and the most committed, passionate, and perfect wife in the world."

She beamed with more light than the sun itself. "Well matched with my husband, I would say."

Benjamin took in a deep breath of the fresh Irish air—cool yet moist on the fine autumn afternoon. This was the first—and least consequential—of a hundred moments about to come. First glimpse of the land, first glimpse of the manor, first meeting with their household, first meetings with their laborers and tenants.

And after all those firsts would come the real work. Benjamin and Lydia were determined to use their title to make as much change as possible, especially for as long as Papa lived and they weren't also responsible for Northfield Hall. They had plans to turn Athenry House into the same shared-profit model, where instead of paying rents, everyone who worked on the estate reaped the profits of the property. They had political ambitions, too, to add more opportunities for the Catholic community in County Galway and fight against any policy aimed at penalizing them.

But if there was one thing they had learned from the first few months of their marriage, it was that revolutions took time. And so first, before any of the work could begin, they had to come to the top of this hill.

Their landholdings spread out below them in an emerald carpet. It was more rural than even the country around Northfield Hall: the ground unfolded in flat, divided fields, with low stone fences curving down towards the manor house. There was only the one road and a few cottages to suggest human habitation. Otherwise, Benjamin could believe all the stories claiming Ireland as the land of fairies.

"It's more beautiful than I imagined," Lydia breathed, tucking her head against his shoulder.

The truth was that their whole life was more beautiful than Benjamin had imagined. Even those first terrible weeks when he had thought Lydia could never love him had sweetened their marriage so that now, as he held her to his side, he couldn't describe the deep need he felt for her. She was a part of him, more essential than any of his limbs. She was his wife, all he had ever dreamed of, and she had handed him more meaning than he ever could have hoped for.

"We'll do right by it," he promised her, pressing a kiss into her hair. "Or we'll die trying."

"Hopefully it won't come to that." Lydia touched her nose to his ear. "But if it does, we'll go out together. Promise?"

"Promise."

Her hand was warm and strong in his. Together, they contemplated the fields. The future. The hard work awaiting them.

Benjamin didn't know what to expect from the coming years. He didn't know if he could win any of the causes that he hoped to champion. But with Lydia's hand in his, he was ready to give it a try.

Their story, in many ways, was just beginning.

AUTHOR'S NOTE

L IKE MANY AMERICANS, I have a mix of Irish in my genealogy, and so for a long time, I have wanted to explore Ireland during the Regency era. On one side of my tree, there are Irish Catholics from across the country, including the Devlins, who ended up joining the revolutionary Fenian Brotherhood in Lawrence, Massachusetts in the 1870s. On the other side, there is an English bishop (and his family) sent to Ireland in the 1810s to represent the Church of England and whose sons ended up clergymen in Northern Ireland through the late nineteenth century.

Somewhere from that convoluted tree came inspiration for Lydia, an Englishwoman with deep ties and sympathy for Ireland.

When plotting the novel, at first, I played with the idea of inventing an impending bill for Lydia to fight. Then I did a little digging and discovered the Insurrection Act, which really was up for renewal in the early summer of 1817. While Lydia overdramatizes it a little bit (it only applied to specific counties), it certainly was used by the English government to investigate and muzzle suspected revolutionaries. The speech from Sir Robert Peel is what he actually said to parliament during the debate on renewing the Insurrection Act, with a few minor edits.

While the Prince Regent did marry a Catholic woman (with *much* scandal attached), I have taken significant artistic liberties with his attitude towards Ireland.

For more of my research into Ireland in the 1810s and the Ribbonists, please subscribe to my newsletter. You'll get monthly research deep dives into your inbox, plus you will unlock the full archive of all my past research newsletters – including the story of how my sister and I recreated the topaz gown our ancestor wore to meet King George IV (f/k/a the Prince Regent)!

Finally, I would like to take a moment to thank everyone who helped bring this book to life. Author Nicola Cassidy gave me valuable notes to keep the characters and story of Ireland authentic. Abby from Victory Editing and my beta readers Sarah Flanagan and Jen Trinh helped shape the story into its final form. Sara Israel from Thimble Editorial provides thorough and thoughtful copyedits. I took Benjamin to therapy with me to figure out the second half of the book, so I'd like to thank Marianna for her insight into his psyche! And finally, I thank all my friends and family for supporting me as I threw my hands in the air saying I was *still* working on rewrites. Most especially, I thank my husband Michael, my own personal cinnamon roll hero.

MORE FROM KATHERINE GRANT

Catch up on The Prestons series:

The Baron Without Blame – A Prequel Novella
He may not know her name, but that won't stop him from proposing a fake engagement...

The Viscount Without Virtue – Book 1
When she discovers her family's enemy is hiding in plain sight, what choice does a lady have but to seduce him?

The Governess Without Guilt – Book 2

One bored governess, one handsome doctor, and unchaperoned nighttime activities. What could possibly go wrong?

You might recognize Robert Hathorne, Duke of Berkwell, and Lady Annabelle Gresham from my first series, The Countess Chronicles:

The Ideal Countess – Book 1
Will a garden scandal lead to a duel at dawn, or happily ever after?

New Year's Masquerade – Book 1.5
With one night left of freedom, will Bernard choose to obey duty or follow his heart?

The Duchess Wager – Book 2
Will the duke lose the bet or his heart?

The Husband Plot – Book 3
What could go wrong when you marry a perfect stranger?

And don't miss Oliver Chow's story in The Hellion of Drury Lane!

Excerpt from The Baron Without Blame

The prequel novella to The Prestons

Ill-timed allergies, a pretty debutante, and a fake engagement - will Martin do the right thing, or follow his heart?

London, 1788

On that marble balcony of Lord Leighster's townhouse, wreathed by an overly-ornate iron railing, it occurred to Martin Preston that human sewage stank no matter in which city one found oneself. It fouled the sights of Calcutta as easily as it did Casablanca, sometimes stinking in town worse than seven weeks at sea. Even at this most magnificent ball in the great imperial center of London, Martin caught its unmistakable whiff above the fragrant springtime garden blooms.

It occurred to him, too, that the thought proved he was in no mood to fraternize at Lady Leighster's soiree. His head was too muddled from his travels, when instead he should be discussing the latest horse races or flirting with a pretty lady. He would do better to go straight home to his dark room and nurse a glass of Madeira. Except Madeira was out, since it arrived from the subjugated Portuguese colonies; and so too was his other old favorite, the smoking pipe, whose tobacco came from the slave trade. He would have to rely on warm milk, then, with a splash of honey.

Small comfort that would be.

Martin took another deep breath, trying to summon the proper spirits to return to the ballroom, when he realized that on top of the garden roses and the city stench, there was another scent. A better scent.

A human scent.

Then came the sneeze. It was louder than any sneeze had a right to be. Martin could practically hear the mucus propelling out the nose.

He wasn't sure which was worse: realizing he was not alone on the balcony or overhearing such a viscerally personal experience. He angled his shoulders away from the noise. Whoever was suffering such a violent eruption surely wanted their privacy. "I beg your pardon. I did not realize this balcony was occupied."

The sneezer sniffled methodically into a handkerchief. "The fault is mine. I did not make myself known."

The voice was female. Light, clear, and a faint flatness to her vowels that made Martin think of the far side of the ocean.

"I'm having an attack of allergies, I'm afraid. I blame Mr. Montague's cologne."

Martin swallowed back any reply. He should not be on a dark balcony alone with this voice.

"I thought you were my mother, which is why I didn't say anything," the voice continued before he could move. "She bid me wait here while she fetches more handkerchiefs from the retiring room. Only I've been waiting for eons. Perhaps she is having a nap."

An unchaperoned female voice. Now Martin really did reach for the door. "I shall fetch your mother for you. Whom may I inquire after?"

Her reply was another sneeze. Now that he knew his companion was female, he could revel in how unladylike the sound was. No wonder her chaperone had shunted her onto a dark balcony; no husband could be caught when one sneezed like a blacksmith.

"Bless you."

"Oh, I so hate allergies!" Her skirts rustled underneath this reply. Martin had an instant vision of Smyrna silk draped over the wide circumference of a pannier. Then – startlingly – he heard a soft thud, followed by a yelp.

Martin didn't dare turn around. "Are you quite alright?"

"Yes," the voice huffed. Then, reluctantly, "I suppose not. My skirts seem to have gotten caught on the railing."

Even in the darkness, Martin blushed. He most definitely should not be discussing skirts with an unchaperoned young lady.

He reined in his thoughts before they could race after images of petticoats and slim legs.

The most proper thing to do was fetch her chaperone. But if he left her alone on this balcony, someone else could just as easily step out and discover her trapped.

Which was how he found himself asking, "May I offer my assistance?"

There was a long, reluctant silence. Then, "I suppose so. Thank you."

Martin turned. He could just make out her silhouette, leaning awkwardly into the wall while her skirt ballooned against the wrought-iron railing. Her gown was pale – a virgin white, perhaps – and shone in the dim moonlight. The rest of her melted into the shadows.

Clearing his throat, he crossed to the railing. His guess was one of her pannier hoops had hooked onto an ornamentation. He knelt, all too aware of her perfume – which brought to mind a summer morning's mist – and tried to lift the skirt off the iron. He freed the hoop, but the silk overskirt still clung to the balcony, and Martin now saw it had been impaled, a long gash like a lightning bolt revealing the ruffled petticoat beneath.

He worked the silk carefully so as not to tear it any further. He had just freed it of the pineapple-shaped spear when the balcony doors swung open.

With a shriek, his companion jumped. She landed even closer to the wall. Most of her skirt went with her, but the triangle of fabric in Martin's fingers ripped away.

Which meant he had a fistful of her dress in his palm when he turned to face the new arrival.

Download The Baron Without Blame to keep reading for free!

About the Author

KATHERINE GRANT WRITES AWARD-WINNING Regency Romance novels for the modern reader. Her writing has been recognized by Foreword INDIES Book of the Year Awards, the Next Generation Indie Book Awards, the National Indie Excellence Awards, the Romance Slam Jam Emma Awards, and the Shelf Unbound Indie Book Awards. If you love ballgowns, secret kisses, and social commentary, a book hangover is coming your way.

Her ideal day includes a cup of tea, a good book, and a board game with her husband. Find out more at www.katherinegrantromance.com

Connect with Katherine on your favorite social media platforms:

instagram.com/katherine_grant_romance/

tiktok.com/@katherinegrantromance

facebook.com/groups/katherinegrant

bookbub.com/authors/katherine-grant

goodreads.com/author/show/19872840.Katherine_Grant